NO LONGER PROPERTY OF
SEATTLE PUBLIC LIBRARY
D0398130

TO THE DARK

Also by Chris Nickson from Severn House

The Inspector Tom Harper mysteries

GODS OF GOLD
TWO BRONZE PENNIES
SKIN LIKE SILVER
THE IRON WATER
ON COPPER STREET
THE TIN GOD
THE LEADEN HEART
THE MOLTEN CITY

The Richard Nottingham mysteries

COLD CRUEL WINTER
THE CONSTANT LOVERS
COME THE FEAR
AT THE DYING OF THE YEAR
FAIR AND TENDER LADIES
FREE FROM ALL DANGER

The Simon Westow mysteries

THE HANGING PSALM
THE HOCUS GIRL

TO THE DARK

Chris Nickson

This first world edition published 2020
in Great Britain and 2021 in the USA by
SEVERN HOUSE PUBLISHERS LTD of
Eardley House, 4 Uxbridge Street, London W8 7SY.
Trade paperback edition first published
in Great Britain and the USA 2021 by
SEVERN HOUSE PUBLISHERS LTD.

British Library Cataloguing in Publication Data
A CIP catalogue record for this title is available from the British Library.

ISBN-13: 978-0-7278-9245-4 (cased)
ISBN-13: 978-1-78029-752-1 (trade paper)
ISBN-13: 978-1-4483-0490-5 (e-book)

All Severn House titles are printed on acid-free paper.

Severn House Publishers support the Forest Stewardship Council™ [FSC™],
the leading international forest certification organisation.
All our titles that are printed on FSC certified paper carry the FSC logo.

Typeset by Palimpsest Book Production Ltd.,
Falkirk, Stirlingshire, Scotland.
Printed and bound in Great Britain by
TJ Books Limited, Padstow, Cornwall.

‘At a mile distant from the town we came under a vast dingy canopy formed by the impure exhalation of a hundred furnaces. It sits on the town like an everlasting incubus, shutting out the light of heaven and the breath of summer. I pity the poor denizens. London is a joke to it. Our inn was consistent with its locality; one doesn’t look for a clean floor in a colliery or a decent hotel in Leeds.’

Barclay Fox’s Journal, 1837

Leeds, November 1822

She sensed him there, behind her in the fog. Jane reached into the pocket of her skirt and took hold of the knife.

From Briggate to Wood Street, then all the turnings and twists through to Vicar Lane, he followed. Growing bolder and closer all the time.

She smiled. Good.

She could run; she knew that. Run so he wouldn't be able to follow. The urge for safety filled her chest, to vanish through the cramped courts and yards.

But she didn't. Jane wanted him to find her. She tugged her cloak closer to her body and stopped, listening.

A small cough. No more than five yards away now. The scuff of a heel on the cobbles. Four yards. Then three.

Jane took a breath and turned.

'Well, well, well.' He took two paces forward. A swagger in his step once he could see her face, his voice like oil. 'Looks like it's just you and me out in this, don't it?' He pulled something from his pocket. A silver sixpenny piece. 'See that? It's yours if you're a good lass.'

Jane stared at him.

'They all like it,' he said. 'Talk about Big Tom for days afterwards, they do.'

The coin danced across his knuckles, twirling from one finger to the next and next, then back again. A trick to mesmerize and distract the gaze.

This was the man she'd been told about. Always the same. She watched his free arm start to move, edging towards the blade in his belt.

One flash of her knife, over before he realized. The empty tinkling of the coin as it landed on the cobbles. He stared at his hand in horror. He only had two fingers left.

'That's for Bessie Colbert,' she said.

Another flick and the blood began to run down his cheek. She leaned close and turned his head, waiting until he was looking into her eyes. 'That's what rapists get. If I ever see you again, I'll kill you.'

She disappeared into the fog. He began to howl.

ONE

Leeds, February 1823

'No, no.' Alderman Ferguson shook his head as he walked, pushing his walking stick down into the packed snow with each step. He started to slip and grabbed the sleeve of Simon Westow's greatcoat to keep his balance. 'Damned weather. I wish it would all melt.'

'It's already started,' Simon said. 'It'll be gone soon enough.'

The thaw had begun that morning. He could hear the slow drip of water from the eaves of buildings, leaving pock marks like smallpox scars in the snow below. After two weeks of being snowed in, things were finally changing. The roads had stayed open, the coaches still travelling between towns, but there had been plenty of accidents. Simon had heard of three horses breaking legs and having to be killed; a good coach horse was valuable property. The skies hung low and grey, but the air was warming. The worst was definitely over.

In Leeds, the snow had fallen a dirty grey colour. The factory smoke and soot that filled the air tainted it before it even reached the ground. Drifts that piled against buildings had a thin black crust, and every path remained treacherous; Simon was grateful for the hobnails on the soles of his boots.

'Maybe it is,' Ferguson grumbled. 'Can't come soon enough for me.' He pulled the top hat down on his head and tried to burrow deeper into his coat. Tight trousers emphasized his spindly old man's legs as he walked up Briggate, away from the Moot Hall. 'I'm ready for spring and some warmth. Aren't you?'

'Always,' Simon agreed. The only crimes since the snow had begun to fall were men stealing food or fuel to feed their families. Nothing there to bring any income to a thief-taker. He was ready to be busy and earning again. Still, he was better off than most; he had money in the bank. He'd enjoyed a good start to the year.

Sir Matthew Fullbrook had asked him to recover all the items stolen from his house while the family had been away over Christmas and New Year. When they returned, most of the family silver was missing.

It took Simon three days to track down the thief, hiding among the poor and desperate in one of the courts off Kirkgate. Laurence Poole. Simon and his assistant, Jane, had cornered him in his room at the top of a tumbledown house. The only way out was through the window, jumping twenty feet or more to the flagstones, and Poole wasn't ready to die yet.

They found everything except a single spoon that Poole had sold to keep himself alive. When Simon returned it, he'd noticed the mix of gratitude and relief on Fullbrook's face. The set was valuable, it was worth a fortune; far more than that, it was his history. An heirloom that had been in the family for generations. Fullbrook settled the bill promptly, in full, with no quibble. He chose not to prosecute, and Poole walked free.

They crossed the Head Row, Ferguson moving cautiously. It was curious how bad weather could age people, Simon thought. Back in the autumn, the man beside him had been striding out, hale and full of life. Now he was frail and old. Cautious and fearful of broken bones that might never set properly.

They parted by George Mudie's print shop. The alderman still had to walk along North Street to his house near the Harrogate Road in Sheepscar. He'd manage, and in a few days the warmer weather would revive him. By spring he'd seem ten years younger again.

Mudie was fitting type into a block. His fingers moved deftly, eyes flickering to acknowledge Simon before returning to his task. The air was heavy with the smell of ink.

'I want to get this set and printed today. Out on the streets first thing tomorrow. A new ballad about a coach disaster on the turnpike where a brave young man saves some of the passengers and wins the heart of a girl.'

Simon laughed. 'And when did this tragedy happen?'

He shrugged. 'Yesterday. Last week. Never. Who cares? It's got death and romance. That's what people want. Once a few of the patterers begin singing it, it should sell.'

'A racket.'

Mudie shrugged once more. 'Show me something in this life that isn't. We're all just trying to make a living.'

He finished and stood straight, pressing his hands into the small of his back, then pushed a pair of spectacles up his nose.

'What brings you here, Simon? Boredom?'

'Waiting for the snow to melt. As soon as that happens, we'll have more crime.' He smiled. 'After all, we're all just trying to make a living.'

Mudie snorted. 'Some enjoy a better one than others.'

It was true enough. Being a thief-taker could pay well, better than he'd ever imagined when he began. But in those days he knew nothing. He was still a youth, barely older than the boy who'd walked out of the workhouse at thirteen to find his own life. All he had was his size and a quick brain. They'd both served him well over the years, the foundation of everything he did. In the early days, he and his wife Rosie had worked together. Then she had their twin boys, Richard and Amos, and stopped taking risks. Most of the time.

Now he had Jane to help. When she first came to him, she'd been a feral girl, living on the streets. Someone who possessed the rare gift to follow without being seen, who could vanish in plain sight. But she was a girl who kept the world at a distance. She built walls around her thoughts and cut herself off. For two years she'd lived with him and Rosie, sharing their meals and sleeping in their attic, but they'd still hardly known her. Since the autumn she'd made her home with an old woman, Catherine Shields, and for the first time, she seemed content.

George was right. He was bored. Two weeks without a stroke of work had left him restless and searching for ways to fill his days. He'd walked around town. He'd taken his sons out sledging in Holbeck and Beeston. Snowball fights on the little scraps of tenter ground that remained as the new factories ate up the land. But they had their tutor each morning.

Simon read the *Mercury* and the *Intelligencer* eagerly, hoping someone had put in an advertisement offering a reward for the return of lost goods. But there was nothing, and he was cast back on his own devices. He didn't read books, he didn't play chess or backgammon. He had nothing but work and his family to fill his life. Twice this week Rosie had chased him out of the kitchen for disturbing her while she was busy.

'You're pacing,' Mudie told him. 'And you're bothering me.'

It was easier to leave. As Simon strolled back down Briggate, he jammed his hands deep in the pockets of his greatcoat and stared at the faces he passed. Some hopeful, most downcast, intent on simply surviving. A man coughed deep and spat to clear his lungs. The air was foul. It had been for years, ever since the factories started spewing their smoke. But the factories made money and plenty of it, at least for a few. For many of the others they meant jobs, the cash each week to keep body and soul together. And every week more and more people arrived in Leeds to seek work. It was as if they truly believed the streets were paved with gold.

But the only thing the cobbles here held was a struggle.

'People are going over to Flay Crow Mill.'

He hadn't seen Jane arrive. But there she was, at his side, matching his pace as he walked. Since winter began she'd taken to wearing an old cloak of faded green wool. With the hood pulled up, no one ever noticed her.

'What's going on there?'

'I don't know.'

Something, Simon thought. It had to be something. And that was better than nothing.

The mill stood down by the bend in the river, out on Cynder Island. It had been there for generations, maybe even centuries, with its hammers for pounding and fulling good Leeds cloth. No one knew how it had come by the name, but the building had been empty and gradually sinking into ruin for a long time. The wooden scoops of the water wheel that powered it had rotted away to nothing. Beyond the shell of the mill the river lapped against the shore, cold and dark.

A crowd had gathered, twenty or thirty people. The usual gaggle of boys and girls, hoping for something gruesome, and men and women with nothing else to fill their days. Simon pushed his way to the front, squeezing into the gaps between people. Jane stayed close to the back, listening for gossip and news.

The best he could make out, melting snow had revealed the body. He could see a pair of trousers and some leather boots. The rest was still covered. Simon held his breath as the coroner brushed slush away from the corpse's face.

For a moment, Simon couldn't believe what was in front of him.

He knew this man with his pale skin and serene expression. He'd last seen him a few weeks ago, not long before the snow arrived. Laurence Poole hadn't been so peaceful then. He'd begged and tried to fight to hold on to his loot from the Fullbrook robbery. By the time Simon left, the man was close to tears of desperation.

He turned away. He didn't need to see more. There was no obvious sign of injury. No bloodstains on the man's coat. Poole hadn't been dressed for bitter weather: just an old, battered wool jacket with swallow tails, plain waistcoat, linen shirt and fawn trousers. The same things he'd worn when Simon found him in his room. No greatcoat. No hat, either.

There wasn't going to be anything worthwhile here. He'd need to look elsewhere for any idea of what had happened. Simon stalked past Jane, letting her hurry to keep up with him. People glanced at him then quickly looked away again. Very likely he had a face like thunder. He really didn't care.

'Who was it?' Jane asked. 'No one mentioned a name.'

'Poole.'

She stayed silent for a few seconds. 'Has someone murdered him?'

'Couldn't tell,' Simon answered. 'I'm sure we'll hear later. But I doubt he wandered out there for pleasure.' Not without a heavy coat to keep himself warm. 'I want to take a look at his room.'

'I saw one of the constable's men in the crowd. He'll be passing the word. That means they'll be coming soon.'

'Then we'd best be quick.'

For two or three years after it was built, Welling Court had been a good address. Set back from Kirkgate up a small flight of stone steps, it had grown up around a courtyard. But those bright days had ended very quickly. Now it was a last refuge for people who had nothing. There was no sun, no warmth, so little hope in the place. The snow had drifted into the corners of the courtyard, thick and dirty. An air of desolation hung over it all.

The room he wanted was in the attic. Simon dashed up the stairs, pulling out his knife as he ran. Jane hurried behind him. The door was locked, but the wood hung so loose in the frame it only took a second to prise it open.

The glass had gone in one of the windows. An old sheet hung in its place, but it couldn't keep out the pinching cold. A bare wooden floor, thick with splinters. One wall had been turned brown by damp leaching through the plaster. Simon touched it and it crumbled under his fingers.

They searched hurriedly, all too aware that the constable might be on his way. They needed to be out of sight well before that happened. If anyone found them here, there would be too many awkward questions.

Two minutes was all they needed. Poole had owned a change of linen and some spare socks. That, along with the greatcoat – pockets empty – and the ancient top hat on a hook behind the door, was all. Except for the notebook and pencil he'd pushed under the bed as if he'd wanted to keep them hidden from sight. Simon scooped them up and thrust them into his coat pocket. A final sweep around the room. Nothing more here; he was certain of it.

They were out of the room and gone without being spotted. A final glance over his shoulder as they rushed down the steps. No sign of any curious faces peering through the windows of Welling Court.

They waited near the parish church, leaning against the wall and eating hot food from Kate the pie-seller.

'There.' Jane nodded towards the three men who turned from Harper Street and marched down the road. Williams, the constable, preening himself in every shop window they passed, and two of his men behind.

Simon sucked the last of the pastry from his fingers and stood. 'We might as well go home and see what Poole wrote in his notebook.'

'Why?' Jane asked. 'It's not our business.'

'I know,' he agreed. 'But aren't you curious?'

She shook her head. 'There's no money in it.'

'The last snow came down less than a fortnight ago. He was underneath it. That means Poole had been buried for a while,' Simon said. 'True?'

'Yes.'

'Soon enough, people will remember that we found him and took back everything he stole from Fullbrook. Once that happens, Constable Williams is going to come and ask questions. I want to make sure I'm prepared.'

Williams hated him; he'd love to bring some kind of charge and throw Simon to the lawyers.

'There's no need for you to be involved,' Simon said. 'He won't even think of you – you know what he's like.'

'I was there when we took everything from Poole.'

'We'll keep that quiet. If I end up needing help, you and Rosie will be out here to do the work.' He grinned. 'You know you'll be able to run rings around Williams and the law.' His face sobered again. 'For now, let's do ourselves a favour and find the murderer. If we manage that, we won't need to worry.'

And there was no paying work. This was a chance to exercise his skill and keep himself safe.

'All right,' Jane said after a moment. But he could see the doubt and reluctance on her face.

It only took a few minutes to reach his house on Swinegate. Inside, he could hear the drone of the tutor as he taught the boys in the parlour. Rosie was sitting at the kitchen table, ledgers open in front of her, pen in her hand as she checked their accounts. Her eyes grew more and more concerned when he told her about Poole's body.

'How long before Williams comes calling, do you think?'

Simon shrugged. 'Hours, maybe. Tomorrow at the very latest.'

The man would relish putting the chains on his wrists and dragging him away. He'd make it into a spectacle. The thief-taker arrested. Simon Westow a murderer. There would be plenty who'd gladly believe it. And if a jury was convinced . . . he caught himself before his thoughts could stray in that direction. It wouldn't do a damned bit of good.

'This was in his room.' Simon gave her the notebook. 'Maybe there'll be something useful in it.'

Rosie grabbed at it and began to leaf through the pages.

'There's a fair bit in here,' she said as she squinted at the writing. 'These could be names and dates, I suppose.' She stared more closely before looking up, concern on her face. 'Half of these don't make sense. They look like they're written in some kind of cipher.'

Why would Poole have a notebook in code? Simon wondered. How would he even learn something like that? What secrets was he keeping hidden?

'What are the last things he wrote?'

Deftly, her fingers traced the words. 'The last thing I can make out is this: *Harker, silver*. There's no date on it.'

They both knew that name. Charlie Harker was the best-known fence in Leeds. A man with enough contacts around England to sell on almost anything. If Simon hadn't found Poole in time, all Fullbrook's silver would probably have been on its way to different parts of the kingdom and ports across Europe. Poole and Harker had probably been haggling over the price.

But Simon knew something else about Harker. He'd killed men who crossed him. Money had moved from hand to hand and the murders had never made it to court. Evidence had been changed. Witnesses suddenly decided to move away from Leeds. But the truth remained. And if such an important deal had fallen through, he could easily have murdered Poole and enjoyed it.

'At least we have somewhere to begin,' Simon said. He looked at Jane. 'I need to make some preparations here. I want you to follow Harker. Stay as close as a shadow. Once you can get him somewhere he daren't lie, ask him about Poole.'

'He'll never admit to anything,' Rosie said. 'If he did, he might as well march himself to the scaffold.'

'I know that,' Simon agreed. 'But there'll be plenty of lies in whatever he says.' He nodded at Jane. 'You'll be able to trip him up.'

'What if he's not the killer?' Her voice was soft, as if she was discovering the question. 'It could be someone else.'

Maybe so, he thought. But Harker made sense. It was obvious, it *felt* right. Still, he'd been in this business long enough to know not to ignore any possibility.

'If it isn't him, we need to catch the murderer soon. Before Williams comes pounding on the door.'

He looked out of the window. Light glistened on the remaining ice and snow. Maybe not having any real work waiting would be a blessing, after all. No distractions.

Simon stood and watched as Jane left. She pulled up the hood of her cloak and moved into the stream of people moving along Swinegate. Thirty seconds and she was gone, vanished in the crowd.

The tutor's voice droned on in the parlour. As he returned to the kitchen, Rosie said, 'What are we going to do?'

'Win,' he told her, and hoped it was true.

TWO

Jane followed the streets without thinking. Along Call Lane and Kirkgate, going past the parish church. Over Timble Bridge with its clamour of businesses competing for trade, then Marsh Lane towards the new houses spreading everywhere.

Before she reached them, she turned down a short, crooked little road where the buildings were old and ill cared-for. Tiny windows of rotting wood, the mortar flaking between the bricks. Paradise, that was the street's name. Maybe it had seemed that way once. Now the name was a grim, taunting joke for a place like this.

Harker lived close to the end. He had a small, walled garden and a back gate that let on to a ginnel. There was no movement behind the glass in the windows, but smoke rose from the chimney. Someone was at home.

Jane found a small niche between buildings. Out of sight and away from the breeze, she could watch the front door and the entrance to the ginnel. Harker wouldn't be able to slip in or out without her seeing him. She'd wait here as long as needed. Simon's freedom might depend on it.

Harker would never even know she was there until her knife was at his throat. When she did that, she'd make absolutely certain he gave her every scrap of the truth. A little pain was a good way to stop a man from lying. If the constable arrested Simon, she'd need evidence that was solid and real to free him. She'd give them a proper murderer in his place.

But if Harker wasn't behind the killing . . .

Time passed. She didn't see anyone inside the house. Her thoughts began to drift.

For a week Jane had had the nagging feeling that someone was following her. Not constantly – she'd only sensed it on four occasions. Once during the day, three times after dark. She knew it wasn't her imagination; the feeling was too clear, too sharp. But she hadn't been able to spot a soul. That worried her; it meant he was good. She ran her fingertips over the scars on her forearm. A rising ladder of lines, the places where she'd cut herself. Her catalogue of failures, the punishments she inflicted.

She eased the knife out of her pocket and felt the smoothness of the handle against her palm. It was comforting. Every night she honed the blade, sitting by the fire at Mrs Shields's house and running it over the whetstone until the edge was so sharp it could almost cut the air.

It was a curious thing: although she hadn't been able to spot whoever was behind her, this time she'd felt no need to hurt herself for it. No desire to trace the blade over her skin and see the blood trickle. Her life had changed.

Jane pressed back against the wall as she heard someone dashing down the street. A skinny boy, clattering along in a pair of clogs too big for his feet and running like the devil was after him.

She'd seen him before, part of a group that slept in the remains of a building near Fearn's Island. He looked out of breath as he hammered his small fist on Harker's door. The man answered, listened to the message, then placed a coin in the boy's hand.

The lad walked away, looking content with himself. From the corner of her eye, Jane saw movement. Harker was going from room to room, closing the shutters on the windows.

Was he leaving? Or did he simply want people to believe he wasn't there? She waited, turning the gold ring on her finger. A twist for luck. It was the only thing of value that she carried, a gift from Mrs Shields to keep her safe. Five minutes, ten, then the single chime as the church bell marked the quarter hour.

She'd just decided that Harker was shutting himself away when he came out of the ginnel, carrying a small leather valise and glancing around before scurrying off towards Timble Bridge and into Leeds. She followed, just far enough away not to be spotted, but close enough to smell the fear oozing from his pores. He turned on to Briggate, caught among the people on the pavement and the coaches and carts on the road. Harker stopped outside the Bull and Mouth, studying the times of the coaches due to leave that day, then pulled out a pocket watch and snapped open the lid. He gave a half-smile that froze on his face as he felt the point of the knife against his spine.

'Thinking about a journey?'

* * *

Simon worked steadily with Rosie, picking out the important papers and hiding them away in the secret drawer in the staircase. When Constable Williams arrived, he'd order his men to search the house. But they'd never find this little cubbyhole, so cleverly hidden away. And there was enough money in there to tide Rosie and the boys over for a month.

'What now?' she asked after everything was done.

'We wait for him to come.'

That was the hardest part. He was a man who was used to *doing*, not waiting. Every muscle in his body was tense. He ached. The expectation ate away at him. The voice of the tutor in the parlour halted, then came the rush of his sons as they dragged the door open and ran through to the kitchen. Lessons over.

They were too big to pick up now. He squatted and drew them close, smelling the scent of their hair and skin. Something to remember when he was in gaol. The cells under the Moot Hall were old and bitterly cold. The stones would be running with damp from the melting snow, puddles of it on the floor. But with a little money to the gaoler, comforts could come in. Food from an inn, extra blankets. He was healthy. He'd survive.

Rosie spooned stew into the bowls. The boys ate hungrily, answering her questions about everything they'd learned that morning. Simon sat and thought, not even pretending to eat, watching them. He felt distant, removed, as if Williams had already dragged him away.

The meal ended, and Rosie sent the boys up to their room to do the work their tutor had set. He didn't stir as she took the food away.

She sat by him, holding his hand. Simon rested his head against her shoulder.

He was thinking of the minutes passing, the tick of the longclock in the hall. It surprised him. He had no high regard for the constable, but he'd expected him to be knocking on the door before now.

Another half hour, and he began to believe the man wasn't coming after all. He didn't understand it. It was common knowledge he'd retrieved those stolen items from Poole. Anyone with a grain of sense would have come to ask questions. And Williams had no love for him. Simon had shown him up a few times. Where was he?

He stood and began to pace, heart racing at every sound outside. And then, he stopped. A knock at the door. But not the thick hammering he'd expected. This was tentative. Smaller. He turned to Rosie. She was already on her feet, vanishing into the hall.

A few muffled words, then he heard the door close again.

'It was a boy,' she said with a frown. 'He has a message from Jane. Come to Paradise.' She gave him a quizzical look. 'Does that make sense to you?'

Simon smiled, relieved. Something to break the spell of worry. 'Yes, it does. Perfectly.'

To the devil with Williams. The man could chase around Leeds after him if he wanted Simon that badly. He took his greatcoat from the peg and put the old beaver hat on his head.

'I'll be in Paradise.'

The door to the house hung ajar. Simon pushed it wide, taking out his knife and gazing around as he entered. A few cautious steps, then he heard noise from the kitchen.

Very softly, he crept through the hall, edging the door open with the tip of his blade. Harker was seated on one of the chairs. His face gleamed with sweat. A small valise sat on the floor at his side. And behind him, Jane, the flat of her knife caressing the back of his neck. She stepped away as Simon entered and Harker seemed to deflate, his body withering after the effort of keeping straight.

'Thank God you're here. She might have killed me.'

Simon ignored his words. 'I see you're packed, Mr Harker. Were you thinking of leaving us?'

'I found him at the Bull and Mouth looking at coach times,' Jane said. 'A boy came here and told him something. A few minutes later he left, trying to make sure nobody saw him.'

'Interesting.' Simon glanced around the room. 'What made you decide to go in such a hurry? It couldn't have anything to do with Laurence Poole, could it?'

'Who?' Harker asked. The lie flared across his face. Simon took a pace closer and the man flinched. 'Poole. No.' He shook his head. 'Is he dead?'

Simon sighed. 'You see, Charlie, the more you carry on like this, the more I think that you had something to do with his death.

I'm sure the constable would like a few words with you about it, too.' He smiled. 'After we've finished here, of course. Now, why don't we pass by all the lies and you tell me why you were really running from Leeds.'

A long heartbeat. Two of them. 'I'm scared. Someone killed Laurence.'

'I already know that.' Simon could feel his patience starting to turn threadbare. 'I saw his body. Why would that scare you?'

'Because they might come for me next.'

Simon watched as Jane moved. She came close, whispered in his ear. He nodded, then she was gone. He heard the latch click as she closed the front door behind her.

'Just the two of us now, Charlie. Time to be honest with me.'

Harker seemed a little more at ease. He raised a hand and rubbed his neck.

'She's cold, that girl of yours.'

'She's killed better men than you. Now, are you going to tell me the truth? Who might come for you next?'

'The men who murdered Laurence.'

Simon's voice grew hard. 'I want some names, Charlie. All you're giving me is fog.'

Harker shook his head. 'I don't know what they're called. A pair of cavalry officers from the barracks out in Sheepscar. You know the type. Young, plenty of money.'

The barracks? Cavalrymen? Involved in thefts? This was new. He tried to hide his astonishment.

'What about them?' Simon asked.

'They met Laurence when he was drunk, and they said he could make money by robbing some of the other officers. Ones who had lodgings outside the barracks. They'd tell him when the men would be gone. He'd only ever steal small things and split the money with them. They thought it was a game, great fun.'

'And you fenced the items.'

He nodded. 'They came here with Laurence once. After that they'd turn up on their own, bring me little things they'd filched at the garrison.'

'Why didn't you turn them away?'

The light in Harker's eyes changed and the colour left his cheeks. 'Because they said they'd kill me if I tried that. They were serious.'

With his history, he'd know if they meant it. And if they scared him, they were dangerous men.

'And you think they killed Laurence?'

'I *know* they did. He told them he wanted to stop. That last time, after you found him with all the silver, he knew he'd come close to ending up in court. He's like everyone else, he doesn't want to dangle from a noose or spend the rest of his life in Australia.'

'When did he tell them this?'

'A bit more than two weeks ago. A few days before we had that last heavy snowfall. The two of them said it was fine. He believed it was all over. The next day someone tried to kill him. After that, I didn't see him anywhere. It made me worry.'

'How do you know all this, Charlie?'

Harker breathed deep. 'Laurence came and told me what they'd done, didn't he? I thought he was making it up at first. He could be like that at times. Loved to tell a tale. But once that lad came and told me they'd found his body, I thought I'd do well to get out of Leeds.' He reached down and patted the bag. 'Save my skin.'

'Why would a boy turn up with news like that?'

'I pay him.' A sly smile crossed his face. 'Always better to have a warning, isn't it?'

'Describe the officers,' Simon said.

One was an ensign, the other a lieutenant. Both in their thirties. Sleek and glossy, with dark hair, moustaches, and the attitude that money bred into some men. There were a dozen or more just like them in any regiment; Simon knew the type. They were the second or third sons in a family. Handed a commission and an allowance to keep them occupied and out of the way.

'Any marks or scars?'

'None that I ever saw.' Harker was growing fretful again. 'Can I go? There's a coach to York at half past five. If I hurry, I can catch it.'

'Leave.' He stood aside, watching Harker pick up the case and dash out. Moving as if his life depended on it. And maybe it did. He was telling the truth, that much was certain. There was more than fear behind his words; he was filled with terror.

A pair of army officers. By definition that made them gentlemen.

They sounded old enough to have served through the French wars that ended eight years before. If so, they'd have seen plenty of fighting. They'd have killed people. Murdering Laurence Poole might well have come naturally to them.

But Simon had no names to take to the commander of the garrison. Not a scrap of evidence. Just the word of a criminal who was hurrying out of the town to try and save his own skin. Who was going to believe a man like that?

Certainly not Constable Williams.

Jane knew she wouldn't find the boy until darkness fell and he made his way back to the old building by Fearn's Island. That was a still few hours away. She drifted through Leeds, crunching through odd remnants of dirty snow and listening to the gossip.

People were talking about Poole. Death was too common to start a conversation, but murder always had the power to set tongues wagging. Simon's name came up a time or two. That was inevitable. Plenty of folk remembered him retrieving Fullbrook's property from the man. They connected him to it.

But no one seemed to have any fresh ideas. Just idle chatter as they passed a few hours in the beer shops. Nothing to set her looking elsewhere.

Half the building had been torn down. Piles of bricks and old timber littered the ground. Enough remained to offer some kind of shelter. The last part of a roof hung raggedly over one corner of the walls. A small fire burned, highlighting the silhouettes.

Jane kept to the shadows, treading carefully as she approached. There were about twenty of them gathered round the blaze. One or two were very young, no more than four or five years old, their eyes alive with fear. They stayed huddled together for warmth and safety. The others were a little older. They'd survived on the streets long enough to have developed a shell. But it was all bravado. She knew that, she'd learned by spending five years out here herself. She'd lived. Half of those in this place wouldn't last long.

Firelight flickered and picked out the boy's face. Jane worked her way around, keeping out of sight until she was close enough to sit by him. His head turned sharply as she settled and he began to rise until he felt the ha'penny she placed in his hand.

'Some questions,' she whispered. He nodded and stood. Before she could move, he started to run. Just a few yards, then he tumbled on to his face. By the time Jane reached him, the children around the fire had scattered like birds. Into the night for safety. Except for one girl. She stood over the boy, staring at him as he whimpered.

'You're safe. I don't want to hurt you,' Jane told him. 'Just questions, like I said.'

'Got to watch him,' the girl said. 'He's sly and he's fast. I knew he'd run as soon as I saw you get close. I made sure he couldn't get far.'

Clever and observant. A useful combination.

'Thank you.' Jane took hold of the boy's arm and lifted him until he was sitting on the cold concrete of the floor. The flames picked out a fresh cut on his cheek and a scrape on his knee. Nothing serious.

'You went to see a man on Paradise today.'

He nodded, bobbing his head quickly and rubbing his ankle.

'Why did you do that?'

'He pays me to bring him news. Anything interesting. A farthing a time.'

It would keep him fed for a day.

'How long have you been doing that?'

'Almost two weeks?' The boy shrugged. 'Something like that.'

'How many times have you been to see him?'

He looked up, his eyes wide and earnest. 'Three times before today. Then I heard about that man at Flay Crow Mill.'

Jane added two pennies to the coin that was already clutched in his fist. He looked at her once more, then jumped to his feet and ran off.

'You work with the thief-taker, don't you?' the girl said.

'That's right.' She was surprised. It was strange enough that a child should have heard of Simon. Even more that the girl would recognize her. 'What's your name?'

'Martha.' She looked to be around eight or nine years old, almost too thin and hungry for this world, a small sack of flesh sewed tight over bones. Pale, dirty hair that hung long and curly around her face. A dress that was too short, only reaching halfway down her calves. Threadbare stockings and her shoes were a ruin of leather.

'You did well.' Jane took two pennies from her pocket and passed them over. She had money, plenty of it; more than she could ever spend. Simon always paid her half his fee and business was usually good.

'I can help you again,' the girl offered. She tried to sound as if the idea had just come to her. But Jane could hear the longing under it all and hid her smile.

'Find me tomorrow if you know anything.' That was as close to a promise as she was willing to give.

Out in the night, Jane breathed. The air was heavy, leaving a bitter taste on her tongue as she began to walk. Up Briggate, Commercial Street, Lands Lane, towards home. Suddenly she sensed it again. Someone was behind her. She couldn't hear any footsteps. But she was certain it was there. He. A man. It had to be a man.

She needed somewhere to hide.

THREE

Simon paused on Swinegate, gazing at the front of his house, wondering if Williams had come calling while he was gone. He only stopped for a second, then he was moving again, taking a deep breath as he grabbed the door handle and entered. Rosie was in the kitchen, still working on Poole's notebook. Richard and Amos were shouting as they played with a ball in the yard.

'No constable yet?' he asked. He'd half-expected to find the man sitting at the table and waiting to arrest him.

'Haven't seen hide nor hair,' Rosie said. 'Nobody's knocked on the door.' She sighed. 'Maybe he won't come.'

Maybe . . . dear Christ, he wanted to believe that. But the connection between Poole and himself was there, out in the open, obvious. Even someone as stupid as Williams had to be able to see it. So why hadn't he been here yet?

He nodded at the small book. 'Have you found anything?'

She shook her head. 'Only bits and pieces. It's code, Simon, I don't know anything about that.'

The minutes passed, the silence broken only by the ticking of the longclock in the hall and the soft scratch of her pen.

'Stop pacing,' she told him finally. 'I've told you before; it doesn't help and it's distracting. If you want something to do, go and play with the boys. Take them somewhere and wear them out so I can finish this in peace.'

Good advice. Anything to stop him thinking and fretting. Down on the scraps of green grass by the river, they ran him ragged. Back and forth for almost an hour until he could scarcely catch his breath. Finally, he spread his coattails and sat on the cold, wet ground. He was exhausted, and happy to see the twins red-cheeked and full of joy. And he hadn't thought about Williams or Poole once.

The boys continued to dash around. He watched them, smiling to himself at the freedom they had. Freedom he'd been able to give them. At their age his home was in the workhouse, every daylight hour and more spent working in the mill. Beaten, abused, feeling like he was going to be trapped there for the rest of his life and wanting to die so it would be over.

But it ended. He closed that chapter when he walked out and chose to live his own life. He'd made sure Amos and Richard would never experience anything like that.

'Come on, boys,' he called eventually and stood. 'Time to go home.'

Still no visit from Williams or his men. Nobody watching the house. But he wasn't about to let himself feel secure. The man could be waiting, ready to bring the hammer down hard.

Simon watched his family eat. He moved the food around on his plate, but barely managed more than a few bites. It tasted of smoke and ashes. Nobody's fault. Just his imagination, but it stopped him swallowing.

'I have to go out,' he said after a few minutes. He couldn't sit here any longer, doing nothing, just waiting. Rosie nodded. She understood.

Outside, the evening air was chilly, still rank with the day's stink. The snow continued to melt and pavements glistened with wetness. Off in the distance, someone coughed. Simon buttoned up his greatcoat and tapped the hat down on to his head.

Barnabas Wade was exactly where he'd expected to find him,

in a corner of the bar at the Rose and Crown on Briggate. He kept looking round, sharp-eyed, waiting for the next coach, the next group of travellers to be fleeced by the opportunity to own shares cheaply.

He scraped a living with guile and a glib tongue, skirting the law but never quite breaking it. His contracts were always solid and legal and carefully written in his favour. Wade had been a lawyer until he was disbarred. He knew exactly which words on paper stood firm as iron.

'Business good?' Simon asked.

'If it was, I wouldn't be ready to stay here all night.' He jingled a few coins in his pocket. Oil lamps flickered in the sconces. The chimney breast was decorated with layer upon layer of old broadside ballads pasted over the stone. 'Shouldn't you be at home yourself?'

'Questions to ask.' He summoned the potboy and ordered a brandy for Barnabas.

'Your good health,' Wade said as he raised the glass in a toast. 'What can I do for you, Simon?'

'What do you know about Laurence Poole and Charlie Harker?'

'I know Poole's dead. You do, too. Or I pity you if you don't. I imagine most everyone in Leeds must know it by now.'

'I've heard.'

'Harker . . .' He shook his head. 'I never had any dealings with him. He handles stolen goods, so he knows every thief in town. More your territory than mine, Simon.'

'Any word on him leaving Leeds?'

'Nothing that I've heard.' Wade cocked his head. 'Why are you so interested in him?'

Simon smiled. 'Just a rumour or two. How about our military friends up at the garrison?'

Wade frowned. 'What is this, Simon? What's going on? Something to do with Poole's death? I was told today it was murder.'

'Who said that?' he asked sharply. 'How did it happen?'

The man shrugged. 'I don't know. A few people were talking about it. He was strangled. A cord round his neck.'

Now he knew the cause. That was one of the worst ways to go.

'Who—' Wade began, but Simon shook his head. He wasn't

about to say anything more. All he'd wanted was to discover how far the news and gossip had travelled. Wade always seemed to know the first inklings of anything.

He stood, made his farewells, and disappeared into the night. A coach pulled out of the Old King's Arms and started up the street, the driver cracking the whip like he was being chased by every hound in hell.

Simon made the round of the inns and beer shops. He found a few people willing to talk. Elsewhere, he stood silently and listened as conversation flowed around him. Laurence Poole was on everyone's lips – the news was still fresh enough to tantalize. More theories than he could ever have imagined. One or two mentioned Harker. Someone believed he'd seen him boarding a coach for Bristol. But nobody said anything about officers from the garrison.

They might as well have been ghosts. Shadows.

But Simon knew they were real. He'd heard the fear in Charlie Harker's voice. He'd seen Poole's body. And there wasn't a single damned thing he could do about it for now.

He could hardly march up to the barracks and make an accusation. The colonel would laugh and turn him away. And he wanted to stay as clear of the constable as possible.

That brought the other big question: why hadn't Williams come to arrest him for murder yet? Did he know something? Was there some clue that Simon and Jane had missed in that room on Welling Court? Going over it again in his mind, he didn't believe it, but they'd been in a rush – maybe there was some small thing they hadn't spotted.

By the time he'd walked down to the bottom of Briggate, hearing the soft lapping of the river ahead of him as it sighed around the bridge palings, he didn't know what to do. If Williams wasn't pursuing him, there was no reason to do anything at all. Poole's death, Harker leaving Leeds. None of it had anything to do with him. Jane had been right about that. It wasn't going to make them any money.

As Simon turned the corner on to Swinegate, he stopped, keeping himself deep in the darkness. A faint figure, a thicker black among the deep blues and greys of the night. Someone was watching his house.

It was child's play to come up behind him. Simon knew every

inch of the ground around here. He could have walked it blindfold. Through the ginnels and the tight squeeze between passageways.

The man wasn't expecting the tip of a knife to prick his neck. He started to turn his head, then stopped as the point dug a little deeper.

Jane pushed back in the shadow of a low arch. She had the knife in her hand, held down against her thigh and ready to strike. She held her breath, listening closely for the smallest noise.

There it was, and once again. She stiffened, judging the distance. Very close, but he was moving cautiously. She still couldn't see him, but she could smell the sour odour of his breath and shrank back against the stone.

Then he was past. Still slow, still hunting. She waited until he'd taken a couple of paces and slid out into the passage. The only light was a sliver from a window above. Just enough to make out the shape ahead of her. A twist of the gold ring on her finger for luck, for safety, and she was ready.

As she raised her knife, he turned and drew in a breath as he saw her. Just as she brought her blade down, he raised a hand to defend himself. The knife sliced through his coat and shirt as if they weren't there. Jane felt it cut deep into his flesh.

Big Tom. He'd come back for his revenge. Except that now he was trying to stifle his screaming, to stop the pain that was searing through his body. He still had hold of his knife, but it was useless in his wounded hand. She batted it out of his fingers and moved closer. One more cut would finish this.

Fear and agony contorted his face around the puckered scar her blade had made on his face. He bellowed and barged forward. A blind panic of fear. Tom was larger than her, much heavier. As he flailed past, he knocked her hard into the wall, banging her head and stealing the air from her lungs. She could hear his boots on the flagstones as he vanished down Lands Lane.

Jane didn't try to follow. He had too much of a start on her. She stood, trying to catch her breath, then bent down to pick up his knife. A curved blade, the edge honed to a deadly sharpness. She weighed it in her hand. It was light, it had a good balance. A fine weapon to pass on to that girl. Give her something to remember.

And something useful. She'd see her soon enough, she was sure of that. Martha would come searching for her once it was light.

As she walked down the street, Jane heard laughter and voices in the Green Dragon, but by the time she slipped into the small yard where Catherine Shields had her house, all the sounds seemed muted. Far away. In this place she felt safe, as if the world couldn't touch her here.

Mrs Shields had known her when she was young, those few brief years when she'd been loved and had a family. Before her mother had thrown her out of the house in order to keep a man. Here, she felt part of something again. She had someone who wanted her.

She sat by the last embers in the hearth, took down the whetstone and sharpened her knife. Stroke after stroke after stroke. She could hear the comforting rhythm of the old woman's soft breathing as she slept in the bedroom.

This was home.

She'd needed time to grow used to that idea, to allow it into her heart. The attic room at Simon and Rosie's house had been nothing more than a place to sleep. She'd always carried the few small things she owned so she could leave whenever she chose. Move on and be free.

But she had no desire to ever leave this place. Its warmth enveloped her. And that thought still scared her a little.

Jane pulled the blanket over herself and thought about Big Tom. If she'd been faster, she could have killed him. One more blow would have been enough. It was the perfect place. Out of the way, with no one to see, she'd have been gone in a second. But he'd escaped.

Perhaps her instincts had grown rusty. She'd have another chance, though. He'd be back once more, after his arm had healed. Eager, desperate for his revenge now she'd humiliated him a second time. When he returned, she'd have to make the end of it.

Next time, she thought as sleep claimed her.

'Who are you?' Simon whispered.

The man swallowed and tried to find his voice. The words came out dry, stammering.

'C-constable's man.'

'And why has Williams told you to watch my house?'

'He . . .' For a moment the man lost the power of speech. He licked his lips. 'He wants to talk to you. No matter what time you came home, he said.'

Simon didn't understand. Williams could have strutted along the street and taken him whenever he chose. For God's sake, the man could have made it a performance, had an audience. It was something he'd ached to do for years. Why this, why so secret?

'What does he want?'

'I-I-I don't know.' The man swallowed hard. 'He said to give you this.'

Very slowly, the man unbuttoned his heavy coat and reached inside, pulling something from his trouser pocket. Simon kept his knife steady, just edging against the man's neck, enough to keep reminding him that it was there.

'Here.' He held up a gold sovereign, King George's fat face on the front. Simon plucked it from the man's fingers. A great deal of money to use as a token. This was becoming stranger and stranger.

'Perhaps we'd better go and see him,' he said.

FOUR

'He has a house in Sheepscar, doesn't he?' Rosie asked. 'Near the turnpike road.'

'Yes,' Simon replied.

Morning, with a thin, pearly light coming through the window. Simon sat at the table next to his wife, across from Jane. He'd finished telling them about the night before and looked from one to the other.

'You can understand why he needs to keep this quiet,' he said to them. 'The Constable of Leeds hiring a thief-taker to solve a murder. The aldermen would never condone it.'

He'd found it hard enough to believe himself.

'I doubt that many people in town would approve, either,' Rosie said. 'At least Williams has the sense to realize that. Why didn't he arrest you? Did he say?'

Simon gave a fleeting smile. That had been his very first question when he sat by the fire in Williams's parlour. The curtains were drawn against the night, everything cosy and warm as he sat with a glass of wine in his hand.

'Because I know you're not stupid enough to kill someone on your own damned doorstep,' Williams answered after a moment. 'I don't like you, that's hardly a bloody secret. God knows I'd love to see you in a cell for something. But I'll credit you with a few brains. You'd have been out of gaol in a day and I'm damned if I want to look like a fool.'

Simon didn't believe that. Still, if Williams wanted to think it, fine. Let him. Better free than staring at the world from a cell.

'Then why am I here?'

The man shifted uneasily on his chair. 'Because I know I don't have a hope of solving this. There are no clues.' At first, Simon thought it was some kind of joke. Williams was asking him to handle this? No, that was ridiculous; he'd never do something like that, he'd never admit defeat that way. Simon stared into the man's eyes. There was no trace of humour behind them. God Almighty, he was deadly serious. Simon took a drink then looked into the glass, through the deep ruby colour of the wine. For once he didn't know what to say. He'd do it. It gave him the perfect chance to continue what he'd begun. But he wasn't going to commit himself just yet.

'Do you know Charlie Harker, the fence?' Williams asked.

'Yes.'

'I thought he might have some information, since Poole was a thief. But he's gone. Someone saw him climb on the London coach. Or it might have been Bristol.'

Simon noted that; it seemed definite that Harker had managed to leave in one piece. But it confirmed that the man hadn't been lying about his fears.

'Why are you so eager to solve *this* killing?' Simon asked. 'We both know there have been plenty of others where you've never found a murderer. You've never bothered to search too hard for them.'

'I suppose that's true enough,' Williams admitted with a sour expression. 'But Alderman Ferguson and Dr Brady are pressing me on this. They're not likely to let it lie.'

That was curious. What would interest that pair about the murder of a thief?

'Why?'

'I don't know,' the constable said. 'But they are. That's enough for me. They want answers.'

Simon sat back in the chair and rubbed his chin. 'What do I gain from helping you with this?' Before he agreed to anything, he was going to make damned sure it was worth his while. Right now, Williams had an air of desperation.

'Ten pounds if you find the killer. I can prise that from the town coffers without too many questions.'

It was far more than Simon had expected – a very handsome sum. A skilled factory hand couldn't hope to earn anywhere near that much in three months. The constable was pressed if he was willing to part with that kind of money.

'And you'll have my gratitude,' Williams added. 'That might prove useful at some time.'

It never hurt to have favours tucked away for a rainy day, Simon thought. The only problem was that he didn't believe too much of what he'd heard. Wheels within wheels within wheels. There had to be more going on than Williams had said, and he didn't trust the man an inch.

The constable put out his hand. Simon shook it.

'We have a bargain,' he said. A lie, but it would suffice for now. Until he understood what was happening.

'What are we going to do?' Jane asked now. The room was quiet, only the sound of the tutor's voice from the parlour as he instructed the boys in mathematics.

'We can start by searching properly,' Simon replied with a grin. 'There's no need to keep it quiet any more. Still, let's not mention that we're working for the constable. If anyone asks, just tell them we're being paid to find out. No need to say who's behind it.'

She nodded. 'Where do you want me to begin?'

Simon would ask people about the soldiers. First, he'd need to find someone in the garrison who could identify them. Easier for a man to do; the soldiers would be more likely to talk to him.

'We need to know where Poole was in the days before he died. How did he end up at Flay Crow Mill?'

'All right.' Without another word, she stood and left. He heard the front door click softly closed behind her.

'Have you found anything more in Poole's notebook?' he asked Rosie.

'No. I still can't make head or tail of his cipher,' she admitted. 'I'm sorry, Simon, but I've never had to do anything like that before.'

'It's fine,' he told her with a smile. 'Why don't you take it to George Mudie? He's good with puzzles. He might enjoy the challenge. We still have a few hours before the boys finish their lessons.'

'Where are you going?'

He grinned. 'I'm off to try my luck with the army.'

There was no point in returning to Poole's room in Welling Court. It would have been thoroughly searched by now. Jane tried to recall where Poole liked to spend his time. She'd seen him in the alehouse by the old cloth hall a few times when Mrs Rigton owned the place. But the woman had been dead for months now, murdered upstairs in her quarters and the killer never found. She'd heard that the business had a new owner, but she hadn't gone back there. For her, the building was filled with too many memories, good and bad.

Now Jane stood on the flagstones, looking up at the windows above the bar; she was aware of someone coming close. Martha, moving mouse-soft.

'What are you doing?'

'Thinking,' she replied. 'Remembering.' Mrs Rigton had given her shelter by the fire all through one long, bitter winter. 'I have to go inside and ask some questions.' She turned and stared at the girl. 'On my own.'

'What do you want me to do?'

'Wait here. I'll have work for you later.' She saw the girl smile with pleasure. 'Do you have a knife?'

'Course I do.' She produced it from under her shawl. Squat, fat, with a wide blade. Jane ran her thumb along the edge, so dull it would hardly peel an apple.

She pulled out the weapon she'd taken from Big Tom and passed it over, hilt first.

'If you're going to be working with me, you'll need something so you can look after yourself properly.'

'But . . .' Martha began, then took a breath and pushed her lips together and nodded. 'Thank you.'

Good, Jane thought. The girl learned quickly.

'Stay here,' she ordered. 'Let me know if you spot anyone loitering around.'

She went before Martha could ask any more questions.

The room was smoky. But the chimney had never drawn properly; that was what Mrs Rigton always said. For a fleeting second, she could almost hear the woman, always full of complaints.

The moment passed. Jane squinted, starting to pick out faces in the gloom. Not too many men in here during the day. As she moved towards a dark corner, a voice made her turn.

'Don't want any of your sort in here. Get out.'

The man standing behind the bar was bulky, with stringy dark hair and a few days' growth of beard on his face. His cheeks had sunk where his teeth had been pulled. His fists were lightly clenched, resting on the wood.

'What sort?' She didn't understand. He couldn't be talking to her.

'Whores coming in here, touting for business.'

She said nothing, but left, feeling all their eyes following her, burning her skin. Her face was hot, cheeks flushed as she closed the door.

'What happened?' Martha asked.

Jane turned away from her, hiding herself. 'Nothing. Come on.'

She stalked off, leaving the girl to follow. She'd been called a whore before, and much worse. Why had it cut so deep this time? Perhaps because she'd once felt safe in there. But that had been so long ago that it might as well have happened in another life.

She tried the other places where she'd remembered seeing Poole. But there was nobody she recognized in any of them.

As the clock on the parish church struck noon, Jane walked down Briggate towards Boar Lane. All her anger and frustration had faded, hammered down in footstep after footstep. Men would always think the worst of women. There was nothing she could do to alter their minds.

Kate the pie-seller was there, shouting out her wares. The tray hung on a rope from her shoulders, the food covered with a cloth to keep it warm. She was a big woman, broad and imposing, the kind to worry most men. But her husband beat her whenever she didn't earn enough money and she accepted it as her due.

'I see you've got some company today,' Kate said.

'Her name's Martha,' Jane replied. 'I'll take two pies. Heard anything lately?'

'About what? Have those, they're still warm.'

'Laurence Poole. Anything at all.'

'Dead, 'ent he?' Kate gave her a withering look. 'And folk don't seem to know who done it. But I heard some friend of his left town right quick afterwards.'

'Who?' She didn't need to ask but she wanted to be certain.

'Charlie Harker. You know him.'

'I do.'

'Took off like a frightened rabbit, they say.' She raised an eyebrow. 'Makes you wonder, dun't it?'

'No other gossip?'

'Just a spat between Caroline Butler and Annie Dunn. Nowt that would interest you.'

That was true. She'd never had time for things like that. Life was too serious, too dangerous to worry about frivolous arguments and love affairs. She began to walk off, chewing the pie and thinking.

'What are we going to do now?' Martha asked. 'Don't you have anything I can do to help you?'

'You don't know the man I was asking about. What I need you to do is what I said earlier; keep your eyes peeled. Tell me if you see anyone following us.'

'Why?' Martha asked quietly. 'Is there someone?'

'Not at the moment. But . . .'

'What?'

'In case.'

It would help the girl to feel useful and keep her alert. Prepare her. But Big Tom would need time to recover before he returned.

There wasn't too much around Sheepscar. A few houses. The toll booth for the turnpike road and the bridge over the beck. Simon saw Whitelock's rape seed mill, with workers bustling around, then Holroyd's dye works, smoke rising from its chimney. Beyond that, beside the road that led to Roundhay, the barracks. It still looked new, built only four years before. It was far enough away from the grime of Leeds for the bricks to still appear fresh and rosy.

The guards stood at the gate in their bright scarlet and pipeclay white, watching Simon with suspicion. But he didn't try to enter. He simply wanted a look at the place. Big, surrounded by a high brick wall, this was home to the cavalry garrison. One block for the men, another for the officers; it even possessed an infirmary and a riding school, someone had once told him. Impressive. But the two beer shops hastily tacked on to the small row of houses across the road weren't the kind of place to attract anyone fastidious. Too dirty and cramped. Too poor. Definitely not a place where he'd find any officers.

He spotted a pair of young women standing on a corner a hundred yards up the road from the gates. They looked cold, with chapped faces, shawls gathered tight around their shoulders, blowing on their fingers as they tried to keep warm against the cold. Simon strolled over to them, hands thrust deep in his coat pockets.

'Waiting for someone?' he asked.

'Maybe,' one answered. She cocked her head and her eyes flashed in a challenge. 'What you got in mind?'

Simon smiled and produced a sixpence, holding it between his fingertips and letting the light catch the silver. 'Information.'

The woman tugged at her shawl, drawing it closer around her face. Her companion looked down at the ground, the toe of her clog poking at the ground.

'What do you want to know?'

'Where do the officers drink?'

She snorted. 'It's not going to be round here, is it? Look at it. Try in town. They used to go to the Talbot. Probably somewhere else now.' Her expression filled with boredom. 'Officers ain't for the likes of us, anyway. Give me a good corporal any day of the week.'

Deftly, she reached out and plucked the coin.

'Do you know where else they go?'

'No.' A shrug. 'Never paid much attention. An enlisted man's good enough for me.'

It didn't matter. Leeds was growing every single day, bursting at the seams. But it wasn't that big. If he poked around he'd find the place. Simon turned away.

'Mister.' Another voice, a little more hesitant. The second girl.

'What is it?'

'The Yorkshire Hussar on Nelson Street. That's where you want.'

Of course, he should have guessed. Simon nodded his thanks and flipped a coin towards her. She grabbed it and removed it from sight in one shimmering movement.

FIVE

It was nondescript, one grimy building in a row of them on the road leading up to Vicar Lane. A painted sign hung over the door, a soldier on horseback waving a sabre. The Yorkshire Hussar. He'd only been in once, and that was years before.

The place was cleaner than he remembered. Dark woodwork that shone, the windows clear and polished to let in the pale February light. The air was scented with a blend of stale beer, beeswax polish, and the fug of tobacco.

'What can I get you?'

The young man behind the bar had thick, sandy side whiskers and an affable smile.

'Tot of brandy,' Simon said. 'There's a nip in the air. Maybe it'll warm me up.'

The man walked over with an awkward, painful limp and poured from the bottle. Simon paid and turned to take a proper look at the room. A coal fire burned in the grate, just enough warmth to take off the chill. Military ballads and army regulations were pasted across the walls and over the chimney breast, discoloured by the smoke.

Only three or four people sat drinking, the types who lived in places like this. Men with ruined faces and desperate hearts.

'Quiet today,' Simon said.

'It'll pick up later,' the barman replied. 'I do most of my business in the evening. Men from the garrison.'

'You own this?' he asked in surprise. The man looked too young, too naive. But when Simon looked again, he could see the wrinkles around his eyes and mouth. Not so youthful, after all.

'Bought and paid for,' the man replied, then reddened a little. 'Well, by my papa. Second son. He made this my inheritance. Up to me to be sure it pays.'

'What happened to your leg?'

'Waterloo.' A reply that explained everything in a single word. The man shook his head at the memory. 'I was a subaltern. Cavalry. Horse shot from under me. Rolled as it went down and broke my leg. The doctor couldn't set it right, damn the bastard.' He shrugged. 'Still, even without an injury, after Boney I'd have likely ended up on half-pay, anyway. That's no life for a man, is it?'

'Does the garrison here keep you busy?'

'They pay the bills. I'm not likely to get rich.' He stuck out a hand. 'Billy Crawford.'

'Simon Westow.'

Crawford stepped back and assessed him. 'I've heard of you. You're the thief-taker.'

Simon smiled. 'My reputation precedes me, does it?'

'In here on business?' He tried to sound as if it was an idle question, but the tone of his voice gave him away.

'Like I said, just seeking a little warmth.' He downed the rest of the brandy. Simon wasn't about to tip his hand; certainly not when he didn't know who he was seeking or how popular they might be in a place like this. He set the glass back on the bar. 'A pleasure to make your acquaintance. I'll return some evening and see what the company's like for cards.'

A fair start, Simon thought as he walked along Vicar Lane. He'd laid the groundwork; he could go back and be welcomed, and the owner wouldn't think it curious or worrying to see a thief-taker in there.

A coach rattled by, one wheel wobbling treacherously as it rattled along the street. He caught a glimpse of the passengers with their terrified faces, holding on for dear life. Another minute or two and they'd be safe at the inn.

Jane sat in the porch of Holy Trinity Church on Boar Lane. Just a few yards away, the carts and coaches rumbled and flew over the cobbles. The crack of whips and the shouts of the drivers. The yelling and conversation of people passing by. All the noises of Leeds to fill her ears.

But she didn't hear it. She sat staring at the wall and trying to think of where else she could search to trace Laurence Poole's last days. So far, she'd come up with nothing. No one could recall seeing him. It was as if he'd drifted towards the end like a wraith, unseen and without substance.

'What now?' Martha asked. She was standing in the corner, looking small against the stone. 'Where are we going next?'

'Simon Westow's house,' Jane replied as she stood. To tell him she'd failed, to hear any ideas, to try and find a direction for tomorrow. 'He's the thief-taker. I work with him.'

'Can I come with you?' A small voice, almost pleading. Jane understood how hard it was for the girl to ask anything. Living on the streets taught you not to do that; it showed weakness. Yet here she was, almost begging.

'Yes,' she agreed after a moment.

Martha's smile vanished as soon as it appeared, but not before Jane had noticed. It was a simple thing to grant, but she needed to be careful. Too much and the girl would be clinging to her all the time.

'We need to prove a connection between Poole and these officers from the garrison,' Simon said. They were sitting around the table in his kitchen. Himself, Rosie, Jane, and the strange little girl standing off near the corner, listening to every word.

'How? I can't find anyone who saw him before he died,' Jane said. 'It's as if he disappeared.'

'Someone must have seen him.'

She said nothing.

'The officers drink at the Yorkshire Hussar. I'm hoping to meet the ones behind these thefts.' Simon turned to Rosie. 'Is Mudie looking at that notebook?'

She nodded. 'He said the code looked simple. He ought to be finished with it tonight.'

Simon turned back to Jane. 'We should know more then. At least we'll have somewhere to begin. You might as well go home. We'll start again in the morning.'

She left, the girl trailing behind her and looking back over her shoulder.

'Who is she?' Simon asked after he heard the front door close.

'I don't know,' Rosie answered. 'She looks like a waif to me. But Jane must trust her if she brought her here.'

'Maybe.'

He put it out of his head. Jane was Jane. Nothing he did or thought would change her.

'As soon as you understand the idea, it's quite simple,' Mudie said. He had the notebook open and next to it a sheet of paper covered in his scribbled writing. Rosie was paying close attention as he explained the code. Simon paced up and down the room.

'Why didn't he put everything into cipher?' Rosie asked.

'I can't tell you,' Mudie answered. 'Maybe he didn't think it was all important.' He paused for a second and thought. 'Mind you, there doesn't seem to be much reason behind any of it.' He pushed the paper towards her. 'It's all there, for whatever it's worth.' Then turned to Simon. 'Someone said you have a client who's paying you to catch Poole's killer.'

'That's right.'

Mudie gave the smile of a man hearing rumours confirmed. 'They told me it was Constable Williams.'

Simon laughed. 'Come on, George. You don't really believe that, do you? The man hates me.'

'He didn't arrest you.'

'Maybe because he knows there'd be no chance of a case reaching court.'

'But you do have a client.'

'Yes.' Simon tilted his head in a nod. 'And I won't say who it is.'

'If that's how you want it.' He downed the glass of brandy in front on him, put the hat on his head and stood. At the front door, he said, 'I won't spill your secrets, Simon.'

'Good.' He glanced at the street. 'Looks like the last of the snow is finally melting.'

Upstairs, one of the twins coughed and Rosie paused, listening for more. She returned her attention to the pages, comparing code and translation as Simon read over her shoulder.

'What's that name?' he asked and pointed at a word.

'Johnson,' she replied after a long hesitation. 'I think it is, anyway.'

'Who is he? Poole hasn't mentioned him before.'

'"Johnson made me,"' she read. 'Sounds as if he could be one of the cavalry officers.'

'What's this place?' she asked after a minute.

'Which?'

Rosie pointed. 'Here. It looks like he's written *dark*, do you see? *To the dark*. I don't know what that means. It's not code, it must be his name for somewhere.' She looked at him. 'Where does he mean?'

Simon was searching in his mind through every Leeds street name he could remember. But nothing with *dark* in it.

'I don't know,' he admitted. 'We'll need to find out.' He read the passage again, looking for any other clues. Nothing at all. 'I'll look again in the morning.'

The world was wet. A light, cold rain was falling, flushing away the final remnants of the snow and turning the earth to mud. Still February, still winter. Jane clutched the cloak tight around her body as she left Mrs Shields's house.

On the Head Row, a bitter east wind lashed against her face. It didn't matter. She kept moving, head up, constantly looking around. One hand rested in the pocket of her dress, caressing the handle of her knife.

She spotted a pair of women trying to walk delicately, pattens attached to the soles of their shoes to lift them above the wet dirt. Pointless pride. They didn't even keep the hem of their dresses dry and clean. Jane wore a stout pair of boots. When she began to work with Simon and he paid her, they'd been the first thing she bought. A pair that fitted properly, comfortable, no holes, and soles that would wear for years.

She still had them, still wore them every day. After so long having to push her feet into shoes that she'd scavenged, too big or too small, these still felt like a luxury, one she valued. Good, comfortable boots and a sharp knife. The tools she needed to do her job well.

Martha was waiting outside Simon's house, standing back in

the shadow of a shed. She came forward as soon as she spotted Jane, hurrying across Swinegate just as a coach roared past.

'How long were you standing there?'

'Not very long.'

She doubted that. The girl looked sodden, bedraggled. She'd been out in the rain for an hour or more.

'Why didn't you knock on the door? They know you. They'd have let you in.'

But the only answer was a brief shake of the head.

Jane listened to Simon and Rosie. By the time she left she felt she knew no more than she had yesterday. Talk and talk about a notebook and code. A few names and places that were already familiar and some that made no sense. *To the dark*. Where was that? What did it mean?

'I didn't understand,' Martha said. They stood outside Simon's house. The rain was fading to a chilling drizzle. Jane pulled up the hood of her cloak and saw the girl lift her shawl to cover her hair. The wool was threadbare, all the colour faded by the years.

'There wasn't much to understand,' Jane told her. 'It means we keep on trying.' That was the only answer.

She worked alone. She always had. Jane liked the freedom of it. If Simon asked, she'd go with him. Otherwise, she followed her instincts and traced her own path. Having someone with her . . . why didn't she just tell Martha to leave?

She hadn't been able to speak the words. Instead, the girl was still here, stroking the shawl Jane had just bought from the old clothes stall at the market. Nowhere near new, but better than the tattered one she'd owned. That couldn't have kept a skeleton warm.

'Thank you.' Her small fingers kept touching the wool, her eyes wide in surprise at the gift.

'Don't make too much of it. You're no use to me if you have a fever or you're shaking from cold. Come on. Don't dawdle.'

First, she'd given the girl a knife. Now she'd bought her the shawl. Why? Why did she feel the need to help her? There were waifs all over Leeds. Dozens of them. Hundreds. She couldn't look after them all. Why did she have this one with her?

But somehow she couldn't bring herself to turn Martha away.

Dusk, and they were returning from south of the river. Questions, directions, walking hither and yon all day between the mills and the foundries in Hunslet and Holbeck. Out along the canal to Knowsthorpe, then back once more.

She'd learned nothing, not picked up a single trace of Poole. She'd need to go back out in the night, when the thieves and the robbers came out and met in the beer shops. They might have some answers. Martha had watched, stayed quiet as she took everything in, placing each piece in her memory.

'What now?'

Jane handed her three pennies. 'Buy yourself a bed in a lodging house and something to eat.'

'Tomorrow?' She could hear the hope in the word.

'Find me.'

She was close to Commercial Street when she felt the prickle. Goose pimples rising on her arms, the tingling along her spine. Someone was close. Someone was following.

She slipped the knife into her hand, listening closely. It couldn't be Big Tom. It was no time at all since she'd sliced his arm open and heard him scream as loud as a girl. He couldn't be looking for her already.

A little further and she sensed movement out of the edge of her eye. Two figures slipping out of the deep blackness of Change Alley. There he was, Big Tom, back again. He held one arm to his chest. A fever of hunger in his eyes, the craving for revenge gnawing at his belly.

But this time he wasn't alone. She didn't recognize the other man, couldn't make out his features in the darkness. But she sensed that he was the true danger, moving with youthful ease and speed.

Jane didn't feel any panic. No fear. She was thinking clearly, completely alive. She'd faced men like this before and beaten them. Without thinking, her fingers turned the gold ring on her finger.

They were trying to push her back towards the wall, to pen her in and remove her choices. But she wasn't about to let them.

'Get that knife off her and we can both have fun before we slit her throat,' Tom said.

He was the weak link. He always would be. You never told people your intentions. Here he was, practically trying to boast. And she already knew he was a coward. Time to make him show that side again.

Jane darted forward, making a quick lunge towards him. A quick intake of breath as he pulled back, then she moved again, edging further and seeing him retreat from her blade.

Time was with her. The men dared not take too long. Not out here where people could pass and the windows of expensive houses looked down on the street. If she held them off for a minute or two longer, she'd be safe. Her mouth was dry; she felt as if she'd swallowed a meal of dust. But she was calm. She was in control. She could keep them at bay and wear them down. And then she'd strike. A pair like this didn't scare her too much.

The other man slid closer. He moved to the side, forcing her to divide her attention. He hadn't tried to attack yet. Just circling and watching. Silent. This one had been in a knife fight before; he knew what he was doing.

She was going to let them commit themselves. It would come very soon. Big Tom had no patience. He wanted things over and done. And he'd be thinking about all those humiliations she'd given him.

He started. One foot pushing forward. It seemed to be a signal. The other man advanced. Jane took a deep breath and swept the air with her blade. It was enough to stop them coming closer for now.

And then . . . she picked out the small noise. For a moment she wondered if she'd imagined it. So soft, like the sole of a shoe crunching lightly over gravel. Coming from somewhere behind the men. Neither of them seemed to notice it.

Once again Jane raked at the air with the knife. She watched for the slightest hint of movement.

It arrived out of the darkness.

Swift. Brutal.

A blur against the night, a figure who leaped and grabbed the shoulder of the young man. Before he could react, a knife sliced his skull and he fell to his knees, keening like an animal and trying to stem the blood running down his face.

Big Tom didn't move. He stood frozen and dumb and stared at his friend in horror. Jane knocked the knife from his hand.

'Get him out of here.' She hissed the words, slapping his face to grab his attention. In the houses all around she could see lights starting to wink and flicker in the gaps between shutters. Another few seconds and people would be looking and shouting.

The young man was still howling and moaning.

She slapped Tom again. 'Get him out of here,' she repeated. 'Before the watch comes.'

Then she was gone, pausing for a heartbeat to look down at the young man. The blood was still pouring between his fingers. He looked as though he'd lost his left eye. Big Tom had started to move. Slow, lumbering, as if he was unsure what to do.

Jane couldn't wait. She pulled her cloak tight around herself and ran. She heard the echo of footsteps close behind but didn't slow until she'd turned the corner on to Short Street, then right once more, to the safety of Butts Court.

She turned and reached out for the figure at her heels, holding her tight by the wrist.

'Why did you follow me?' Jane tore the shawl off Martha's hair. 'Why?'

'I wanted to see where you lived.' The girl sounded small, cowed.

For the third time: 'Why?'

'I . . .' Martha began. Then: 'Those men . . . Are they the ones you wanted me to watch for?'

'Yes. Come on.' She began to walk. They were still too close to where it had all happened. Jane hurried away, moving briskly, not waiting for the girl.

No more words until she went through the gap in the wall of the yard behind the Green Dragon, and Leeds seemed to become a distant country. She was safe here. *They* were safe here.

Jane unlocked the door. Everything was soft and quiet inside. Things were *normal*. The gentle rhythm of Mrs Shields's breathing, a sound as soft and rounded as a bird. The glow of the banked fire. She pushed the poker into the coals, feeling the warmth as the flames rose.

'Sit,' she ordered the girl.

Two glasses of cordial. Martha sniffed at hers, suspicious, waiting until Jane drank before she put it to her lips.

'Why did you want to know where I live?'

'Just to know.' The girl turned away from her, looking at the room. After a while, she asked: 'Is he going to die?'

'No. But I think you've blinded him in one eye.'

Martha's face showed nothing. No pain. No regret. 'Were they going to kill you?'

'They were going to try.' And now they'd never know if they were good enough.

The girl stared. 'Did I help?'

'Yes. You did.' Jane waited a moment before she added, 'Thank you.'

Had Big Tom dragged his friend away before the watch arrived? Or what tale was he spinning them now? She'd need to be out early, asking questions to know if they were safe.

And if not?

Jane had her money hidden behind a stone in the wall. Plenty of it. Hundreds of pounds, more than anyone could imagine she'd possess. She could go. Start over somewhere else with a new name. Leave the only place she'd ever felt safe and wanted.

She glanced across at the girl. She'd need to vanish, too. But it would be easier for her. No one had seen her face. No one knew her.

'Sleep,' she said.

'I wanted to repay you,' Martha said. 'You've done so much for me. The knife, the shawl.'

Debts, obligations. She had no time for them. Jane didn't want anyone to have power over her, and she didn't want anyone to feel beholden.

'You never owed me anything.' She brought a blanket from a chest under the window. 'If you think you did, it's paid in full. Now go to sleep.'

SIX

She reached the market at first light. People were already crowding around, hunting through the sparse offerings of late winter. Butter. Onions. Withered apples and pears. Leeks and dried beans. Over in the Shambles a cleaver fell with a thump as a butcher cut up a carcass. A dry morning, no cloak today, but Jane was hidden under her shawl. She wandered through the crowd without being noticed.

There was plenty of gossip. Who'd left who, how they'd shouted and screamed at each other. But nothing about a fight on Albion Street during the night. For half an hour she walked and listened. Not a single whisper.

She'd barely slept. Worry had coursed through her body, jolting her eyes open and making her pulse race. Whether Big Tom had been quick enough or sharp enough. But it seemed he'd used his brain for once. Jane breathed deep with relief.

Before she left the house, she'd woken Martha. They left together. Jane had given her a few coins and told her to keep her distance for a few days. They parted in their different directions, and this time she'd doubled back to make certain the girl wasn't following her.

For now, they were free. For now. They'd been lucky. But all it took was a single word. It was safer for them not to be seen together.

At Simon's house, she sat at the table, watching the boys as they stuffed themselves with bread and cheese. They were full of life and joy, the things she half-remembered when she was their age. But it was like she was looking into their world through a window and she was locked outside.

She had a home now, but all those years when she might have been happy had disappeared. Sometimes the regret welled up inside, so big that she believed it might consume her. But once it died down again she knew there was no point in sorrow. It had happened. It had made her who she was now. Without it she wouldn't have all that money hidden away.

'Any luck yesterday?' Simon asked.

'Nothing.'

'That girl isn't with you today?'

'No.' No need to say more than that.

'Rosie went through Poole's notebook again. She found two more things. Have you heard of Michael Peacock?'

She frowned, then shook her head. 'Who is he?'

'He owns a shop just on the far end of the bridge. Anything second-hand. He piles junk outside the door during the day.'

She could place it now. Dusty, grimy windows that looked as if they'd never been cleaned, white cobwebs and the hard, dry bodies of flies clustered in the corners of the panes.

'Why would Poole know him?'

'He's a fence. Doesn't handle much, only small items.'

'I thought Poole used Charlie Harker for that.'

'There must have been some things Charlie wouldn't take,' Simon said. 'Go and talk to him.'

'You said two things.'

'I'll handle the other one.'

Yesterday's drizzle had washed away the final traces of the snow. Now it was just a dirty memory, another rough winter. The sky folded heavy with factory smoke, the air vibrated with the sound of looms and machines.

Holbeck thrummed. He could feel the heat snaking from the Round Foundry as he passed, following the road beyond the mills then turning down towards the moor.

William White, the other name in Poole's notebook, lived down here, in a cottage set back down a winding path through a long front garden. Simon had met him a few times, a tinkerer who possessed a gift with machinery.

Many of the manufactories round here called him in when they had a problem their own engineers couldn't solve. He had a way of seeing things that went beyond the obvious. A man who could follow a puzzle through a machine and find the answer.

It gave him a good living, enough to let him afford this place, cultivate his wildflower garden and support a wife and five children. But the house was curiously silent as he approached. As he rapped on the door, Simon could hear the hollowness inside. He glanced through the window. Empty. Nothing but bare, swept boards.

Another house stood across the street. Two storeys high, long windows upstairs to let in the light to the workshop. The quick, rhythmic clack of a loom that stopped as Simon knocked. Ten seconds, then a man was squinting at him through a pair of spectacles.

'Yes?' He had a pinched, worried face, with thin, bloodless lips. Still a full head of dark hair although he looked to be in his fifties.

'The house over—'

'Gone,' the man said before he could finish. 'They left just after the start of the year. He had an offer to be a mechanic for some factory in Bradford. Packed up and moved out. Good luck to them, too,' he added, although it was envy, not sincerity, that blossomed in his voice. Understandable. These were hard times for hand-loom weavers. More and more of the work was going to the factories. It probably wouldn't be long before this man took his place there, too.

'Thank you.' Simon tipped his hat and walked away. It must have been a good offer for Billy White to take it. He valued his independence and he'd spent years working on his garden. Each spring and summer it became a beautiful wilderness of colour. Leaving that must have taken some persuasion.

But it meant that whatever questions Simon had would go unanswered.

The night before, he'd gone back to the Yorkshire Hussar, sitting quietly in the corner and watching. A few officers from the garrison had been there, but none who fitted the description Harker had given. And nobody by the name of Johnson.

During the evening he sat in on a few hands of cards, losing just enough for the men to warm to him before he left. They'd remember his face when he returned. The money was nothing, an investment. But it could lead him to the men who'd killed Laurence Poole. And before it went too far, he'd find out what was really going on in Constable Williams's game.

He'd thought about it, tried to examine it from every angle. But there were pieces missing. Whatever they were, he knew he was caught up in something political, a twisted, grubby little spectacle. All Simon knew was that he'd do every damned thing he could to avoid being sucked in too deep. He wasn't going to lose his life or his liberty over this.

Probably no one ever would. The garrison carried influence in Leeds. The officers were all gentlemen from good families. Who was Poole? A thief, common, a nobody. Even if Dr Brady and Alderman Ferguson wanted the truth, that didn't mean it would ever come to a trial.

He crossed Leeds Bridge, smelling the ripe stink of the water long before he could see it. Full of chemicals and death these days. That was what many people claimed, and he believed them. Yet he could still see men on the shore with their fishing poles, hoping for a bite on the line and a supper that cost them nothing.

'So Williams really has employed you?' George Mudie's grin was so wide, it looked as if it might split his face.

'That stays between us,' Simon told him. Time to give the man some of the truth. At least that was the way it looked on the surface; no mention of the niggling doubts underneath. It was the only way he'd grant the favour Simon needed to ask. 'Not a word to anyone.'

'I promise.' He laughed again. 'It's rich, you have to admit that.'

Evening and the print shop was closed; there was just a single lamp glowing at the desk near the back of the room. Mudie poured himself another glass of brandy and sipped.

'How are you going to find these cavalrymen?'

'I have a few ideas.'

'I daresay you do. And once you've found them, how are you going to convict them?'

'That's Williams's job. I bring him the evidence, and my part is done.'

'It's the same question, isn't it, though, Simon? How?'

For now, he had no answers; instead, he ignored it.

'You do some work for the garrison, don't you?'

'Occasionally. When they're having an event where they invite people. I print the posters for them.' Mudie's voice turned wary. 'Why?'

'Is there anything coming up soon?'

'The late winter ball. They have one every year. It gives the women a chance to order new gowns from the dressmakers.'

'When do you need to go to the barracks?'

'I didn't say I needed to go there at all.'

Simon smiled. 'But you do.'

Mudie sighed. 'What do you want? It had better be above board.'

'To go with you.'

'And?'

'That's it.'

He shook his head. 'No, it's not. I can see it in your eyes.'

'All I'm going to do is ask a few questions while you conduct your business,' Simon told him. 'I'll leave with you, as soon as you're done.'

'What's the catch? If you're asking me like this, there has to be one.'

'I can't get in there on my own. The sentries on the gate would never let me through.'

Mudie stayed silent for a long time, turning his glass on the table.

'Fine.' He paused and raised a finger. 'But nothing illegal, nothing that's going to jeopardize my business with them. Understood?'

'And accepted. Thank you.'

'Be here at nine tomorrow. And look presentable.'

'I shall.' He pursed his lips. 'To the dark. Do the words mean anything to you?'

Mudie shook his head. 'No. Why?'

'They were in Poole's book. I've been trying to make sense of them, that's all.'

'Just one poster?' Simon asked as they walked along North Street. A cold day, dry again, but with a thin, chilling breeze flying out of the east.

'It's a proof,' Mudie explained. He was bundled up against the weather in a thick greatcoat with a cape over the shoulders, gloves, and a warm beaver hat that nestled over his ears. His best coat and a neck stock that glistened white in the light. With tight trousers and high boots to protect himself from the mud, he looked every inch a prosperous modern businessman, carrying the poster rolled in oilcloth. 'They look at it, tell me if they want me to change anything, then I print it up for them.'

'How long are you likely to be there?'

'Could be anywhere up to an hour. They're never in any rush with civilians. The colonel in charge of the garrison has to give his approval, so . . .' He shrugged.

At the gate, Mudie stated his name and business. They let him pass, and Simon followed without a word. No one challenged him or questioned his presence. Everything as smooth as he could have hoped.

Inside the walls, the parade ground seemed to stretch all the way to the horizon, a huge expanse, lined on all sides with buildings. Stables, where troopers were tending to their mounts, quarters for all the men, other buildings bustling with people coming and going.

'I'll see you at the gatehouse in an hour,' Mudie said. 'Make sure you stay out of trouble.'

Where to start? That was the question. Talking to the troopers was a possibility. But he had no idea what kind of loyalty they felt towards their officers. Better to find a civilian. They must employ a few.

He found a group of them in the kitchens. Women scrubbing the breakfast dishes, gossiping and laughing as they worked. He smiled as they made a joke or two at his expense, allowed himself to blush at their bawdy comments, and suddenly he was welcome.

A few minutes of their chatter and he could start to ask his questions, leading them along, aware that the clock was ticking. By the time he emerged, he knew about Johnson. He was a lieutenant, and the women didn't care for him one bit. He went around with an ensign named Murdoch.

'He's easy to spot, is that one,' one of the women said. 'He reckons the sun shines out of his arse. If yon one were any more full of himself, he'd likely explode all over the yard.'

That was enough to set the women cackling. He listened; there could be a useful nugget in with the scandal.

By the time Mudie arrived with a satisfied look on his face, Simon was waiting in a nook, sheltered from the wind. They'd crossed Sheepscar Beck and started back along North Street before either of them spoke.

'A worthwhile morning?'

'Fair,' Mudie replied with a smile. 'They only asked for one small change and that'll take me no more than a minute. Confounded them and said it would be difficult, so they offered to pay extra.' He sighed with contentment and gave a short laugh. 'If only all my customers were this easy . . . what about you? Did you find what you needed?'

'Enough.' He'd discovered what he came out here to learn, and he'd managed it without arousing suspicion. Now he needed to flesh out the little he'd learned about Johnson and Murdoch. That should be easy enough. They were bound to have accounts at some of the shops in Leeds. A pound to a penny the proprietors were having difficulty squeezing money from the pair of them. They'd probably have little love for the men.

He'd set Rosie on that search. The shopkeepers all knew her, she spent money with them, always paid her bills on the nail. A good customer. She knew how to ask questions and tease out information so that people never realized they'd let anything slip. Yes, this was an ideal job for her.

'Sounds like we're both happy,' Mudie said. 'And no trouble?'

'None,' Simon told him. 'Exactly the way I promised.'

SEVEN

Jane hadn't known Michael Peacock's name, but she'd known his shop her entire life. Everybody who crossed Leeds Bridge passed it and glanced at the windows.

A bell tinkled as Jane opened the door and entered. The air felt old, musty, as if no one had disturbed it in years. Dust motes floated and glinted in the muted light. She looked around. A dozen or more walking sticks sat in a bucket, books rose in awkward piles from the floor. Cheap picture frames were stacked against the wall. So many things that there was hardly a path between door and counter.

The man who stood by the counter was younger than she expected. Still old enough to have deep lines on his face, but his hair was a rich, deep brown, hanging almost to his shoulders. Thin as a cadaver, clothed in a black suit, so dark that the pure white shirt and stock appeared startling in contrast.

'Can I help you?'

Peacock had warm eyes and a winning smile. He didn't look as if he belonged here. He seemed too . . . clean, she decided. Too tidy and ordered for a place as jumbled as this.

'Are you Michael Peacock?'

A quick shake of his head. 'That's my father. Do you have business with him?'

'Yes.'

'He should be back in' – he reached into a waistcoat made of black silk and silver brocade and pulled out a tarnished pocket watch – 'about an hour. Would you like me to give him your name?'

'I'll come back.' She hesitated. 'Who buys all the things in here?'

'People.' He stared at her, seeing the old cotton dress and the faded colours of her shawl. 'People like you who don't have money.'

She was still curious. 'Who sells it to you?'

'People who need the money.' He shrugged. 'Or there are dealers. We buy from them sometimes. Why?'

'I just wondered.'

'My grandfather opened this place almost fifty years ago. We keep it going.'

Jane nodded. 'I'll come back in a little while.'

Outside, the day felt fresh. She walked along Dock Street, south of the Aire, past Ericsson's timber yard, beyond the boatwright and Fearn's Island, around the bend in the river. The wind was sharp, still peppered with winter, the sky as dull as lead shot.

No rush. By the time she returned, it felt as if an hour had passed.

A different man stood in the shop. Michael Peacock, it had to be. He had the look of his son, but a quarter of a century older. Less hair, and what remained was grey. The lines on his cheeks and forehead were deep furrows. Knuckles gnarled by age.

'Martin told me a young lady had been in looking for me,' he said. 'Was that you?'

'Yes,' Jane said. 'I want to ask you about someone called Laurence Poole.'

For a moment, panic flashed across his face, then he had control again.

'The man who was killed at Flay Crow Mill?'

'That's him. Someone said you knew him.'

'I suppose I did.' He rubbed his chin. 'Not well, exactly. He'd come in now and then to try and sell me things. Just small, no real value to them.' Peacock's eyes roved around the shop. 'You see those pins over there?' They sat on the table, long hatpins with cheaply decorated tops. 'I gave him a penny for the lot. It's all they were worth. They've been here a year at least. No one wants them.'

'When did you last see him?'

'Why?' His eyes narrowed and his voice grew harder. 'Who are you, girl?'

'I work with Simon Westow. The thief-taker.'

The words were enough. Simon's name commanded respect, maybe even a little fear.

Peacock smiled. 'You should have said so from the start.'

'When did you last see Poole?' Jane asked again.

'Just before that last big snow. That's why I remember it. It was that day or the one before. He looked scared the whole time he was in here. Tried to hurry me along.'

'What was he selling?'

The man pursed his lips. 'Nothing I wanted to buy. Even for the farthings he was asking. It was all rubbish. I sent him away.'

'How often did he come to you?'

'I don't know,' Peacock answered after a few moments. 'I never thought about it. He just appeared when he had something he wanted me to buy. Things Charlie Harker wouldn't take. Sometimes it was twice a month. Usually less than that. I don't know.'

'That last time he was in the shop, did he say much?'

'No.' Peacock's voice was firm now. 'As I said, he was after me to give him a price on the things he'd brought. He acted like he had to be somewhere else and he was late.' He looked up and shrugged. 'I'm sorry. That's all I can tell you.'

A quick final encounter. All it showed was that Poole had been terrified, and that was already easy to guess. A thought struck her. 'Have you ever had anyone in from the garrison?'

'Soldiers?' He laughed. 'Maybe one or two of the troopers who are curious. They poke their heads round the door and go away again.'

'Any officers?'

'In here? Never.' Peacock shook his head. 'Why?'

'No reason.'

She wandered around Leeds. By evening she felt she'd been in every beer house and gin shop in town. Her feet ached, and her throat was dry from asking questions.

No sign of Martha. For once, the girl had listened to her. Good. She didn't need anyone trailing in her footsteps. It was easier to work alone. Not to have to explain everything. Not to feel responsible.

'Murdoch and Johnson have accounts where you'd expect,' Rosie said. She counted the places on her fingers. 'Tailor, shirtmaker, bootmaker. At the stables for saddles and bridles.'

She'd put on her good clothes for the job, relishing the chance to wear a new gown and do some work. A dress of deep blue velvet that Simon had never seen before. It had a high waist and puffed sleeves, all trimmed with fine lace the colour of a summer sky. She'd put her good woollen cape over that, all topped with a broad-brimmed hat which boasted an extravagant plume. He'd watched as she examined herself in the mirror and nodded before she went hunting for information.

'How much do they owe?' Simon asked.

'More than they can pay,' she replied with a smile. 'The bootmaker's already dunned them three times and never had a reply. He's about to turn a lawyer on them.'

He heard the creak of floorboards upstairs and glanced at the ceiling. Just the boys shifting in their sleep. It was nine in the evening, a sky like pitch outside, the warmth from the stove keeping them comfortable in the kitchen. The oil lamps glowed, casting deep shadows into the corners.

'Peacock didn't know them at all. None of the officers go in there,' Jane said, then told the others about Poole's last visit to the shop.

'He must have been trying to put money together to run,' Simon said.

'But he had nothing of value in his life to sell,' Rosie said, then sighed. 'It's hardly much of a memorial, is it?'

'Why would Johnson and Murdoch want to kill him?' Simon asked. He looked at their faces.

'Maybe he cheated them,' Rosie suggested.

Simon shook his head. 'If he'd done that, he'd have had the money to get away.'

'Unless he spent it,' Jane said.

'On what? You were with me when we searched his room. He didn't own anything.'

'I don't know, then.'

'He went into Peacock's shop. Not long after that, he was killed and the snow came to hide him. He must have done things, been in places. What? Where? Who saw him? Someone must have spoken to him. We'll see what we can find tomorrow. I have business tonight.'

He stood and kissed Rosie. In the hall he put on the heavy greatcoat and small-brimmed hat, glancing at his reflection in the long mirror. He looked respectable, with his well-cut jacket, trousers taut over his thighs and calves, and a shine on his boots. Like . . . no, not like a businessman. Never that. His eyes were too sharp, too suspicious to ever be anything but a thief-taker.

'Where are you going?' Jane roused him from his thoughts.

'The Yorkshire Hussar. I'm going to play cards with some soldiers from the garrison.'

'Murdoch and Johnson?'

He grinned. 'If they're there and they want to lose their money. Come on, I'll walk up Briggate with you.'

The night was alive with people. Groups moved from beer shop to dram shop, singing and laughing. The whores stood their pitches at the entrances to courts, joking and teasing for business. Lights glowed behind shutters and reflected in puddles on the pavement. Someone played a fiddle, a rousing jig that carried in the winter air.

Jane didn't speak. No need to talk. She was thinking about Big Tom and his friend. Throughout the day she'd listened carefully, and never a peep about them. She was safe from the constable. Big Tom would return, wanting blood. That was as certain as tomorrow. And she'd take care of him when he did. This time she had to, no half measures.

She felt the nudge and turned.

'You were miles away,' Simon told her. 'I'll see you in the morning.'

'Where do you want me to look?'

'Wherever you can think.' He shook his head. 'I don't really know.'

With a wave, he was gone. She had no sense of anyone as she walked over the brow of the hill and cut through Green Dragon Yard to Mrs Shields's house. There, sitting by the door, was the girl.

'I didn't have anywhere else to go.'

'I gave you money.'

'Someone took it.'

She didn't believe that.

In the Yorkshire Hussar, Simon paid for his brandy and looked around for a game of cards. He spotted one of the men from the night before and raised his glass in a toast. The man waved him over.

He could see the others at the table. A grim-faced bunch, looking as if they'd already lost their entire family fortunes. One of them wore an ensign's uniform. Simon introduced himself.

'Murdoch,' the man replied.

Perfect. One of the pair he was seeking.

The cards were dealt. Simon played poorly, making a mistake or two, letting the others win. It gave him a chance to study the ensign. The women who worked at the barracks said he was arrogant. He certainly didn't seem that way now. He stared at his cards as if looking might change them and toyed with the small pile of coins in front of him.

Murdoch snorted and threw down his hand, raising his arm for another drink. Rum. A fresh deal, and Simon played with care. He'd been taught by some of the best players in town, men who'd made their livings at the card tables. He knew how to finesse, how to gamble, how to shuffle and make the cards work for him. The men at this table were amateurs, not even good ones. It would be easy enough to win the whole pot, but that wasn't why he'd come. He wanted to know Murdoch a little better.

The deal passed to Simon.

Over the course of an hour, he took the ensign down to pennies. Some careful work with the deck, things no one would notice. He made sure the others all won, only small amounts, not enough to seem suspicious, as Murdoch's frustration grew. Not just a bad night for him, a dreadful one.

Finally, Simon placed the cards on the table. 'That's enough for me for now.' He stood. 'Gentlemen, I wish you well.'

Now he was hoping that Murdoch needed the chance to win back some of his money. The man's face had grown more and more desperate as they played.

'Before you leave—'

Perfect. He'd taken the bait.

Simon turned his head. 'What?'

'One last chance,' Murdoch said with a sad smile. 'My pockets are empty.'

The others were already buttoning up their coats and pulling on their gloves. They'd lost interest, all of them content with a little extra money and no desire to risk it now.

'All right,' Simon agreed. 'On the turn of a card suit you?'

He took two sovereigns from his trousers and laid them on the table, letting the light wink on the gold.

'I only have eight pennies.' Murdoch counted them out.

'If you have the higher card, you walk away with the sovereigns.'

'And if I don't?'

Simon smiled. 'Then you'll be eight pence poorer. After you.'

The room was absolutely silent. Everyone was watching, some pressing close, others craning their necks to try and see.

Murdoch reached out and cut the deck. He held up the card for them all to see, then turned it towards himself. The nine of clubs. He smiled with relief. A good card. Not easy to beat. The odds rested in his favour.

Simon ran his fingertips along the edges of the cards, searching for the one he wanted. The tiny notch he'd put in the surface when he was playing. For a moment he couldn't feel it. Then it was right there. He took a breath and lifted. A glance. The queen of hearts.

He showed it to the room and watched as Murdoch's face fell. Conversation began again, a sudden buzzing like machinery all around them.

'Here.' Simon pushed the eight pennies and one of the sovereigns across the table.

Murdoch raised his eyes in astonishment. 'Why? You won.'

'I won't see a man penniless. You're in the cavalry so you must be an honourable fellow. I'm sure you have money coming. You can pay me back once you have it.'

'That's very gracious.' The coins vanished into his uniform. He extended a hand. 'Neville Murdoch. Don't worry, I'm good for the debt.'

'I've no doubt about it, Ensign Murdoch. I'll bid you a good night.'

A sovereign, Simon thought as he strolled home. To most people it was a great deal of money. Once, back when he was in the workhouse, it would have been an impossible fortune to him. Now he was prepared to let it go. He shook his head, surprised at himself and how life had changed.

The money was an investment. It brought him close to Murdoch, and that meant Johnson was a single step away. Once they learned he was a thief-taker, he knew they'd sniff the possibility of money and cultivate his friendship. He'd lead them along until he was ready to pounce. Simon smiled to himself as he walked home, barely even feeling the February cold against his face.

EIGHT

Martha sat close to the fire. Mrs Shields was in her chair, wearing her nightgown, a shawl and quilt wrapped around her body. The thinness of her wrists and her ankles poked out.

'I don't understand.' Her voice was soft and quizzical, and her expression gentle as she looked at the girl. 'Why would you want to follow Jane?'

Martha didn't take her eyes from the flames.

'Because I can learn from her. She has a job.' A small pause. 'She's clever.'

Jane stalked into the kitchen. She didn't want to hear any of this. She wasn't clever. She didn't want anyone saying so. All she did was use the only talent she possessed. Nothing more than that. She could hear the low voices in the other room but blotted out what they were saying.

Martha shouldn't be here. She needed to keep her distance. Jane had told her that.

This was *her* home. Hers and Catherine Shields. They had their private bond of history, from the time Jane was small. Martha wasn't any part of that. She didn't belong here. She was the outsider.

She strode back into the living room, feeling the warmth from the fire as she entered.

'If you lost your money for lodgings and food,' she said, 'I'll give you more.'

'Can I stay here tonight?' Martha asked. 'Just tonight, that's all.'

But one night could stretch on and on.

Jane reached into her pocket and counted out money. A shilling, two. More than enough to buy her a good, warm room for a week. One she didn't need to share and enough to feed her for a few days.

'There.' She opened the girl's hand, poured the coins into it, then wrapped the small fingers around them.

'Tonight,' Mrs Shields said with soft finality. 'It's too late to send anyone back outside. You can stay until morning. But that's all. What you and Jane arrange after that is up to you. But there isn't room for three of us to live here.' A serene, sad smile. 'I'm sorry.'

'Thank you,' Martha said. 'Thank you.'

The old woman held up one finger. 'There's a price. In return you have to tell us about yourself.' She patted a cushioned stool and glanced at Jane.

'I . . .' Martha closed her eyes and remained silent for so long it felt endless. Jane watched the girl's face, astonished to see so much pain creeping out from behind the mask. It was there in the way she pursed her mouth, squeezed her eyelids tightly together, seeing everything and wanting to see nothing at all. 'I hurt my sister. I had to run away.'

'Child.' Mrs Shields reached forward and stroked Martha's cheek. The girl flinched at the touch, drawing back, then moved forward again, letting the fingers slide over her skin. 'What did you do that was so bad?'

'I tried to drown her. Held her under the water.'

The old woman's eyes flickered, but her face showed nothing. 'Why would you want to do something like that?'

'She killed my cat. Just because it scratched her. It was only a kitten. It didn't mean anything – it didn't know any better. It was only playing. She put it in the water barrel and held it down until it stopped moving. I wanted her to know what that felt like.'

'Did your sister die?' Jane asked.

'No.' The girl looked down at the flagstone floor. 'But I daren't go back after that. My father . . .' Her words faded to bitter silence.

Mrs Shields brought a heavy wool blanket and a worn cotton nightgown from a chest. 'Put this on and settle down.'

Martha stood, thin and pale. The gown lapped around her feet and out across the floor.

'What about tomorrow?' she asked.

'Tomorrow is tomorrow,' Mrs Shields told her softly. 'Worry about that then. For now, just rest. You'll feel better in the morning.'

First light and smoke already lay over the town.

'I don't think Leeds will ever be clean again,' Mrs Shields said, looking at the sky. She stood in the flagstone yard, the door to the house pulled closed behind her. 'Not properly. I remember the way it used to be when I was a girl.' She drew in a breath and let it out in a slow sigh, then took a sip from the glass of cordial.

Jane stood beside her. She'd slept poorly, always aware of Martha, the smell of her, the sense of her body close by, her presence in the house.

'I'm sorry. I didn't know she'd be waiting for me to come back.'

'Don't worry, child.' The old woman smiled at her. 'But be careful around her.'

'Why? Do you think she was lying?' Jane kept her voice low.

Martha had still been asleep when they came outside, but she didn't want the girl overhearing.

'No.' The woman was careful with her words. 'I'm sure she told us the truth.' She hesitated. 'At least, the truth as she chooses to see it. I don't know if it was everything, though. She wants something from you, child.'

'I know. She said that.'

Mrs Shields shook her head. 'No, I don't think she understands quite how much she wants.'

'She can't stay here any more. You've told her.'

'I don't like to turn her away, but you need to keep some distance from her. Not just out there.' She reached out and placed a fingertip on Jane's head, then her breast. 'In here and here, too.'

'I will.'

By the time she reached Simon's house, Jane could feel the fast rhythm of machines thrumming all around Leeds. Catherine might recall a time before industry was here, but it was all she'd ever known. The only air she'd ever breathed.

What was she going to do about Martha?

'Ensign Neville Murdoch owes me a sovereign,' Simon said with relish. 'That's a fair start.'

'It doesn't bring him any closer to the dock,' Rosie said. 'You still need to prove he killed Poole.'

'I'm going to try. I intend to deliver him and his friend to the constable.'

'What do you want me to do today?' Jane asked. She couldn't help with the cavalrymen – they both knew that. It was a man's work.

'There's one more name that George Mudie found in Poole's notebook,' Rosie said. 'It was in code – I don't know why. Walter Carter. He's like Peacock, unimportant. But it looks like Poole sold things to him a few times.'

'Yes.' She kept her voice dull. 'I know who he is. I'll go and talk to him.'

Simon wouldn't be seeing Murdoch until the evening, if the ensign went to the Yorkshire Hussar at all. He drifted up Briggate, past the shops that catered to the people with money, and across to the far side of the Head Row.

The buildings along here were plain. No fancy goods in the shop windows. A street of trades. Men worked and sweated. These were small businesses, one man or two, three or four employees if they were doing very well. Workshops, not factories. Just people trying to survive by their skills.

The smell of ink had seeped into the plaster of the wall and down through the floorboards in Mudie's shop. The heavy press sat at the back of the room, the man feeding in sheets of paper and pushing down hard.

'I wanted to thank you for breaking that code,' Simon said.

Mudie shrugged. 'Nothing too hard, and it was a pleasant way to spend an evening. My mind doesn't get enough exercise these days. Did you get much from it?'

He'd been a journalist once, first for someone else, then running his own newspaper until it went out of business. He still loved a story, a mystery of any kind.

'A few things.'

'Are you likely to earn Williams's ten pounds?'

'In good time,' Simon told him.

'Which means you've hardly got anywhere. Don't try and fool me, I've known you too long.'

'I'm making a little progress.'

'Didn't you say that Alderman Ferguson and Dr Brady were putting pressure on our friend the constable over this?'

'That's what he told me.'

'Have you stopped to wonder why?' Mudie asked.

'Only briefly.' Another lie. But all in a good cause. The question had nibbled at him, but he still didn't know what was really going on between the constable and those two.

'You should, Simon. Think about it: what interest could they have in the death of a thief like Poole?'

'It's a chance to embarrass Williams. I've heard that he and Ferguson have had words a few times in meetings.'

'Maybe that's all it is.' The man frowned and shrugged. 'But if you happen to run into one of them and could steer the conversation without giving anything away . . .'

He was right, Simon thought as he picked his way between the puddles on Briggate. He needed to go to the source, to find out what their interest was in this. That way he might make it through this quagmire. A coach flew out of the Rose and Crown, a whirlwind of noise and whips, careering round the corner, never stopping as it knocked over an old man. People rushed to help him back to his feet and pick up his hat. No real damage done. This time.

Ferguson would be at the Moot Hall for the meeting this morning. Simon pulled out his pocket watch, glanced at the time and smiled. He might even be walking along North Street at this very moment.

Time for a little stroll.

'Westow,' Alderman Ferguson said in surprise. 'Do you have business out this way? We don't often see you here.'

'All done.' Yet another lie; they were stacking higher and higher. 'I thought I'd stretch my legs for a few minutes. Another meeting at the Moot Hall?'

'They come around too quickly,' Ferguson answered with a grimace. 'All hot air and fraying tempers. But we're there to run the town. It's a civic duty.'

And one they all managed to make pay handsomely. Simon turned, strolling back into town beside him.

'Why don't you resign if you don't enjoy it?'

A wheezing chuckle. 'You know me. I'm like the rest, Westow. I like the power.'

At least he was honest enough to understand that and admit it.

'Bad business about the thief who was murdered at Flay Crow Mill,' Simon said. 'Have they found the killer yet?'

It was blatant, completely obvious and clumsy. But he could think of no other way to drag it into the conversation.

'Not that I've heard.' He banged his stick down on the road. 'But Williams is neither use nor ornament.' He glanced at Simon. 'Did you know this Poole, then?'

'I had one or two dealings with him.'

Ferguson gave him an appraising look. 'That's right. Fullbrook's silver. Any idea who'd want him dead?'

'None at all.' One more lie for the pile. 'But I didn't really know him well. Pity.'

'Why?'

'I'd like to see it solved.'

They walked in silence for a while, following the short rise that led towards the Head Row and Briggate. Suddenly the buildings started to close around them. Street after street of houses hurriedly thrown up on empty land.

'Why the need to find out who killed him?' Simon asked. 'There have been plenty of deaths where no murderer's been found.'

'That's exactly my point, Westow. We've had far too many of them. Time it stopped.'

'How will you do that? A different constable?'

'If that's what it takes.' His voice turned dark. 'And it probably will.'

That was the answer. Williams was fighting for a job that paid him well, one where he didn't really have to work. Find the killer and he'd win. Ferguson would give up on the idea of a new constable, at least for now. Williams had very carefully shaded the truth when he'd enlisted Simon. But life was no more than a selection of lies and truth, most of them coming in different tones of grey.

Neither Ferguson nor Williams gave a damn about Laurence Poole or his killers. The only one who did was Simon. He was trapped in the middle of a political battle.

Who was the stupid one now? he wondered. He'd allowed himself to be caught up in a row between two other men as they jostled for position against each other.

At least he'd learned what he needed. More than he expected. With a wave, he left Ferguson at the Moot Hall. Let him indulge in his games. Simon had work to do.

He felt angry. But a little rage was good. It stoked the fire inside, the furious roar. Suddenly he cared more about Poole than he had before. He was going to bring those cavalrymen to justice.

Not in order for Constable Williams to keep his job and wipe the smirk from Ferguson's face. Not even for ten pounds.

Not even really for Poole himself. But it was the only way he'd be able to calm the feelings beginning to surge through his veins.

Walter Carter lived in a building in Pack Horse Yard. A low, dark passageway led in from Briggate. At the other end Jane could slip out to Lands Lane. All around there was noise. Carts and coaches rumbling over the cobbles and shaking the ground. The yells of people as they walked and talked.

At night there was always music from the public house. Singing clubs that met in the upstairs room. She'd heard them from time to time. Raucous and out of tune, going at the old songs with pleasure but no skill.

Carter was a man who seemed to snuffle around his rooms. Dressed in clothes that had fitted him well ten years earlier but looked tight and uncomfortable now. A face speckled with blackheads like dots across his skin. His hair was receding, turning from sandy red to grey. He looked like a man on the cusp of old age. Except for his eyes – they were young and lively.

'Well, well, the prettiest girl in Leeds has come to see me.'

Every time Jane came here, he used the same lines. Trying to make her blush. That was what he claimed, at least. They were words. They meant nothing. She let them wash over her.

'Laurence Poole,' she said.

'What about him? He's dead.'

'You knew him.'

'I—' He started to object, then nodded. 'Yes. I knew him. He'd bring me things he'd stolen.'

NINE

Jane studied his eyes as he spoke.

'What else?' she asked. 'I know there's something, I can see it on your face.'

'He came in here a few weeks before they found him at Flay Crow Mill.' A long hesitation, as if he wasn't sure whether he wanted to say more. 'He gave me something to look after for him. He said he'd come back for it.'

'What was it?'

He shook his head.

'Simon is looking into this,' Jane said. 'You can tell me or he'll come and visit you.'

A deep breath and a defeated sigh. With a nod, he dug into a pile of papers and packages in one corner of the room. He came out with a small parcel wrapped in brown paper and neatly tied with string. 'This.'

It was square, like a box, solid, impossible to guess what was inside.

'Did he say what it was?' Jane asked.

'No. Just to keep it safe and he'd come back for it.' He held it out. It was lighter than she imagined; it seemed to weigh no more than a bird in her hands. 'But he never did.'

'I'll take it,' she told him.

'I liked Laurence,' Carter said. 'We'd have a drink together sometimes. Down at the Palace or up at the Fleece. He could make me laugh.'

She listened. The man needed to talk, to remember Poole. Let him. There might be some tiny nugget of gold in there, something useful. But all he had were memories; there was nothing fresh to learn from them. Still, she waited until his voice faded, like a clockwork toy running down, then left him to his grief. That was better in private, anyway. But she had the sense he was still holding something back from her.

'He's out somewhere,' Rosie said. She tousled the hair of one of the boys as they ran around in the kitchen. 'No tutor today. He's ill. So I have to look after them.' She smiled. 'Could always be worse.' She looked at the package. 'What is it?'

Her eyes widened as Jane explained. Rosie brought a knife from the pocket of her dress. She cut the string and peeled away the paper.

It was a box. Plain, small. She eased off the lid. Inside lay a small, bound book. About the size of her palm, perhaps half an inch thick. The leather of the cover was cracked and old, starting to peel. Rosie turned the first page.

Jane stared and caught her breath. She'd never seen anything like this. It was . . . more than beautiful. Beyond any words she knew. The people painted on the page looked alive, as if they might walk out and embrace her. Even the writing was unlike anything she'd ever known. Some letters thick, others thin as spider legs. One word that shimmered as if it was made from gold.

She wanted to reach out, to touch the paper. But it looked too fragile, too delicate; she was afraid she'd damage it.

Without thinking, she heard her voice echo Rosie's words: 'What is it?'

'I don't know.' Rosie's answer was hesitant, full of wonder. 'It's . . .' But she couldn't put it into words, either. 'About the only thing I can say is that this didn't belong to Laurence Poole.'

'Who'd know?' Jane asked.

'George Mudie,' Rosie answered after a moment. 'He might.' She looked at the boys. 'Coats and boots on now,' she ordered. 'We're going out.'

Like a whirlwind, they left the room, shouting and tumbling as they dressed. Rosie eased the book back into its box and looked up.

'Are you coming with us?'

Jane shook her head. She needed time to think. Some time by herself to consider what she'd seen in that book. It was the first time an object of any kind had touched her. Pierced her. She felt as if all the air had been driven from her body and she needed to consider why.

'What are you doing here?' Simon stood as Rosie entered Mudie's shop and began to walk towards her. He'd returned to warm his bones after seeing Ferguson. The boys crowded round his legs. His voice changed from curious to urgent. 'Has something happened?'

'This,' Rosie said, and held out the box. 'I don't know what it is. I wanted George to take a look at it.'

Mudie cocked his head. 'What's inside it?'

'A book,' she replied, then stopped and corrected herself. 'Open it up. It's not anything I've ever seen before.'

Simon watched as Mudie placed the box on the printing press and opened it. A single glance inside and the man took a step away.

'You handle it.' Mudie held up his hands. He'd wiped them on a rag but they were still black with ink.

Simon examined the tattered leather of the cover. It didn't look like much, scuffed and worn. But it felt old, as if thousands of fingers had touched and rubbed across it over the years.

'Open it,' Rosie said.

He did as she said, his chest tight as he slowly turned each leaf. It was a small book, not more than twenty pages, but every one of them was exquisite. Painted, the colours bright, the lettering elaborate and black, different from any printing he'd ever seen. As he reached the end, Simon stared at Mudie.

'Well, George, what is it?'

Mudie exhaled as if he'd just come out of a trance. 'I'm not sure. But I can tell you that it's all done by hand and those words are in Latin.'

'What's Latin?' Rosie asked. She waved at the boys to sit and be quiet.

'It's an ancient language. The Catholic church uses it. I'm certain that book' – he nodded at it – 'wasn't written recently.'

'How old?' Simon asked.

'Hundreds of years.' He sounded stunned, with something close to reverence in his voice. 'It must be worth a fortune. Where did it come from?'

'Jane.' Rosie told them where she'd discovered it.

'Poole must have stolen it,' Simon said. 'That's the only explanation.'

'Then why haven't we heard anything about it?' Mudie asked. 'For Christ's sake, Simon, it's the most beautiful thing any of us are ever likely to see in our lives. Someone has to be missing this.'

Simon held the book in his hands. It was everything Mudie claimed. Delicate, remarkable. And it had to be valuable. Worth more than anything he'd ever touched.

Why hadn't someone reported it stolen? Where had it come from? And how had it ended up with a man like Poole? Was this book the reason he'd been murdered? If he'd intended to run from Leeds, why hadn't he tried to retrieve it before he was killed?

'We need to find out who owns it,' he said.

Mudie gave him a withering look. 'How are you going to do that? Put an advertisement in the *Mercury*? I know you're working for the constable, but do you really want it all coming out in public, with everyone asking awkward questions?'

Simon smiled. 'I was thinking of something more subtle.'

'Thank God for small mercies.' He rubbed his hands on the rag once more. 'If I ever get these clean, I want a proper look at that. I'd love to spend an hour just going through it.'

'Maybe you will, George.'

Simon slipped it back into the box and made sure the lid was firm. Out on Briggate, he was acutely aware of the package in his hand, how much it was worth. He said nothing until they were home. Then he wrapped the box in oilcloth and hid it away in the secret drawer in the stairs, pushing the wood until it locked with a satisfying click.

Only when it was safe and out of sight did he breathe more easily.

'We have to return it to its owner,' Rosie said.

'How?' he asked. 'We can't do anything until someone realizes it's gone.'

'You told George you had some ideas.'

He shook his head. 'I was lying. I don't have a clue.'

'Then you can think while I go shopping. Play with the boys – that'll clear your head.'

She kissed him on the cheek, picked up her basket and vanished through the door. In the kitchen Amos shouted and Richard tried to yell louder.

The book. Images of it filled Jane's mind as she walked. The shiny gold, the brilliance of the colours. So alive. She didn't know what it was. She didn't care; it didn't matter. It existed – that was enough. It meant she'd be able to see it again. Maybe even touch it if she dared, to reach out and feel all of that for herself.

The day flowed around her and she was barely aware of it. Darkness began to close in. For a moment, she wondered about returning to Simon's house, to have the chance to see the book once more.

No. That would wait for the morning. Better to go home. Maybe Mrs Shields would be able to tell her something about it.

As she walked up the Head Row, Jane realized she hadn't thought about Martha all day. Good. And it seemed the girl was keeping her distance.

By the time she entered Green Dragon Yard, night had arrived. A thin blaze of light leaked from a window, enough to cast deep shadows across the flagstones.

She stumbled, boots kicking against something on the ground. Without thinking, Jane grasped her knife and looked around. No, she had no sense of anyone at all.

She knelt, hands moving over clothes until she found flesh,

fingers across a skull, a face, then the neck. Dead. Gently, she turned the head until it caught the edge of the light.

Jane bit down on her lip until the blood flowed. It was the only way to stop herself from screaming.

TEN

The Yorkshire Hussar was busy. Dozens of conversations spilled and spiralled through the air. Simon moved between them to the card tables at the back of the room. No Murdoch, but he saw two of the men who'd won a little at cards the night before.

Simon claimed an empty seat, settled in, and looked at the hand that was dealt. Tonight, he'd let the others win; he had no quarrel with them and it would divert attention from him. Ensign Murdoch might come in later. Perhaps this time Lieutenant Johnson would be with him.

He played the game, sipped on a glass of brandy, but his mind wasn't on the cards. It kept slipping back to the book that Poole had left with Walter Carter.

He'd never paid much attention to words. There were men who read for pleasure, but he'd never been one of them. That book, though, was remarkable. All the work that had gone into making it . . . the sense of devotion and faith seemed to rise from every page. It shone.

How had someone like Laurence Poole ended up with it? And if he had something so valuable, why was he trying to peddle rubbish even Michael Peacock wouldn't buy? That book could have bought him a gentleman's life. It made no sense at all.

'Westow.' The man speaking his name brought him back to the here and now.

'Sorry.'

'Your bet.'

He shook his head and placed the cards face down on the table. 'Too rich for me.'

He downed the rest of his drink in a gulp and stood. His mind wasn't sharp enough for cards tonight. He was far too distracted. Tomorrow he'd come back when he was thinking clearly. Maybe Murdoch would show his face then.

Jane tried to breathe, but it caught in her chest. The pulse was pounding in her neck, her heart racing. Bile rose into her throat. She forced it back, standing with one hand pressed against the cold stone of the wall.

The body was cold. The crust of dried blood around the missing eye gave his identity away. Big Tom's friend. He'd been alive when Jane left him. She made herself explore further, fingers rubbing against the flesh of his throat and feeling where it had been sliced open.

Tom had murdered his friend and left the corpse here. Brought it to where she lived. To the one place she felt safe. He couldn't kill her himself, so he'd try to have her hung for murder. Panic started to fill her mind. What if he'd already told one of the night watch? The constable might be on his way. She lifted her head and listened, almost expecting to hear boots on stone.

But they didn't come. There were only the usual noises of the night.

Questions rattled through her. How long had he been dead? How had Tom moved the corpse? Jane made herself take a deep breath. None of that mattered. He was here now and she needed to be rid of him.

She couldn't let anyone find the body here. She couldn't bring murder to Mrs Shields's home.

She was scared, terrified. She had goose pimples on her arms and her skin was clammy and cold. Her palms were sweaty. Jane rubbed them against the thin cotton of her dress and took hold of the body.

She had to move him. There was no other way.

She pulled. Strained and tugged. All she could manage was an inch. He was too heavy to shift. She tried again. Two inches this time. Then a foot. Every muscle burned. She was on the edge of tears. Ready to give up, to say it was too much for her, but she couldn't. She had no choice. She had to continue. To keep the law from Mrs Shields. Jane shut everything else out of her mind. The only thing in the world was the dead man in front of her. She tried again, and again and again. She managed to drag him ten yards. Then she had to stand, panting as if she'd run for miles. It had seemed to take forever. He was so heavy, so awkward. She didn't know if she could move him much further. But she had to. She needed him away from the house, to stop any suspicion. Jane bent again and gripped his clothes.

After a few minutes, she arrived at a rhythm of sorts. Ten paces at a time. She forced herself, pulling until she believed every muscle would snap. Whenever she looked up, she seemed to have covered no distance at all. The house was still too close. A short break, gasping for air, then more, taking the corpse further and further away. And every moment she had to remain alert for voices and the sound of men walking.

But the only thing around her was the night. Off in the distance, people shouted and laughed. No one strayed anywhere close to her. Down and along, ten more paces and stop to rest. She'd lost track of how long she'd been pulling him. The moments all seemed to blur together. Half an hour? Longer? She'd made progress, gone from Green Dragon Yard now and over into Butts Court. But not far enough yet.

Jane tried not to look at the corpse. She didn't want to remember the dead face. It was easier to think of him as something not human. He was just a weight, a thing. A jumble of bones inside a broken, bulging bag of flesh. She hauled him, stopped. Moved him, stopped again. Over and over until she thought her heart might burst from the strain.

Another short rest, then she forced herself to do it again. Flexed her fingers to ease the cramp in her hands. Forced her jaws together, grabbed him and pulled. Ten more paces and a pause to catch her breath. Once more. She was close to Basinghall Street now. A few people were passing just yards away, even in the middle of the night. She needed to stay out of sight.

Jane dragged the body into a doorway and rested. She was trembling from the effort. Arms and legs shaking, beyond her control. For a minute she couldn't stop it. All she could do was stand, barely able to stay upright.

Gradually, her body began to obey, to move the way she told it. Very slowly, her fingers unclenched. She was sodden, wringing with sweat. It trickled down her back, it was under her armpits, inside her stockings. Jane began to walk away, trying not to hurry as the feeling of relief overwhelmed her. She was dizzy and her head swam until she needed to stop and lean against the wall to steady herself.

A minute, just one minute, standing still, becoming part of the darkness, and the world began to ease back into focus. Every part of her body ached. Her shoulders, her back, her arms. Her fingers, where she'd been forced to clutch him. Thighs and calves. Each step was painful as she retraced the path to Mrs Shields's house. Then she was home. She was safe.

'You, too?' he asked.

The oil lamp sat on the kitchen table. The flame flickered as Simon entered. He saw Rosie sitting with the book in her hand, staring at one of the pages with quiet reverence.

'It's . . .' She struggled for the word. 'Wonderful' was all she could manage.

'It is,' he agreed.

'Did you have any luck tonight?'

Simon shook his head. He ran a finger over the edge of the pages. 'I'm damned if I can understand why no one's realized this is missing.'

'Perhaps you should talk to Constable Williams.'

'Maybe.' He'd considered it as he walked home. Williams might know something. But he'd hold back from that. Beyond himself and Rosie, only Jane and Mudie knew about the book. That was enough. He could trust them. Outside that small circle he was wary. And he certainly didn't trust the constable; he wasn't about to give the man any type of hold over him.

Rosie's gaze was rapt. 'How much is this worth, do you think?' she asked.

'I couldn't begin to guess,' he told her. 'More than we possess.'

She wrapped it very carefully. 'We know it's been stolen.' She sighed. 'It didn't appear out of the air. Sooner or later, someone's going to want it back. We're thief-takers, Simon. No one's going to be able to prosecute Poole for this. But they'll pay us to return it.'

'There's a part of me hopes they'll never notice,' Simon said. 'Do you understand that?'

'I do. This is going to be worth a great deal to us, though.'

He could hear the hunger in her voice.

The book lay on the table between them. Simon had watched Jane open it and go through every page, staring, devouring each one of them, placing them tidily away in her memory.

'Do you think Poole was killed for that?' he asked.

'He might have been. But that's just one of the questions,' Rosie said. 'The first one is where did it come from? If you can discover that, we can follow the trail and find the other answer.'

Jane raised her head. 'If those cavalrymen who killed him were looking for this, wouldn't we have heard by now?'

Simon rubbed his temples. 'Yes,' he agreed after a while. She was right. They'd be asking questions of everyone and trying to tear Leeds apart to find something as valuable as this. 'I'll need to talk to Williams anyway, and let him know what's happening. I won't mention the book. Not yet.' He paused and corrected himself. 'I'll send him a message to meet, anyway.' He chuckled. 'After all, I can't be seen walking into his office.'

Rosie looked up at Jane. 'Where's that girl who was with you?'

Before she could answer, a fist pounded against the door. Simon led Mudie through to the kitchen.

'All of you together *and* the book,' he said with satisfaction. He held up his hands, as clean as they were ever likely to be. 'I won't put any ink on it, I promise. May I?'

He turned the pages slowly, mouthing the Latin words.

'I saw the curate from St John's Church yesterday,' he said when he'd finished. 'The conversation happened to turn to printing and prayer books.'

'Just happened?' Simon raised his eyebrows. 'This wasn't printed, though, was it?'

'No,' Mudie said with a sigh of happiness. 'Everything here is written or painted. All done by hand. It must have taken, I don't know . . . days, weeks. Possibly even months. If I understood what he said, this is what they call a Book of Hours.'

'What's that?' Rosie asked.

'It's the services of the Catholic church. The prayers. A rich man would pay monks to make one. As a gift for his wife, possibly.'

'We don't have a Catholic church in Leeds,' Simon said.

Mudie raised an eyebrow. 'Very good. We haven't for centuries. Which means this book is at least that old. Quite possibly more.'

'My God,' Rosie said. She exhaled slowly. 'Could it have been stolen from a church?'

Mudie shrugged. 'I've no idea. We only have three in Leeds. Real churches, I mean. I've never heard of any of them owning something like this. And none of the chapels would want it. This is much too fancy for their taste. No, this has been in some rich family for generations. They just don't realize it's missing yet.'

'How would Poole know about it?' Simon asked.

'Maybe he didn't,' Jane said. She stared at the book on the table. 'Maybe he was in a house taking other things and came across this. Anyone can see it's worth money.'

'It makes as much sense as anything,' Mudie agreed. 'Now, I have a business to run. With a little luck, the clients are already queuing outside my shop.'

'We know a little more about the book,' Simon said. 'That's something.' He stroked the ancient leather binding.

'None of it helps us, though,' Rosie said. She shook her head in disbelief. 'Can you imagine being rich enough not to know this was missing?'

'Poole knew it was worth money,' he said. 'That's why he left it with Walter Carter. It's a perfect hiding place; no one would expect him to have anything of value.'

'Yes,' Jane said.

'So when he had this, why was he trying to sell scraps to Peacock, things no one wanted to buy?' Simon asked.

'He needed money to run from Leeds.'

'To leave, yes. I suppose he was going to collect it before he left on a coach.'

'Why didn't he just sell it to Charlie Harker?' Rosie asked.

Simon shook his head. 'Harker wouldn't have enough money to buy this book. If he and Poole hadn't managed to agree a price for the Fullbrook silver, Charlie couldn't have afforded this.'

That was the irony, he thought. Poole had something worth a fortune, but there was no one in town with the money to buy it. In London, perhaps . . . even there it would stand out and be difficult to sell. But Laurence was dead before anything like that could happen.

'Keep trying to find out what you can about Poole before he died,' he told Jane. 'You did a good job with Walter Carter.'

She nodded and left.

'I've never seen her look at anything the way she did that book,' Rosie said. 'Did you see how she took it all in? I think she'd have eaten it if she could.'

For once, Jane desired something. Such a human trait. Good, he thought. About time, too. Coveted, that was the word the preachers used. As if wanting something lovely might be a sin. 'Let her. Have you noticed she's become more human since she started living with Catherine Shields?'

And she was still the best at this work that he'd ever known. Now Simon had to push himself harder to keep pace with her discoveries.

Someone had discovered the body at first light and called for the watch. Jane listened to the gossip as she wandered up and down Briggate. No doubt that he'd been murdered, what with one eye gone and his throat slashed. Gordon Baker. That had been his name. Through the blood and the sorrow of death, someone had recognized his face. Maybe someone would mourn him. It wouldn't be her. Good riddance; that was all she could think.

Nobody mentioned the yard behind the Green Dragon or Mrs Shields's name. But there was no reason they should. There was no connection with Baker that anyone knew, and the corpse had been found nowhere near the house. Jane's body still ached. She'd been sore and stiff when she woke. It had eased a little as she walked to Simon's house, heart in her mouth, keeping her distance from Butts Court and Basinghall Street. She didn't want anyone to see her near there.

But she was safe. That was the important thing. She'd beaten Big Tom once more. Baker's death would remain a mystery. They wouldn't be coming after her or Catherine Shields. She'd done her duty. It was the very least she owed the woman.

Walter Carter hadn't told her everything. Jane had sensed it when he gave her the package. There was something else about Laurence

Poole that he knew and was keeping to himself. Some last secret piece.

He was easy to follow as he left Pack Horse Yard. He never suspected a thing. Jane walked with the shawl over her hair, a purposeful look on her face. No one would ever recall what she looked like or that they'd even seen her. She was one more ghost moving along the street. Her breath bloomed and steamed. The air was crisp enough to redden her cheeks.

Carter followed the road down to the Calls and entered a warehouse that overlooked the river. Very strange. He wasn't a man to come calling in a place like this. What business could he have here?

She slid back into the shadows to wait. A little time and patience and she'd have her answer.

Five minutes passed, ten and more. The parish church clock chimed the hour, and then quarter past.

Finally, Carter emerged, clutching a box. A little bigger than the one that had held the book. A glance around and he began to scurry off like an animal seeking its burrow.

Jane slipped between passers-by, her eyes fixed on him. Across the bridge, seeing the barges lined up three and four deep by the warehouses. By Dock Street she was right behind him, close enough to nudge him and make him turn in annoyance.

'Down there,' she said. He opened his mouth to object until she showed him the knife under her shawl. Ericsson's lumber yard lay a few yards along the road in between the small businesses importing this and that, each with their offices and tiny wharves. But hardly anyone passed on the cobbled road. A cart waited, no one in sight. The horse had its head down, munching on a small bundle of hay.

'You've been busy,' Jane said. 'Collecting something?'

Carter pulled the box closer to his body. 'It was waiting for me.'

'In a warehouse.' Jane stared at him. Carter's gaze darted around, as if he was hunting for some way to escape. The day was chilly, but he had a thin sheen of sweat on his forehead.

'Yes.'

'What's in it?'

He swallowed, shook his head, but didn't answer.

'If it belongs to you,' Jane told him. 'You must know what's inside.'

He held the box tighter, trying to push it out of sight beneath his coat.

'Open it for me. Let's see what you have.'

'Not here,' he said.

She let the light flash on the knife blade. 'Here,' she told him.

With each layer of wrapping that came off, Carter seemed to grow smaller.

He pulled away the final piece of paper. It revealed a piece of silver, a tiny jug of some kind. She could see a mark on the base. The metal was smooth, almost like silk under her fingers.

'Whose is it?' Jane asked. 'Poole's?'

Defeated, he nodded. 'He was going to come back for the package he left with me. He told me this was going to be mine for taking care of everything for him. He said it would be enough to keep me for the rest of my life if I was careful.' He looked wistfully at the jug. 'He was telling the truth, wasn't he?' Carter turned to her. 'What was the other thing?'

'A book,' she replied.

'A book?' he asked in disbelief. 'What use is a book? I thought he was going to sell it.'

She didn't try to explain. How could she begin to describe it? She'd never be able to make him understand when she couldn't make sense of it herself.

'Why did you come to collect this now?'

'Because . . .' he began, then hesitated and tried to collect his thoughts. 'I was going to wait until people forgot about Laurence. Nobody would notice. But after you took that package, I thought I'd better do something before it was too late.'

'What else is there around town?' Jane asked.

'That's all,' he said. He looked at her with wide eyes. 'Can I have it?'

She shook her head. 'You know it belongs to someone else, the same as the book. Did he tell you where he stole them?'

'No.' Carter's voice was empty, just a husk. All his hopes, his good future had vanished.

Jane had one more question. 'Why did you give me that package? The one with the book.'

'You took me by surprise. I thought maybe you knew and you

were testing me.' He was a man filled with regrets. 'And you work with the thief-taker. I decided I'd better give it to you, just in case.'

'You can go home now,' Jane said.

'Why?' he asked. His eyes glistened; he was close to tears. 'I don't have anything from all this, do I? I can't even sit and look at that jug.'

'Maybe Simon will give you some of the reward when it goes back to its owner.'

'Do you think so?'

'Perhaps,' she said. 'I don't know.'

A pat on the arm and she left him.

Jane watched Rosie turn the jug in her hands.

'It's been well kept. Not from Fullbrook's, the only thing missing there was a spoon. Carefully polished. It looks like it's part of a set. For tea or coffee.' She weighed it in her hand. 'Poole was busy, wasn't he? And Carter said there was nothing else?'

'That's right.'

'Did you believe him?'

'This time? Yes.'

ELEVEN

'Carter swore to Jane that the book and this are all Poole left.'

Simon picked up the silver jug and turned it in his hands. Beautiful workmanship. Probably a hundred years old, maybe more. He peered at the hallmark, then dipped a nib in the ink and copied it on a sheet of paper.

'What do you think it's worth?' she asked.

'Enough to make me wonder why no one's realized it's missing. The same as the book.'

'Maybe they're from the same place,' Rosie said.

'That's my guess.' Simon folded the paper and placed it in his pocket.

* * *

Jane wandered around Leeds, going all the way from Little Woodhouse out past Fearn's Island. She kept the shawl raised over her hair as she moved through the crowds. Gordon Baker's murder was still on everyone's lips. But with no suspects and no clues, she was safe. She'd succeeded.

If she'd come home early, before Big Tom left the body there . . . she couldn't let herself think about that. Jane ran her fingers over the ladder of scars on her forearm. Luck had smiled on her last night. That was enough.

'I've come across this before.' Nicholas Kent the silversmith tapped the paper and pushed a pair of thick spectacles up his nose. A piece of plate lay in front of him, a small part of the delicate decoration complete. A design of vine leaves and flowers so real that Simon imagined he could touch them. An apprentice swept his bench with a small, fine brush, gathering up every last particle of silver. It was far too valuable to waste.

A few years before, a man had stolen some silver from Kent's workshop. A sugar bowl that was still waiting to be worked. Simon had tracked the thief all the way to Halifax and brought him back to face trial. Condemned to death, he was granted a reprieve before he reached the gallows, the sentence commuted to fourteen years in Australia. The thief was out there still, if he'd managed to stay alive.

'Where's it from?' Simon asked.

'Leeds,' Kent replied with a smile. 'You didn't know that, did you?'

'No. I've never come across the mark before.'

'It's from a long time ago. If you tease that design apart, you have the letter B twice.' He illustrated with a thin finger. 'You see? Those are his initials. BB: Benjamin Bootham. I've only seen three things he made, all of them spoons. Wonderful work.'

'That's very helpful. I didn't know the hallmark at all.'

'It's rare,' Kent said. 'I don't think he produced much. Where did you find it?'

'I saw a piece in York.' Yet one more lie, but safer than the truth, especially if the man's work was so uncommon.

'Where was it? In a sale room? What was it? Another spoon?'

'A milk jug.'

'Really?' Kent said in disbelief. 'I've never heard of him executing a piece like that. Where did it come from, do you remember?'

'I never thought to ask,' Simon told him. 'I liked the look, that was all. Then it slipped my mind until I came home.'

At this rate his lies would reach all the way to heaven, but it was for the best.

'You live and learn,' Kent said. 'Whoever was selling a Bootham piece must have made himself a pretty penny. I'm surprised I never heard about it. Gossip like that usually travels.' He sighed. 'Ah well.'

'I appreciate the information, Nick.'

'If you have the chance to see another Bootham, take me with you, Simon.'

A Book of Hours that was probably priceless and a rare and valuable silver jug. Poole had stolen them both, that much was obvious. When, though? And where?

Jane was right: he hadn't been murdered for these. If that were the case, they'd have heard about the search for them. Why was he dead, then?

Questions Simon couldn't answer. He needed to befriend those two cavalry officers and dig down to the truth. Maybe they'd both be at the Yorkshire Hussar later.

'So far I'm hearing plenty of questions,' Williams said. 'But no evidence against Poole's killers.'

'It'll come,' Simon told him. He hoped he was right.

The house was closed against the February night. A fire burned bright in the grate, oil lamps were lit and the heavy curtains drawn.

The reply to Simon's note had come in terse, cryptic terms: *Eight. I want to know your progress. W.*

'It had better. And I need it quickly. Ferguson and Brady aren't about to give up. They're still breathing down my neck.'

'I'll try.'

'Do better than that, Westow. Remember, I'm making it worth your while to succeed.'

'I haven't forgotten.' The promise of ten pounds was sharp in his mind. But so was everything else.

* * *

'Westow, good to see you again.' Murdoch shook his hand and smiled. 'You won't mind if I keep that money a day or two longer, will you? I can double it playing cards tonight and repay you with interest. How would that sound?'

'Excellent.' Simon gave a small bow.

Murdoch introduced the man at his side. 'This is Peter Johnson. My comrade and good friend. *Lieutenant* Johnson. His father thought it was worth the money to buy him a proper commission.'

Well, well, Simon thought. There was more than a twitch of envy behind that remark.

'Do you play cards, Lieutenant?'

'I do.' He had a broad, greedy smile and small, dark eyes that gave little away. A slippery handshake. There was something about the man that made Simon's hackles rise. He wouldn't trust him in a hundred years. 'And I'm a damned sight better than Neville. You won't be leaving me in your debt.'

'Then I wish you luck.'

He was going to need it. Simon intended to use all those tricks he'd so painstakingly learned and part the man from some of his money.

'What do you do, Mr Westow?' Johnson asked as they settled around the table.

'I'm a thief-taker.'

The lieutenant raised his eyebrows. 'Not a common trade. That must be an interesting profession. Plenty of rogues?'

'It's more straightforward than you'd imagine,' Simon told him with a simple smile. 'Something is stolen and the owner places an advertisement for its return. I take it back and receive a fee.'

'What about the criminals?'

Simon shrugged. 'That depends on whether the victim wants to prosecute. Most of them don't want to spend the time or the money going to court.'

Johnson took a cheroot from a case and went through the ritual of lighting it from a candle on the table, puffing until he had a wreath of smoke around his head.

'There must be opportunities to . . . guide things a little.'

The man tried to sound casual, as if he was making idle conversation. But he wasn't wasting any time. Straight to the heart of the matter.

'I daresay that's true enough,' Simon agreed. 'For anyone inclined to such things.'

The cards came around. A few easy hands, watching and learning the lieutenant's style. He was cocky about his ability to read the game, impulsive in his betting. He didn't lose anything, but he wasn't a winner, either. Murdoch was more cautious, feeling his way into things. Simon wagered a little, made sure he won, and sat back.

The deal passed to him. At first, he was kind, not skinning Johnson for much, just enough to make it sting. He let Murdoch make enough to settle his debts. Ten hands and Simon passed the cards to the next man at the table.

'I'll take a rest for a while.'

'Splendid idea,' Johnson agreed and started to rise. 'We'll join you if you don't mind, won't we, Neville?'

The lieutenant bought glasses of brandy for the three of them. They stood by the window staring out at Nelson Street. The carts and drivers had gone home for the day. All that remained were the coaches, roaring out of town to make time on the highways, and a few sedate private vehicles, the horses trotting, the owners hidden inside behind heavy leather curtains.

'I'd be interested in hearing more about your work, Mr Westow,' Johnson said. 'You must lead quite a life.'

'Not really. No more than you gentlemen. You fought with Wellington?' They were both old enough, into their thirties. By rights they should both have been captains by now, if not majors. They probably lacked the funds to buy the promotion.

'Yes, up through Spain all the way to Paris.' Murdoch sighed. 'Then it was half-pay for a year until Boney returned. We've both been lucky since then, still on the proper strength. Better than many who served.'

'And the military life suits you?' Simon asked. 'I suppose it must.'

Johnson grimaced. 'The cavalry is an expensive business. Supply your own damned horses and equipment. The army doesn't pay for any of it. And a man needs his pleasures as well. Allowances from the family don't stretch too far.'

He was coming to it. Maybe it wouldn't happen tonight, but he was edging closer and closer. All Simon had to do was push him a little.

'Then what do you do?'

Johnson looked at his friend for a moment, then nodded.

'We have a little enterprise,' Murdoch said.

'Bold fellows. I admire initiative. What is it?'

'We used to work with someone from the town. Unfortunately, he's no longer available.'

'Really? What happened to him?' Simon asked.

'He had an accident.'

What happened to Poole was definitely no accident, but he held his tongue.

'You didn't say what kind of business you have.'

'It's not exactly a business.' Johnson wrinkled his nose at the idea he'd be involved in anything so vulgar. 'More an adventure that pays.'

'That sounds intriguing.'

Johnson raised his glass in a toast. 'We enjoy it. Perhaps we can discuss it more another time.' He nodded towards the card table. 'A few more hands?'

He could have taken them for all they had, but Simon was content to sit back and observe, come out a pound ahead and be anonymous. A little after eleven he took his leave, feeling satisfied. Things were moving. No sense in trying to rush them. There would be a shift soon enough. Johnson sounded eager to forge ahead.

As he made his way home, Simon thought about the Book of Hours and the silver milk jug again. Who owned them? For the love of God, how could people have failed to notice they were missing? They were unlike anything else Poole had ever taken. Too valuable and rare to sell in Leeds. He suddenly recalled the cryptic words in the notebook. *To the dark*. What did they mean?

He was wrapped in his thoughts, a heartbeat too slow. By the time he felt someone close, it was too late – they were already there. Footpads, a pair of them. One in front, the other behind. Knives out. Far enough away that he couldn't cut them.

Who? The faces were hidden in shadows under the broad brims of their hats. Young men by the look of them, with lean bodies. But their movements were awkward and unpractised. They were nervous, new to this game. That made them unpredictable. Dangerous.

Simon took the knife from his belt and slid a second from its hiding place up his sleeve. He took a pace to the side, able to see both of them now. Neither of the men spoke. He could feel the fear coming off them in waves.

No one had sent this pair to kill. They were only robbers, fresh to it, chancing their luck at night. But this time they'd bitten off more than they expected. Simon wasn't some drunk, too scared to defend himself.

Simon darted towards one of the men, watching him dance back towards the middle of the street. The other didn't move, didn't try to take advantage of the opening. Good. A blow from someone as green as this pair could kill just as effectively as an assassin's knife.

'I'm Simon Westow, the thief-taker,' he said. 'I'll give you a chance. You can run off now and forget this ever happened or you can spend the rest of your lives regretting it in Australia. I will prosecute you, if you're still alive.' Simon gave time for the words to sink into their minds, astonished at how confident he sounded. This was his night for gambling. Could he bluff them? 'It's your choice.'

He waited and let the silence weigh down on them. Give them time to consider the future. Finally, the first man turned and loped off. Another moment and the second joined him, glancing over his shoulder to make sure Simon wasn't following.

He leaned back against the wall and took a deep breath. His hands slid the knives away into their sheaths. This time he'd won. This time. But he was growing too old to stake his life on words and brashness. One quick move, one bit of bravado . . . he didn't want to contemplate it.

Yet he knew that in a day or two, probably much less, he'd have completely forgotten about the whole episode. It would be a moment that passed and faded to nothing.

TWELVE

'Over on Cankerwell Lane,' Barnabas Wade said. 'By Sunny Bank.'

Simon knew the area. Up from town, and out along Woodhouse Lane on the road to Headingley and Skipton.

He walked up Briggate with Wade. The man always moved as if he was in a hurry to be somewhere. Long, eager strides that left Simon rushing to keep up with him. A thin, cold drizzle was falling. Wade had the collar of his greatcoat turned up and the brim of his hat low to keep the rain off his face.

'The Atkinsons have money,' he said. 'They're related to the family who were merchants here for a few generations.' He sighed and gave an envious look. 'And I know for a fact that they go away every winter.'

'Go where?' Where would people go, and why? He didn't understand that.

'South,' was the only answer Wade could give.

Simon had asked if he knew of any wealthy families who might be away for more than a day or two. Wade had rattled off the names. He kept watch on the rich in the vain hope one of them might buy some of the shares he peddled. It had never happened. Simon knew it never would. But Barnabas was a creature who treasured his dreams.

The Atkinsons seemed the most likely possibility. Their house was set apart from Leeds. Cankerwell Lane was back from the main road. Peaceful and hidden. A perfect place for Laurence Poole to rob.

'What about servants?'

'Simon, I have no idea,' Wade said in exasperation. 'If you want to know, why don't you go and find out for yourself?'

Out past the farmland, beyond the isolated gentility of Queens Square and Providence Row. A little further and he turned down the hill that was Cankerwell Lane. A few houses, then open land tumbling all the way down to the Bradford Road and Park Square. From up here it was easy to see the smoke rise from the chimneys of the manufactories then hang, stifling, over Leeds.

Down towards Sunny Bank, Wade had said. The big farm was spread out ahead, its buildings square and solid. Up here, away from all the industry, the air was clean, the town nothing more than a faint, dull insistence in the distance. He breathed deep, tasting the sweetness of it.

The Atkinsons owned an imposing house. It was perched halfway up the hill, standing at the end of a long drive, acres of open parkland stretching out behind.

He walked to the front door, boots crunching on gravel. No tracks from coach wheels, no hoof marks. It didn't look as if anyone had been along here in a while. He hammered on the wood and heard the sound echo through the house.

Nobody answered. Simon walked around the building, noting the shutters closed on the windows, upstairs and down. At the back, the small yard was empty and felt as if it had been that way for months.

A small window next to the kitchen door was broken, the pane of glass in fragments on the cobbles.

He had his answer. Poole had been here and this was how he'd entered. No need to follow. He'd seen all he needed.

Back on the road, Simon took his bearings. He saw a pair of labourers busy mending a cartwheel behind the farmhouse at Sunny Bank. They glanced up as he approached.

'You were up at the Atkinsons,' one of them said. He was stocky, with a thick, muscled body. A mat of dark hair covered the backs of his hands. His jacket was tied around the waist with string, and gaiters covered his trousers from calf to ankle.

'Nobody home,' Simon said. 'I was hoping there might be a servant.'

'You'll not find anybody in't winter,' the other man told him. 'They 'ent never here then, are they?'

He was the opposite of his companion, thin but hard. A whipcord body. Sunken cheeks where most of his teeth were gone. Hair cut short, just a little longer on top. Wrists hardly any thicker than twigs, but Simon knew the man would be strong.

'Where do they go?'

He shrugged and turned back to his work.

'Pack up the whole house,' the stout man said. 'Servants, too. Come back middle of March. Been that way for years.'

'When do they leave?'

'See in the New Year here and leave right after that.'

'Any idea where they travel?'

'Never asked. Wouldn't mean owt to me, anyway.'

He thanked them and strolled off. A track led over to Little Woodhouse, a collection of tranquil houses that gazed down on the town, then a path between the hedgerows back towards Leeds. How long since he'd been out here? Three or four years at least, but it had barely changed. The way the town seemed to alter right before his eyes, growing and growing, it came as a relief to know that a few things remained constant.

Then Leeds consumed him. It took him in its maw, filling his nostrils and his throat with its smoke and its stink and its dirt. It was an ugly, dingy place. But it was home, and he had his bargain with the place: he understood it and it accepted him.

Now he knew where it had happened. What else had Poole stolen from the Atkinsons? It was impossible to know until they returned. But he could report a possible burglary to Constable Williams. That would be an excellent way to muddy the waters.

Gordon Baker had become yesterday's news, discarded and forgotten. She'd beaten Big Tom once again. But it wouldn't be enough. It would never be enough until he was dead. He was still out there. Hiding, healing. Jane turned the gold ring on her finger.

Another hint that had come to nothing. An alehouse along the York Road, just past the junction with Marsh Lane. A rumour that Poole had sometimes visited a friend there. But the landlord didn't know the name and shook his head at the description.

Close to Low Fold, Jane stopped, wondering where to go next. She'd exhausted everything. This tip had seemed unlikely, but it was all she had.

'What are you doing?'

She whirled. She already had the knife clutched in her fist, ready to wound.

Martha stood quivering, wide-eyed, too scared to move.

In a single, swift movement, Jane slid the blade back out of sight. 'Don't do that. It's dangerous.'

'I didn't—' The girl stopped and closed her mouth.

'You know now.'

'I've heard things,' Martha said. 'It was him, wasn't it? The dead body.'

'Yes.' Jane gathered her shawl and pulled it closer around her head. The wind was sharp, cutting against her cheeks. She began to walk back towards Leeds. Let the girl keep up if she wanted to know more.

'Did I kill him?'

'No. Someone else slit his throat.' No need to tell the girl how she knew.

'Did that man do it?'

'Yes.'

Martha stayed silent. She hurried, glancing up at Jane. 'Nobody said a word about us. I didn't hear anything.'

'I know.'

'Does that mean we're safe now?'

Jane kept walking, a steady, even pace. 'Probably.'

'Can I work with you again?'

All the questions had been leading to this. Martha already knew the answers to everything else.

'Yes,' Jane said reluctantly.

'What do you want me to do?'

But there was nothing they could do. Jane had followed all the leads, traced every whisper. Still she had nothing about Poole. He might as well have completely disappeared from Leeds in the days before his death.

She stopped suddenly, thoughts rushing through her mind. 'Come on.' She began to hurry.

'Did Poole date the entries in his notebook?' Jane asked.

'No,' Rosie replied. She buttered another slice of bread and placed it in front of Martha. Richard and Amos were already eating, sitting on the other side of the table. They tried to hide their curiosity as they glanced at the girl with a mix of awe and fear. She was a little older than them, but smaller, thinner, with a layer of grime on her skin, so different from their clear, scrubbed flesh and clean clothes.

'Is there anything that comes from the days before he died?'

Rosie stood, cocking her head as she thought. 'I don't think so,' she answered slowly. She wiped her hands on a piece of linen and left the room. Martha had finished the bread and was looking around hungrily for more.

Rosie returned with the notebook, leafing through the pages, Mudie's decoding of everything in her other hand.

She shook her head. 'No, there's nothing to indicate when he did something. Why?'

'I can't find any trace of him right before he was killed. Nobody saw him. Either he was hiding in his room or he left Leeds for a little while. He told Harker he was scared of those soldiers who were after him.'

'If he vanished, why would he come back?' Rosie asked. 'He knew it was dangerous.'

'Perhaps he didn't go too far,' Jane said. 'Carter still had the book. He wouldn't have left without that, would he?'

Rosie nodded. 'You're right.'

The same overheated room. Curtains closed, the fire bright and stifling. Constable Williams sitting with his glass of wine, the decanter on a small side table.

'I got your note. You said you'd found something.'

'The Atkinsons,' Simon said.

Williams snorted. 'Which ones? There are three lots of them in town.'

'Cankerwell Lane.'

'That's Robert and his wife. What about them?'

'I had to go out there. No one around and the window by the back door is broken.'

The constable sighed. 'I'm surprised it hasn't happened before. The house is empty every winter. I'll take a look.'

'It might be a good idea,' Simon said. He didn't let his face show anything.

'Tomorrow. The day after if the men are busy – there's probably no rush. I thought you meant you had more information on Poole's murder.'

'It's coming. Bit by bit.'

'Hurry it up, Westow. Alderman Ferguson was asking me questions about the investigation again today. I need something to tell him.'

'Very soon.' Although the way things looked, it might not be what he hoped to hear. So far he had no evidence to link Poole and the cavalrymen.

Soon, but not tonight. He waited for an hour at the Yorkshire Hussar, but Murdoch and Johnson never appeared. Simon finished the dregs of his brandy and started down Briggate.

No one bothered him on the way home. No hopeful robbers

coming out of the shadows. The streets were quiet. He seemed to have Leeds to himself for once. A coach left the Rose and Crown, its lamps lit in a vain attempt to cut through the darkness.

He locked the door and fastened the bolts. Home. Safe. Another long day.

Rosie was sitting in the kitchen. A candle gave a pool of light, enough for her to read the notebook on the table. Her fingers traced the translations Mudie had made. He stood behind her, lifting the hair off the back of her neck and kissing the skin lightly. She put a hand over his.

'Found something?' he asked.

Rosie shook her head. 'Jane had an idea, but there's nothing in here to help.' She told him about it as she closed the notebook and folded the sheet of paper. 'We're back where we began.'

'Maybe we're not.' He began to pace around the floor, chewing on his lip. 'Poole wanted somewhere to hide . . .'

'What are you thinking?'

'The Atkinson house,' Simon told her and counted off the reasons on his fingers. 'He already knew it was empty. It's out of the way – no one would think about it. He could come and go in the darkness without anyone seeing.'

'If he was safe there, why would he come back to Leeds?'

'I don't know,' he admitted. 'But he must have had a very good reason.' He continued to pace.

'Go and take a look inside. It might tell you something.'

He grimaced. 'Damn it. I was with Williams tonight. I told him about the broken window at the house. He's going out to check.'

'You know he doesn't like mornings,' Rosie said. 'If you're early, you can be in and gone before he even stirs.'

THIRTEEN

Simon put his lips close to Jane's ear.

'Not a word now until we're inside. You know how sound carries in the dark.'

The first hint of dawn was rising to the east, a thin line of blue on the horizon. Cold, too. He was wrapped in a heavy, caped greatcoat and gloves, but he could feel it on his face. His breath steamed in the air as he started down Cankerwell Lane. Nothing stirred around them.

He'd stopped at Mrs Shields's house, tapping lightly on the door until Jane opened it, knife in her hand and suspicion in her eyes. One look at him and she dressed, ready to leave in less than a minute. No questions. There would be ample time later.

Ragged clouds flitted across a sliver of moon, leaving just enough light to pick out their path. Along the road, down the drive, to the yard at the back of the house. He reached through the window and unlatched the door.

Inside, the house had the heavy, dull smell of desertion. A place that had been neglected and unaired for too long.

'What are we looking for?' Jane kept her voice low.

'Any sign that Poole spent time here. Plates, a bed slept in. Anything at all.'

'Can we have a light?'

'No. There's a farmhouse down the hill. Even with the shutters closed, we can't risk them seeing anything. Oh,' he added, 'Williams and his men might be here this morning, so we need to be quick. You search upstairs.'

He began in the kitchen. A few crumbs of cheese on the table. A knife and board for bread. A small keg of beer had been breached. Put it all together and it was enough to convince him that Poole had used this as his bolthole.

Simon went through the other rooms, all too aware of the rising daylight beyond the window.

Five more minutes and he gave a soft whistle. Better not to tempt fate. Half a minute later Jane came down the stairs.

'Someone slept in one of the beds. More than once. There's a jug of water on a dresser in the room.'

'Any sign of where he might have found the silver?'

She shook her head in reply.

He led them back out, making sure the door closed properly, then kept to the shadows until they were out of sight of Sunny Bank. No talking until they turned back on to Woodhouse Lane, as if they'd been holding their breath. All around them, the world was waking. In the distance an early coach approached. Hooves thundered, metal and wood and leather creaked as the driver let the horses enjoy the final gallop into town.

Then it was past and they were alone again.

'Someone had been eating and drinking in the kitchen,' Simon said. 'It must have been him.'

'Why would he leave the book and the jug with someone else?'

'Safety. It was too dangerous to carry them with him. You saw his room; it wasn't a place to leave anything valuable. He was being sensible.'

She nodded, but her eyes were still cloudy. 'Why would he only take one piece of silver?'

'He probably took more and sold it.' Simon shrugged. 'We won't know until the Atkinsons return.'

'Then he should have had money,' Jane said. 'He was selling scraps at the end.'

'I don't know,' Simon admitted. 'Not yet, anyway.'

They reached the Head Row. A stream of people flowed around them, heads down as they made their way to work.

'At least we know where he was staying before he was killed,' Simon said. 'That's a start. We're learning more.'

Jane sat by the window, sipping a glass of Mrs Shields's cordial and eating a withered apple left over from the autumn. The fruit was tart, cutting through the sweetness of the drink.

There was still so much she didn't understand about Poole. Questions that troubled her. Why had he returned to his room on Welling Court? How had he ended up dead at Flay Crow Mill?

'You're miles away, child.' Mrs Shields stood close, staring out through the glass.

'I'm thinking,' Jane said.

'The answers often come when we least expect them. When we're thinking of something else.' She smiled and placed a hand on Jane's shoulder. So light it was barely there. But comforting. It was warm, it felt intimate. She'd spent too many years starved of any sort of affection. She reached up and placed her fingers on top on the old woman's. She knew her skin was coarse, ingrained with dirt, but Mrs Shields didn't pull back. She never would.

After a minute, Jane stirred. 'I need to go.'

'Will Martha be with you today?'

'I expect so.' She turned to look at the old woman. 'Why?'

'Just be careful around her, that's all.'

'You don't trust her?'

'I told you: I think there's more that she hasn't told us. I want you to look after yourself.'

'I will. I promise.'

Jane left with the warning running through her head. She had plenty of secrets of her own. Gordon Baker's body by the entrance to this little garden. Things left unsaid so Catherine wouldn't worry. Jane had taken care of them all.

She raised the shawl, tucking her hair underneath, and looked around. A dry day but brisk, cold enough to keep her moving to stay warm.

Without thinking, she headed toward Flay Crow Mill.

The remnants of the buildings smelt of decay. Moss and mould grew on the damp wood. Most of the paddles that had once powered the mill wheel had gone, and those still left were swollen and warped by the water. And all around, Cynder Island was nothing, a dank piece of land that jutted into the river.

It had begun here. She paced out the distance to the far side of the building where Poole's body had been found.

No mystery as to why they'd chosen this place for the killing ground. It was isolated, yet still part of Leeds. Only one street led here. Jane glanced at the buildings. She knew someone who lived up there . . .

The note from Williams was terse: Poole stayed at Atkinson's.

Simon crumpled the paper. At least he knew the constable's men had been out there.

He needed to find the cavalrymen and push them harder. Prod them in the right direction but let them think they were leading him. To learn about their involvement with Poole and find the evidence Williams needed.

At the barber's shop, he settled back and let the man shave him. The hot, wet towel felt luxurious against his cheeks, and he closed his eyes as the razor scraped away the heavy stubble until his face was smooth once more.

Stepping out on to Kirkgate, Simon almost walked into Lieutenant Johnson. It was as if he'd thought of the man only to summon him from the air, all smiles and genial good graces. The cavalryman looked splendid in his uniform; Simon saw two girls sneak admiring glances as they passed.

'Well met, Westow. Great minds think alike. A good shave always makes me feel like a new man.'

Simon ran his fingertips over his chin. 'Presentable, at least.'

'Come and take a drink with me,' Johnson said. 'I started thinking the other night. There might be a place in our enterprise for you. A little money never hurts, does it?'

'Of course not,' Simon replied.

The Bull and Mouth seemed like an odd place to talk. With coaches arriving and leaving, it was bustling, people constantly moving around and yelling. But Johnson appeared at ease there, sitting at the table with a glass of rum in front of him.

'I trust that anything we say will be in confidence.'

'Of course,' Simon agreed.

'Good. Very good.' The man hesitated, playing with his drink. 'The thing is the law wouldn't approve of what we choose to do.'

'The law doesn't approve of many things.'

'True. Very true.' Johnson smiled and nodded his head. 'You understand, excellent. Perhaps we have a slightly different view of things in the army. Your business must bring you into contact with thieves and their fences.'

'All the time.'

'Tell me, Mr Westow, do you ever bend the law?'

'It's happened.' So far he hadn't even needed to lie.

'What would you say if I told you we flouted it? Broke it?'

'Then I'd say be careful you're not caught. The consequences can be drastic.'

'We're very cautious. And we take time to choose our targets.'

'For your sake, I'm pleased to hear it.'

'The man we had working with us in Leeds was a great help.'

'You said he was no longer available.'

'He died.' Johnson grimaced. 'Extremely unfortunate.'

'How did it happen?' He tried not to place any special emphasis on the question.

'Honestly, I wish I knew.' The lieutenant placed his hands flat on the table, palms down. 'We'd disagreed, but I never wished anything bad to happen to him.' He shook his head in shock and sorrow.

It sounded reasonable, but Simon knew better than to believe a word of it. And he needed something more.

'Has anyone else close to you and the ensign died?' He tried to keep his tone light.

'Never. This man was a good fellow.'

'And you're seeking someone to replace him.'

'Exactly.' The lieutenant brightened.

'Someone willing to break the law.'

'Yes.'

'That's asking a great deal,' Simon said. 'I'd need details.'

'Of course,' Johnson agreed.

'And where risk is involved, there has to be reward to make it worthwhile. I'm sure you understand.'

'Perfectly.' Johnson smiled. 'You won't be disappointed. The last man we dealt with was satisfied, although before he died he said he intended to leave Leeds.'

'Then why were things ending?' He needed to keep probing, to surprise Johnson into some small mistake.

'He intended to leave Leeds and try his hand elsewhere.'

Not quite, Simon thought. Laurence Poole was terrified and then he was murdered before he could go.

'I think we might be able to find some mutual interest,' Simon said after a while.

'Excellent.' Johnson shook Simon's hand. The cavalryman was hooked. Now Simon had to play the line like a good fisherman. 'As I said, we were appalled when our friend died. Without him, we haven't been able to keep things going. Times have become a little tight.'

'Perhaps they'll ease quite soon.' Simon pulled out his pocket watch. 'You'll excuse me. I have an appointment.'

'Of course.'

'I'll be in the Hussar tonight.'

'We will be, too.'

Simon walked up Briggate, crossed the Head Row and into Mudie's shop.

'I need a paper and pen.'

'On the desk. You look very pleased with yourself, Simon.'

'Things are moving.'

He scribbled a note and folded it twice.

'When do I hear the tale?' Mudie asked.

'When it's ready to be told.'

A boy stood on the corner, watching people as they passed. Simon's hand twitched in his pocket, then he held up a ha'penny.

'Want to earn it? And another to go with it?'

'What do I have to do?' The boy's voice was full of suspicion. He watched Simon through hooded eyes.

'Take this note over there.' He gestured towards the Moot Hall. 'Give it to Constable Williams.'

'Why can't you take it yourself? It's only a hundred yards.'

'If you don't want to do it, I'll find someone else who needs the money.' He whisked the coin out of sight.

'No. I mean . . . I'll do it, mister.'

'No questions,' Simon told him. He handed over the coin and the paper, watching as the boy dashed across the street, dodging between carts and coaches. Two minutes and he returned, holding his hand out for the second coin.

'Gave it right to him.'

'Good job.'

Now he had to hope the boy was telling him the truth.

FOURTEEN

Robbie Flowers stood by the window. The glass was grimy; it had probably never been cleaned in all the years he'd lived here.

Jane was at his side, staring down at Flay Crow Mill. From up here, she could see there was order to the arrangement of the buildings below. But the years of neglect were even more obvious. Three roofs caved in, a hole in the fourth.

'You didn't see anything?' she asked.

He shook his head. 'Why would I look down there? I've seen it often enough.'

'Maybe you heard a noise.' She glanced at his face, realizing with surprise that she was looking directly into his eyes. Two years ago, he'd been a full head taller than her.

'There's always noise.' He pointed. 'Listen, it's there. People working on the river. Day and night.'

In the corner, an old woman moaned and tried to push herself out of the chair. But she was firmly tied in place. Flowers's mother. Her mind was gone; she saw the past instead of the present. But her legs still worked. Given half a chance, she'd be out and away down the stairs.

Jane had found her by the Moot Hall once, standing, staring at the building. She'd helped her back here. Flowers worked in one of the warehouses on the river, a clerk checking the daily shipments in and out. He had no one to look after his mother while he was gone. No money to pay for a companion for her. He had no choice but to tie her in the chair to stop her wandering.

Jane had been waiting outside the door when he returned today.

'I'm sorry,' Flowers said. He turned away, untying the knots that held his mother in place as he spoke gently in the old woman's ear. She'd soiled herself; Jane could smell it. She knew the man would clean his mother, then feed her, read to her until the light grew too dim.

'Thank you.'

'You need to talk to Mrs Robbins. She has the room underneath here.' He gave a soft smile. 'She's a nosy old cow.'

'I don't know her.'

'Just say I sent you. That'll be enough.'

Mrs Robbins was an old woman starved of company. Flowers was right. Saying his name took care of everything. She lived in a bare room, just a single chair heaped with old coats, blankets, anything to keep her warm. She burrowed into it like an animal seeking its shelter.

'Yes, I saw that,' the woman said, then dipped her head for a second. 'I saw something. Two of them and they had another one with them. Between them. Dragging him, like.' She narrowed her eyes to picture it in her mind. 'Couldn't see much. Just little moments. It were dark, dead of night.'

'When was this?' Jane asked.

'That night before the last big fall of snow. I was going to go down in the morning and take a look, see what was what, but it were too deep by then. I thought I might slip and break something.'

'Did you get a good look at the men?'

'No.' She shook her head, lank grey hair flying around her face. 'Too far and my eyes, they aren't what they were. And it were dark, I told you that.'

'Of course.' Jane smiled at her. 'What can you remember?'

'They had shiny boots. I saw a flash of light glint off one. At first, I wasn't sure what it was, then it happened again. Couldn't see nothing else after that, they went round the far side of the mill, by the river.'

Jane let the woman continue until she'd given all she knew. It wasn't much. She couldn't identify anyone, not even a description. Finally, she took four pennies from her pocket and placed them in Mrs Robbins's hand. 'Thank you.'

Outside, the wind caught against her face and chilled her to the core. The snow might have gone, but winter was keeping its grip today. She traced the path the old woman had described, following it all the way to the water. At least it seemed that Poole had already been dead when they dumped him; perhaps that was some small blessing.

A pity the woman hadn't been able to see more. Even a glimpse of a face would have helped. Still, boots with a shine that reflected the light. The kind of thing a cavalry officer would wear. That was as close to proof as she was likely to find. But it wasn't enough. She knew that.

One more item for the list, though. It confirmed what they suspected, and it was more than they'd known before.

She wandered back towards town. No one bothered talking about the body in Basinghall Street any more. Life had flowed on and left him behind.

Kate the pie-seller was standing by Leeds Bridge, catching customers just as they reached town, hungry and weary. She'd found a good spot; her tray was almost empty.

'You'd better make it two,' Kate said with a smile. She was looking somewhere beyond Jane.

She turned. Martha, keeping her distance.

'I suppose so.' She walked back to the girl and gave her the food.

'I saw you down on the bridge,' Martha said. 'I looked for you earlier.'

'You've found me now.'

'I was thinking about that man.'

No need to say his name. Jane remembered his face all too clearly, however much she tried to push it away. The weight and heft of him as she dragged his body down the night streets. She'd never be able to forget that.

'You shouldn't waste your time on him.'

'No one's going to come after us, are they?'

'I told you: we're safe.' Big Tom would return, but he wanted Jane. He wouldn't bother about Martha at all. She realized she hadn't given him a thought during the morning. He was fading from view. That was foolish. She needed to keep alert. Be ready. When the chance came, she had to take it. Next time there could be no hesitation, no holding back.

'What are we going to do this afternoon?'

'Find people,' Jane said. 'Talk to them.'

Dark had fallen and a fine, light snow was coming down as Simon entered the Yorkshire Hussar and shook off his hat and coat. He paid for a glass of brandy and strolled over to the card table. A couple of the men ducked their heads in greeting, and he saw Murdoch and Johnson. The buttons of their uniforms shone bright in the glow of the lamps, and the smoke from their cheroots made a pale cloud over their heads.

A hand or two of cards, feeling his way into the game. Simon bet small amounts until the deal passed to him. Then he began to work the deck. Enough to make the cavalrymen feel the squeeze, but without ruining them.

He never glanced around, never seemed curious about the rest of the room. But he hoped that Williams had done as he'd asked in his note and put a pair of men in here.

Finally, he passed the deal to someone else and stood. Murdoch and Johnson followed him to an empty table. A man sitting close by shifted down the bench with a quick, furtive look at Simon.

'Your good health. And to a prosperous future.'

'Indeed,' Johnson agreed. 'You've thought about my suggestion, I take it?'

'I'm intrigued,' Simon said. 'I think it has possibilities. But I told you, I'd like to know more first. I'm worried about this man who died.'

'Why?' Murdoch raised his head. 'He's gone, it gives you an opportunity.'

'How did he die?'

Johnson took a small sip of his brandy. 'Violence, I'm told. A waste of a good life.'

'And this happened after he decided to stop working with you?'

'What are you trying to imply, Westow?' Murdoch asked. He curled his hands into fists.

'Nothing,' Simon replied calmly. 'If I'm going to be a part of something, I want to know all about it. Wouldn't you?'

'Indeed.' Johnson turned to his friend. 'We're dealing with a sensible man, Neville. But there's little I can tell you, Mr Westow. You can probably find out more than us. The poor fellow's name was Laurence Poole.'

'I knew him,' Simon said. The lieutenant was brazen, naming Poole. But at the same time he was cautious; he'd said nothing to incriminate himself. From the way he was talking, he never would.

A quick hint of a smile. 'I thought you might.'

'I don't recall how he died,' Simon said. 'Found in the snow, I remember that.'

'He'd been strangled, I heard.' Murdoch's voice had a sharp edge.

'Do you know who might have done it?'

'No.' The reply was sharp as a shot. The ensign would say nothing more. Better to change the topic.

'What do you require of me?'

'I'm sure you've developed skills in your profession,' Johnson said.

'A few. But that's not an answer.'

'We'll be able to put them to a use that's profitable for us all.'

'That's fine.' Simon pursed his lips. 'But I do still need to know more before I agree.'

'You will,' Murdoch said. This time he had an edge to his voice and the smile had vanished from his eyes. 'I told you. But not here. We're not fools, Westow, and I trust you're not, either.'

'You'll have gathered that I'm careful,' he said.

'You'd better be. We don't do business with fools.'

They weren't going to give anything away in here where someone might overhear. Whatever he'd hoped for wasn't going to happen; they were warier than he'd expected. Brighter, too. Nothing to be gained by staying. It might even look better if he seemed annoyed. Simon drained the glass and stood. 'Then we'd do better to meet somewhere else. Or,' he added, staring at them, 'let the matter drop.'

He saw Johnson wince. Good. 'No need for that,' he said hastily. 'But another time might be an excellent idea. Tomorrow, perhaps? We can all sleep on it.'

'I'm free,' Simon said. 'Where and when? The choice is yours.'

'You know the barracks?'

'I do.'

'A road runs past there. Go about half a mile farther on there's a large oak tree. It's a good spot to meet. Shall we say eleven o'clock?'

'Very good.'

'Then I'll wish you a good night,' Johnson said with a smile. 'Until tomorrow, Mr Westow.'

On the way home he kicked at stones just to hear them skitter down the street. He thought he'd been clever, asking Williams to put a couple of men at the Hussar. But the cavalrymen had outfoxed him. So far, they'd kept themselves in the clear on Poole's death. On everything.

He knew the spot they'd mentioned. It was isolated, impossible for anyone to come close without being seen. No witnesses, and if it came to court, his word against a pair of upright cavalry officers. That wouldn't be any kind of contest.

He'd been too quick to make assumptions about Murdoch and Johnson. They were deadly; he already knew that. But they were sly, too, shot through with cunning and intelligence.

He was going to need to tread carefully to trap them.

Rosie was already asleep, the house dark as he let himself in, dropped the latch and shot the bolts behind him. In bed he stretched, trying not to think about the morning.

FIFTEEN

'There's nowhere close,' Jane said. She remembered the place, the way the tree stood alone above the road.

'There's a copse a couple of hundred yards along,' Simon said.

'It's winter, it's going to be bare. I don't know if there'll be anywhere to stay out of sight.'

'Do what you can.'

He trusted her. She knew exactly what he needed. And he felt safer knowing she was close. Not as near as he'd like, but it would be the best they could manage.

Jane left half an hour before him. She'd be one more girl tramping along the road with her shawl over her hair. She'd have time to find a place where she could settle to watch.

None of the snow that fell overnight had stuck. The roads were scoured bare by the wind and rutted with the cold. Hard and rough enough to turn an ankle if he wasn't careful. Simon passed the barracks, feeling the stare of the sentries.

He didn't expect a trap. The men were coming to talk business and they seemed serious about it. But he was prepared, anyway. Always ready, just in case. One knife in his pocket, a second in his boot, and the last loose in its sheath up his sleeve; a single movement and it would be in his hand.

He arrived early; by his watch it was still five minutes before the hour. No craning his neck to try and spot Jane. She'd be out there, keeping herself well hidden. He waited patiently, only turning his head as he heard the sound of hooves. Murdoch and Johnson were in full uniform, approaching on horseback.

Of course, that made sense; they were cavalry.

They arrived at a sedate trot, the two of them chatting as they rode, holding themselves high in the saddle as if born to it. The men reined in, one on either side of him.

A clever move. Up in the saddle they had height, and the sheer size of the beasts was intimidating. He had to look up to talk to them.

'A pity you don't ride, Westow,' Johnson said. 'There's some good gallops out towards Harewood. Blows away the cobwebs in the mind.'

'If you say so.' He patted the neck of a horse. A coat like velvet, warm, alive. 'Why don't you dismount? It'll be easier to talk.'

A smooth movement and they were both standing on the ground. Scabbards knocked against their legs.

'Better?' Murdoch asked with a grin.

'Much. Well, gentlemen, what's so secret about your plan that we need to meet out here?'

'It involves theft,' Johnson said.

'I suspected it might,' Simon replied.

'From other officers,' Murdoch said. 'Does that shock you as dishonourable?'

'It doesn't mean anything at all to me. Who does the stealing?'

'You.'

'And who sells the stolen items?'

'You.'

Simon raised an eyebrow. 'That sounds as if I'll be doing all the work. What do I receive?'

'One-third of the proceeds.'

He snorted. 'The rest goes to you, I take it?'

'That's correct,' Johnson said. 'We tell you where to go, what time the place will be empty, so you'll have no problems. And exactly what to take.'

'I'm still the one taking all the risks. If I'm caught . . .'

'You won't be caught,' Murdoch said. 'Do what we tell you and there'll be no danger.'

'How valuable are these items?' Simon asked. 'How often will you expect me to commit a burglary?'

'They're small but worth enough to make it a good proposition. How often?' He shrugged. 'As the chance occurs. Don't worry, it won't be often enough to arouse suspicion.'

'The idea has possibilities,' But Simon wasn't going to accept it quite so readily. 'But I'd be doing a great deal for just one-third of the money.'

'That's our offer,' Johnson told him. 'You can take it or you can leave it.'

'Then for now I think I'll leave it.' He tipped his hat to them. 'Gentlemen.'

Before he'd taken a pace, Murdoch had drawn his sword, bringing it down like a barrier.

'You're welcome to reconsider that decision,' Johnson said. All the friendliness had vanished from his voice. 'But I'd advise against saying anything about this to anyone. For your own sake. We're bad enemies to make.' A nod and the blade vanished.

Simon began to walk away, forcing himself not to look back. Suddenly he heard hooves and stiffened. But they were moving away from him at a gallop. He stopped and exhaled very slowly. For a moment, as Murdoch drew his blade, he'd wondered how things might play out. He'd have no chance against two men trained in arms, and knives against swords . . . they could easily have left him for dead.

He waited by the bridge, near the turnpike toll booth. Sheltered from the endless wind, it was a comfortable spot, with the constant burble of water from Sheepscar Beck as a background. He'd been there ten minutes when he heard footsteps.

'How much of it did you see?'

'Everything,' Jane said. 'But I was too far away to hear what you were saying.'

'They want me to do what Poole did for them.'

'Why did one of them take out his sword?'

Simon smiled. No more than a few minutes had passed and it didn't seem as terrifying.

'That was Murdoch, the ensign. I turned down their offer.'

Jane frowned. 'Why? I thought we wanted to catch them.'

'Don't worry, we will. We're negotiating. Another day or two and we'll come to an agreement. After that we can make a proper plan. The problem is I don't think we'll be able to have them for Poole's murder. They're too slippery.'

'What's the point, then?' she asked. 'What does the constable say?'

'I hope he'll be happy to snare a couple of cavalrymen for robbery. Even if he can't bring them to court for Poole, it will appease Ferguson and Brady.'

They began to walk back towards Leeds. Soon enough, he could smell the heat, the oil, all the stink of the factories.

'Do you still want me to see if I can find out more about Poole?' she asked.

'No.' Simon sighed. 'We've done what we can there. We know he was in the Atkinson house.'

'The shiny boots that woman saw at Flay Crow Mill—'

'Don't prove a thing, unfortunately.'

Nothing to do. No direction, no aim. Jane wandered. She stopped here and there, sitting, half-hearing the chatter as people talked. With no work, she felt as if she had no use in the world. She needed to be doing things.

Big Tom. She wanted to find him. But she had no idea where to begin. And it was safer not to ask questions. No drawing attention to herself in case someone remembered the body on Basinghall Street.

At least Martha hadn't found her this morning. This was a day for being on her own. For watching, brooding. She drifted, letting the crowds carry her around town. On Vicar Lane she saw a dog chase a rat into the road. A coach barrelled through, crushing the rodent against the cobbles. A few moments later, a cat darted out and carried off the body in its jaws. Nobody else seemed to notice.

Without even trying she could pick out the children in the shadows behind the market stalls. Waiting for some food or fruit to fall, ready to run and grab it. A trio who picked pockets. One to distract, the other to dip, then hand it on to the third who ran off, only to reappear a few minutes later.

Somewhere, in a house nearby, the man who'd trained them would be waiting. They'd deliver the goods to him. And he'd already be bringing along the younger ones to replace them when they were caught.

She'd seen it for years. She'd never had the light touch needed to become a dab herself. Or enough speed. Her skills were different. They kept her alive and out of the prison hulks or the vessels transporting convicts to Australia.

Barely a handful of faces she remembered from her years of living on the streets were still here. They saw each other sometimes, but always kept a wary distance. That was better than opening the door on the memories of those times.

She'd told Mrs Shields so much of what happened during when

she was out here. The old woman had listened, never judging. A long, gentle hug when Jane's voice faded off to nothing, the arms so light around her that for a minute she wondered if they were really there.

She was happy now. Content. Accepted and wanted. She'd forgotten what that could be like.

Jane shook her head. Thinking this way never did any good. She had to find something better to occupy her mind.

By three she believed she'd walked every inch of Leeds. All the streets, the little lanes and courts on both sides of the river. Her legs ached; her feet were sore despite the comfortable boots. Nothing. No familiar faces to ask. Not even any worthwhile gossip wafting on the breeze. The only good thing was that the walking had kept her warm.

Slowly, she began to make her way home. Night was coming, the air was growing colder. Soon it would be dark. She'd learn more after dark, once the thieves, the whores and the drunks were out. The kind of folk who would trade their hoard of secrets for a few coins.

Jane fretted through supper. A bite of bread, a nibble of cheese, until Mrs Shields asked what was wrong.

'I'm restless. Nothing more than that.' Finally, she pulled the shawl tight around her head. 'I just need to be out.'

'Look after yourself, child. Be careful.'

Leeds offered another world after darkness fell, one where she was comfortable. There was plenty of danger, but only for the unwary, those who weren't alert to the possibility of violence. Music spilled out into the cold air. Loud voices, pools of sound that shifted as she walked. Jane gathered her shawl under her chin and kept her other hand tight around the knife hilt.

Twice she felt a hand reach towards her pocket and turned, keeping the blade steady. The first time, it was a young man who ran off as if the devil was after him. The second was a child, probably no more than six, all the innocence already burned from her eyes. Jane shooed her away.

A man tried to touch her. He stopped as soon as he saw her face. Over in the shadows a woman gave a husky chuckle.

'There's something about you terrifies them.'

'Good.' Jane stared.

'You work with that thief-taker, don't you?'

'Yes.' The question left her uncertain; she didn't like people recognizing her.

'I knew Simon Westow. Years back when he was starting out. Before he met that lass he married.'

'I'm Jane.'

The woman took two steps forward until the light from a window across the street fell on her face. She had her mouth covered with a fan. As she lowered it, Jane could make out the smallpox scars on her skin. A regiment of them from her cheeks to her neck.

'You can call me Caroline.' She smiled. 'Ugly, aren't they? You can be honest. I saw the way you looked. Everyone does.'

Jane didn't know what to say. How the words might come out.

'Don't worry.' Caroline laughed. 'I've heard it all. I'm used to it. I've had these most of my life. One of the reasons I ended up out here.' She waited a moment. 'You're looking for something.'

'Laurence Poole,' Jane said.

'Dead,' she answered without hesitation. 'His friend's left Leeds. If you work with Simon you know that.'

'I do.'

'Talk to Dorothy Ryan,' the woman said.

'Who?'

'Poole would see her sometimes. Always wanted to make people believe he wasn't paying for it.'

'How often?'

Caroline shrugged. 'I don't know. Ask her.'

'I don't know where to find her.'

'I'll take you.' She paused. 'It'll cost you tuppence, mind. You got that much?'

Jane took two pennies from her pocket and handed them over. Caroline led the way, fan raised to cover her face. She walked with assurance through the darkness, stopping at the entrance to a court fifty yards down Kirkgate. Welling Court, Jane realized. Where Poole had a room.

'What's your name again, pet?' Caroline hissed.

'Jane.'

'Come here. Meet Dorothy. She'll tell you about your man.'

Jane kept a hand on her knife, senses pricking, alert for anything.

But after the introduction Caroline faded back into the blackness of the night and she was facing a woman who stepped into the small pool of light.

'Laurence Poole.' Her voice was a rasp. She held out a small, pale hand, palm up. 'What's it worth?'

Two more pennies that disappeared into the folds of clothing.

'That'll buy you some information. Not much, mind. You know where we are?'

'I do. He lived up there.' Jane pointed up to the top floor.

'He'd come down for me sometimes. Take me up there and do it. Out of the weather. Stayed with him a night or two when it was right bitter.'

'When did you last see him?'

'That evening before we had that last big snow. It was just starting when he was here. You remember that?'

'I do,' Jane said.

'He came running in—'

'Running?'

'He was in a hurry. He said hello as he passed. A few minutes later he was off out again.'

'Did he say anything?' Jane asked.

'Told me he might be back later. But I didn't see him again after that.' A hint of sorrow and regret in her voice, but not much. It had happened, and nothing she could do would change that.

'What about before that? A week, maybe two?'

The woman narrowed her eyes. 'That'll cost you more.'

Two more pennies and Dorothy licked her lips before speaking. 'I know I didn't see him for at least a week. Any more than that . . .' She shrugged. 'I can't be sure. It all blurs. Why?'

'I wanted to know, that's all.'

'That's everything I can tell you.'

One more piece in the puzzle. No need to tell Dorothy she'd probably been the last person to see Poole alive. Apart from the murderers.

Jane walked home, cutting along Commercial Street, then up Basinghall Street, past the spot where she'd left Baker's body. Suddenly she felt it, the jolt along her spine. That sense of someone watching, someone following. Not close. But still there.

Big Tom. Who else could it be?

Jane swallowed; her throat was dry. She tamped down the fear. Refused to panic. She was ready. She'd beaten him three times now. She had the knife in her hand, ready. Jane walked along the familiar streets, through the yard behind the Green Dragon, and then to the safety of home. He was still out there. But she was here, where he couldn't touch her.

SIXTEEN

The next night Simon stayed clear of the Yorkshire Hussar. Let Murdoch and Johnson feel a little worry. It would do them good to be off balance.

He stayed at home, playing with Richard and Amos after their lessons, or talking to Rosie. The hours passed happily, and he scarcely noticed them going.

Jane came, telling him about Dorothy and Poole. It added a little more. But it was far too late for Laurence. He was fading to bones in an unmarked grave in the churchyard.

He sensed they'd be waiting long before he arrived. And there they were, heads jerking up and smiling as soon as he entered the Yorkshire Hussar. By the time he'd bought a glass of brandy they'd found a seat for him.

Leaving them to stew for a day had been the right thing to do.

They were friendly, no trace of resentment in their manner. But they needed him far more than he needed them, and they knew it. He was even more of a gift to their scheme than Laurence Poole had been. They needed to court him, to woo him into working with them.

The deal moved from player to player. Simon lost a little and won it back. Murdoch and Johnson were both down. Nothing desperate, just enough to nibble at them.

The deck reached Simon. He riffled through the cards then shuffled as he talked to the others. It looked so casual, hardly worth noting. But his fingers were deft and quick. A careful arrangement as he began to deal.

Their money didn't go to Simon; he wasn't that foolish or vain. It was distributed around the other players. He passed the cards to the next dealer, stood and stretched.

Very soon, exactly as he expected, Johnson and Murdoch joined him at the bar. All their joviality had vanished. Glum expressions and slumped shoulders; it looked as if they'd lost more than they could easily afford.

'That money I owe you—' Murdoch began.

Simon waved it away. 'I told you – pay me when you can. We've all had a bad run at cards before.'

A nod of acknowledgement and thanks.

'I've been thinking more about your proposition, gentlemen,' Simon said.

'And?' He could hear the hopeful note in the lieutenant's voice.

'And my decision still stands.'

Johnson lit a cheroot and stood, staring at the tip.

'What would it take to change your mind?' he asked.

'I'd want half,' Simon replied.

A long, weighted silence. 'You expect a great deal.'

'Of course I do. If I'm doing all the work and taking the risks, I deserve it.' He paused just long enough for them to believe he'd finished. 'I might well deserve more than that.'

'You'd be damned lucky to get half,' Murdoch muttered. But the look that passed between the pair of them told him that he'd already won.

Simon raised his glass in a toast and swallowed the dregs of the brandy. 'I've said what I came to say. I'll wish you both a good night.'

'Westow.' The voice stopped him before he'd taken two paces.

'What?'

'All of this stays strictly between us,' Murdoch warned.

'Naturally.'

'If word should ever leak, it would be the worse for you.'

The words were enough for Simon to keep a knife in his hand as he walked along Briggate, and he didn't breathe easy until he'd locked his door and pushed the bolts home. All the lights were off, the boys asleep in their room. Amos had kicked his blanket halfway off and Simon lifted it back in place, tucking it in around him. He pushed his face against the boys' hair, drawing in the scent of his children. Soon enough they'd be grown, with lives of their own. He needed memories to hold close later.

A final look around the house before bed, the usual check that it was secure.

The note had fallen off the kitchen table, lying under a chair. He picked it up and read by the light of the candle.

Make it soon. Very soon. Ferguson is applying pressure. Williams.

A second read, then he put the paper into the firebox of the range. Tomorrow he was going to be busy.

Dr Brady's consulting rooms were in Park Square, in a small, elegant house. The estate had been built thirty years ago, before the arrival of the manufactories, when this was the western edge of Leeds and the air came fresh and clean off the Pennines and down the Aire Valley. Now big brick buildings with their chimneys lined the river, more of them every year, and the people who paid to be aloof breathed the same air as everyone else.

'Your name, sir?' the clerk asked. He was a thin man with a furrowed brow and hair that was hurrying away from his brow.

'Westow,' Simon answered.

Brady was prosperous. He didn't have a seat on the council, but he was a power in Leeds. He had the ear of every important man and woman in town. He was someone who helped wield power from the shadows. The physician to society.

'Mr Westow.' The man wore an expensive suit of the finest worsted, trousers cut tight against a pair of well-toned thighs, the coat expertly tailored to show off his figure. But he was the kind of man for whom no shave could be too close, no suit too perfectly cut. He had a high opinion of himself and believed everyone else should think the same. Especially his patients. 'Come through.'

Buttoned leather chairs, a dark, heavy desk and bookcase, and a deep Turkish carpet on the floor. It had cost a small fortune to furnish this place. But those who came here would expect nothing less, and Brady was never one to disappoint.

Simon had heard the rumours of the doctor's affairs with a couple of rich men's wives; Rosie swore at least one of the stories was true. But somehow, no scandal ever stuck to him. Instead, the women were intrigued and the men were envious.

'I'm surprised we've never met,' Brady said.

'It happens. We have a mutual acquaintance, Alderman Ferguson.'

'Henry.' A genial smile. 'Yes, of course. He's mentioned your name once or twice. You're a thief-taker, I believe.'

'That's right.'

The man arched an eyebrow. 'I'm sure you must have a store of tales. Now, what can I do for you?'

'I keep feeling a pain in my side.'

It was easy enough to fake. He had a scar there, a knife wound that was the best part of ten years old. Enough to spin a story.

'I'm not convinced this is the cause,' Brady said after he'd examined it. He had a soft, gentle touch and clean, pale fingers. 'I can't find anything distended and there's no tenderness.'

'Maybe I imagined it.'

'Perhaps you did,' Brady said. He sat behind his desk. 'Or it was never anything at all. An excuse to see me, perhaps. Either way, it'll cost you the usual fee.'

Simon smiled. 'Of course. You're in business.'

He chose the word deliberately; a barbed reminder. Strip away the expensive trappings and the medical terms, and Brady was just another tradesman, no different from him. No matter the profession, money was the fuel that powered the engine.

'And is it *business* that brought you here?'

'In a manner of speaking. I was talking to the alderman the other day. He seems to have it in mind to replace Constable Williams.'

Brady gave an enigmatic smile. 'I don't see what that has to do with me.'

'No? You don't have the same aims?'

The doctor spread his arms. 'I'm not a politician, Mr Westow. I'm a physician. As you can plainly see.'

'One who's listened to by all the important men in Leeds.' He grinned. 'And their wives, I've heard.'

An angry grimace flickered across the man's face. 'Don't believe all the gossip that flies around. But I still don't understand why you want to talk to me. You'd do better speaking to Henry Ferguson.'

'We've had a few words. I was interested to find out where you stand.'

'I imagine you can guess.' He stood. 'Now, if that's everything . . .'

'One more question: who would you like to see in Williams's place?'

He was asking Brady to reveal something. Maybe he would, or he might choose to keep his mouth closed. It all depended on how eager he was to show just what he knew. Even those in the shadows like to step into the light sometimes.

'Do you know Charles Porter?'

'I can't say I do,' Simon answered. 'I've seen him but I've never spoken to him.' He doubted he could even give a fair description of the man.

'He's upright. Quite devout. A church warden in Armley.'

'Very sound. Does he have anything to qualify him as constable?'

Brady chuckled. 'Does Williams?'

That was fair, Simon acknowledged. The man had been given the post as a pension for decades of service to the corporation. He'd done no work, that was hardly a secret, and he'd used the office as an opportunity to make money, like so many before him. What Brady really meant was that Porter would be pliable; he'd do exactly as he was told by the people who gave him the position.

'Do you want someone who'll be serious about the job?' Simon asked. 'Or simply putting on a show of being serious?'

'It's about time we had a man who'll act, don't you think?' Brady replied. 'Look around, you can see how the town's growing. There's more crime than ever. I'm sure you must have seen that in your work.'

Simon thought of the two failures who'd tried to rob him on Briggate. 'Oh, yes. I have.'

'We need someone who'll clamp down on things, who'll recruit a night watch that isn't made up of frightened old men.'

'Someone to bring order.'

'Exactly.' Brady nodded his agreement. 'Hardly such an outrageous idea, is it?'

'Not at all.' And it wouldn't affect his business one jot. The professional thieves were cautious and clever. They kept away from the streets. People would still be paying him to have their stolen items returned.

'After all, Westow, you'd be familiar with order. You grew up in the workhouse, didn't you?'

So Brady did know all about him. Simon wasn't sure whether he should be flattered. The man meant the comment as an insult, a way of putting him in his place. A sting to repay the crack about business. But it didn't work. Simon's past was his own. He couldn't alter it; he wouldn't want to. He took pride in all that pain; it had shaped him, given him the determination to succeed and handed him the anger at those who loved to exercise power. Let the doctor believe he was scoring points if that was what he wanted.

'I did. It was instructive.' He paused, allowing the silence to grow for a moment. 'Still, a town is nothing like a workhouse. I'm sure you understand that.'

'We have support. But we need a good reason to have Williams dismissed.'

'That's understandable,' Simon said. 'Maybe you'll find it.'

The enigmatic smile returned. 'I'm sure we will. And good day to you, Mr Westow. It's been interesting to meet you.'

'For me, too.'

'But don't forget to pay the clerk as you leave.'

With no handshake and half a guinea lighter, he came out on to Park Square. Another grey day. How long until spring and some warmth in the air? He spotted a small movement over by St Paul's church.

'I saw you leave the house and followed,' Jane said.

'I had someone to see. Trying to stir things a little.' As they returned to Swinegate, he explained the visit.

'I've never heard of this other man. Porter? They want him as constable?'

'That's the idea. I can't say I know him, either. I'll get Rosie to ask a few questions. The women will have the gossip. They always do.'

'Yes,' Jane said.

'I told you we probably won't be able to take Murdoch and Johnson for Poole's murder. We don't have any real evidence, and they won't admit a damned thing.'

She nodded.

'I think I can give Williams the cavalrymen with the proceeds of a robbery,' Simon continued. 'Unless the army takes them for a court-martial.'

'Yes. What about Poole, though?'

'This way we can give him a little justice, too.'

'How can you work it?'

Simon grinned. 'Very carefully. I have something for you to do . . .'

SEVENTEEN

Things were starting to turn, but they still had a long way to go. Talking to Brady had sharpened his thoughts.

'I'll ask around the shops and have a word with the women about Porter,' Rosie said. 'I should be able to give you chapter and verse this evening.'

Another gown he didn't recognize, this one the colour of good claret and made of fine wool. A hat in a matching shade. She wrapped a shawl the shade of old roses over her shoulders and stared in the mirror as she adjusted her bonnet just so, then left the house. By the time she came back she'd probably know more about the man than he'd ever learned about himself.

Tonight he'd return to the Yorkshire Hussar. If Murdoch and Johnson were there, he'd insist on another talk to make certain they gave in to his demands. They would, with reluctance; he'd seen the defeat on their faces.

This afternoon he'd go out into the cold with his sons. A good long walk up to Woodhouse Moor and let them run and play on the open ground. Allow himself to breathe and remember the things that were important in life. Young, smiling faces. Two boys who trusted him without thinking. A reminder that there was honest innocence in the world.

Jane sensed Martha before she arrived. Hearing the boots running along the cobbles, small feet hurrying on the setts. She slowed her pace until the girl was beside her.

'Where are you going?'

'I have to talk to some people. The same thing I always do. You've seen me do it.' She wasn't about to give away all her business.

'Are we looking for someone?'

Jane shook her head. 'Not this time. We have to find out about a man called Charles Porter.'

The girl stood still. Fear filled her eyes and she clutched her elbows tight around her body.

'What is it?'

'Does he live in Armley?'

'I don't know.' Simon hadn't told her. Simply given her the names of two men who'd worked for Porter in the past. 'Why?'

Martha was quiet, looking down at the ground, the toe of her boot digging and pushing at the dirt.

'My mother . . .' Jane waited. No more words came.

'Did she work for him?'

A quick nod. 'She did his laundry. He came to our house one day. I don't know why. He . . . I saw them together. I walked in; I didn't mean to. She was facing the other way, bent over with her skirt up. She didn't see me.'

'What about him?' Jane asked. She kept her voice soft. She knew, but she still needed to hear the words.

'He turned his head. I was standing there. He . . . did this.' She stroked a cut across her neck with her fingers. Her eyes were filling with tears. 'I ran off.'

'He can't hurt you now.' A gentle nudge in her back, guiding her down towards the bridge. Some food from Kate the pie-seller. A warm pie in her belly would help. The woman glanced at the girl then left them alone.

They leaned on the parapet, staring down at the filthy water. Somewhere off to the south Jane could make out the steady booming rhythm of a mechanical hammer. The sound of the factories filled the air. The birdsong of Leeds.

'Why do you want to know about him?' Martha seemed a little easier, less panicked. She'd finished her pie and licked every last crumb from her fingers. Hunger was a hard habit to break.

'Simon asked me.'

'Has he done something wrong?'

'No.'

'Then why does he want to know?'

Jane weighed whether to tell her. But the girl deserved the truth. 'He might become constable. A thief-taker needs to know about people.'

'If he becomes constable, he could kill me and no one would do anything.'

'He won't.' Porter would have long since forgotten about her. It would be history to him. Not that Martha would believe that. It was a nugget to pass to Simon.

'But—'

'He won't.' If the man had really wanted to kill her he would have done it long before now.

Martha stayed fretful, shivering away out of sight as they went around and Jane asked her questions. They didn't walk as far as Armley, but to Kirkstall and a row of cottages set back from the canal towpath.

The trees were bare and dark, the grass thick and tangled on either side of the track. Jane halted, lifting her head and sniffing.

'Is something wrong?' Martha asked. Her eyes were wide.

'What can you smell?'

'I don't know,' the girl answered cautiously. 'Nothing.'

'Yes,' Jane said. 'That's exactly it. Nothing.'

None of the rancid stink of Leeds. She'd been out here before, all over the countryside that surrounded the town. But she'd never noticed this. The air was scrubbed clean. Full of the scents of earth, of so many things she couldn't identify. She had to stop, to breathe deep over and over again to take it all in.

Somewhere close by a bird was singing. A little way off, another joined it with a different tune. Jane listened, feeling as if the world had fallen away for a few moments. All around her there was beauty.

Then it passed, evaporated. The magic faded. She was back in the here and now, standing on a muddy trail as the tree branches slowly dripped.

'We need to go,' she said.

A wasted trip. The house was empty, the people had moved on elsewhere, following the work and the money. But without coming out here, how could she know? By the time they approached Drony Laith, she'd forgotten all about it.

The new mill was almost complete, with tall brick walls, a strong slate roof, windows set high to let in the light. She could hear the carpenters inside with their saws and chisels. A few months before there'd been a wood here, the place where she'd buried all her money among the roots of a tree. She'd believed it would always be safe. But times changed. All around her, Leeds was uprooted, shifting and spreading. Now her money was hidden behind a stone in Mrs Shield's house.

Martha was still scared. The mention of Porter's name had shaken her to the core. Her face was pinched with worry and her shoulders were slumped. It was real, not some act to bring sympathy and attention.

'Come home with me. You'll feel safer there.'

The girl's face brightened into a half smile. She pulled the shawl closer around her head and hugged her elbows tight against her body.

'Just tonight, though,' Jane told her. She hoped Mrs Shields would understand.

'What did you manage to find?' Simon called out as he entered the house. He could smell the scent Rosie wore when she went shopping, he knew she was home. He ushered the boys through to the kitchen, making them scrub their hands and faces before feeding them bread and cheese.

'Eat upstairs,' he ordered. 'You mother and I have things to discuss.' He waited for their protest, then added, 'Now.'

'It seems a few people know Mr Porter in town,' she said as she ladled hot stew into a bowl.

'Do they have good opinions of him?'

Rosie pursed her lips. 'He settles his bills, although he's slow to pay in full. And for a man of God, he certainly seems to enjoy flirting with women. There are mutterings that it's been more than that in an instance or two. No one seems to have proof, but I came up with a pair of names if you want me to find out more.'

Simon grinned. 'Maybe later. All that from a single afternoon?'

'From an hour,' she corrected him. 'People are always happy to share juicy tattle.'

'Do they think he's a strong-willed man? The type to bring order to Leeds?'

'No,' she replied simply. 'Nobody holds him in especially high regard.'

Porter would be another Williams. The only difference is that this one would wear Ferguson and Brady's colours and do everything they demanded. It was probably stupid to expect anything else. Those men craved power and the chance to exercise it. They wouldn't want to employ anyone likely to challenge them. By the sounds of things, Porter was exactly what they needed.

'It's useful to know in case he becomes constable. But he's not there yet. Williams could hang on if he makes a good arrest.'

'Simon—'

'Don't worry, he'll have the opportunity to take Murdoch and Johnson. If he can't make the charges work against them, let him lose office. From the sound of it, there's not a great deal to choose between him and Porter, anyway.'

'Just be careful.'

'I will. And I have you and Jane to help me.'

He was still thinking, trying to put together a plan when Jane arrived, the girl trailing behind her like a puppy hoping for a home. Simon listened as she explained what Martha had seen between Porter and her mother. While she spoke, the young girl moved to a corner, staring down at the flagstones on the kitchen floor as if she wanted to vanish through them.

'Jane's right,' Rosie said. She walked over and took hold of Martha's hands. 'You're safe now. If he wanted to do anything, he'd have done it a long time ago. How long ago did this happen?'

'Two years. Perhaps it was a little longer than that.'

Rosie caught Simon's eye and lifted her gaze towards the ceiling. He knew she wanted the girl to stay, to take the attic room where Jane used to sleep. They already had the twins; what more did she hope for, a daughter as well? Jane earned her keep many times over. This one . . . she was too young, she didn't seem to have any particular skills.

But his wife kept staring. What could he do but agree?

'Martha,' Rosie said, 'we have an empty room under the eaves. You could stay for a day or two.'

'Do you mean it?' She was cautious, as if it was a temptation that might be withdrawn in a moment.

'Yes,' Simon agreed. 'A proper bed. Sheets, blanket. But first you'll have a bath.' If she was going to stay in his house, she'd be as clean as his sons.

EIGHTEEN

Another mouth to feed. Simon had noticed Jane's disbelief when they offered Martha the attic room. Still, Rosie seemed happy. She'd fussed around the girl, bathing her, feeding her, settling her for the night in clean sheets and warm blankets.

'What are we going to do with her?' he asked, but his wife said nothing. She washed the girl's dress and hung it near the range to dry overnight. 'We can't take in waifs.'

'It's only for a few days, Simon. She's not going to live here.'

He wondered how true that would be.

Voices blared from the door of the Yorkshire Hussar. Inside, two men were arguing, others forming a circle around them. Eyes agog, waiting for the first blow. It never came. Billy Crawford, the landlord, pushed his way through the crowd, brandishing his cudgel.

His voice brooked no argument. 'You want to fight, you do it outside.'

Like scolded boys, the pair left, two or three friends with them. A murmur of talk; the moment had passed. Simon ordered his glass of brandy and stood near the card table, watching the players.

No sign of the cavalrymen. He sipped at his drink, then a second, but still they didn't arrive. After an hour he drained the glass and walked back out into the night. A bitter wind whipped down from the west, enough to make him tap the hat down on his head and turn up the collar of his greatcoat.

From the corner of his eye, Simon noticed a slight movement, a scuttling in the shadows. Probably just a rat. But he slipped a knife into his hand from its sheath on his arm. Always better to be ready.

He strolled down Briggate like a man without a care. Yet he was listening closely, alert for any footfall behind him. People walked on the other side of the road; a lonely whore stood by the entrance to a yard.

They came out of Byrd's Court, a few yards before the turning on to Swinegate. They thought they were quick, but Simon was faster. He had one of them by the hair, the flat of his blade against the man's neck, before they understood what was happening. The other man held up his hands and stepped into a pool of light that leaked from a window. Lieutenant Johnson.

'It's us,' he said. 'We came to talk to you.'

Simon let go of Murdoch. The ensign stumbled forward, rubbing his throat.

He'd known exactly who it was; he'd identified them by the way they moved. But he wanted to teach them a lesson. A street was different from a battlefield, and he wasn't an opponent to threaten.

'Gentlemen. My apologies. I didn't know.' He made a show of replacing the knife in its sheath. 'It's late, it's dark . . . I hope I didn't hurt you.'

Murdoch shook his head. 'Christ, though, you can move,' he said.

'If you're slow out here, you die. What can I do for you? Do we have our agreement? Half to me?'

'For now,' Johnson said. 'I'll warn you, though. Cross us and we'll come and test your skills properly.'

'As long as you keep your side of the bargain, there'll be no need.'

'We'll be in touch with your instructions, Westow.'

Simon tipped his hat. 'I look forward to it. Goodnight to you both.'

As he walked away, he wore a faint, satisfied smile. They thought they were good because they had cavalry commissions and came from proud families. But they weren't trained for these kinds of battles. He'd let them off lightly and given them something to think about. They'd be wary about crossing him in future.

Morning, and Simon came downstairs to find the girl sitting at the kitchen table. Upstairs, Richard and Amos slept on in their tangle of blankets. Rosie was moving around, dressing and brushing her hair.

'I haven't eaten anything,' Martha said, in case he might accuse her of stealing food.

'Are you hungry?'

She nodded, eyes following his hands as he cut some cheese and passed it to her.

'I want to help you and Jane. I need to do something to thank you for . . .' Her eyes swept around the room. 'For everything.'

'My wife might have some tasks for you.'

She couldn't keep her feelings from her face. 'Yes.'

He was gone in a few minutes. By the time he reached Briggate, Martha had vanished from his mind.

The town was awake. A hint of brightness in the sky after so many grey, dreary days. Men and women on their march to the factories, a few laughing and joking, others with dead eyes and slumped shoulders. Already he could sense the pulse of the machines and the looms starting up for the day – something felt more than heard.

'Are you going to stand there gawping all day?' He turned at the sound of the voice and broke into a grin. 'I thought that was you, Simon.'

Nathaniel Brooks. He started to shake hands then drew Simon into a hug, arms so tight and strong they were almost crushing him. They'd been in the workhouse together. Where Simon had gone to work in a mill, Nate had been apprenticed to a blacksmith.

Now he owned a small workshop on the far side of Quarry Hill. One apprentice and two assistants, forging nails by the hundredweight to feed the housing boom. Success had put a paunch on him, but his muscles were still hard, bulging through his shirt.

'It's been too long. What brings you out this way? Don't say it's friendship because I won't believe it.'

'Some work. I'm putting a little money in your pocket, Nate.'

Brooks let out a roar of a laugh, loud enough to make his men stare.

'I'll dine out on that for years – Simon Westow is spending his money honestly, my boys. Not that they'll ever believe me.' His face sobered. 'What is it you need?'

Simon explained, drawing quick illustrations on a scrap of paper. Brooks listened, frowning and chewing on his lip.

'I can make those easily enough,' he said. 'Not too different from manufacturing nails.'

'That's why I thought of you.' Simon grinned. 'That and old times. Not that our old times are worth the memories.'

Beaten in the mill, beaten by the master in the workhouse. Barely enough food to keep body and soul together. Yet they'd both survived. More than that, they'd flourished. Luck, pure luck, and determination.

'No,' Brooks agreed with a thin sigh. 'They weren't.' He glanced at the drawings. 'I can have these for you tomorrow. We might need to tinker with the tips a little until you're satisfied, but that's easily done.'

'How much?'

Brooks waved the question away.

'How much, Nate? It's business, you're doing the work. You deserve to be paid.'

'Two shillings. And before you say a word, that's the going rate.'

Simon passed the man a florin.

'Done.'

Simon sat in the kitchen. Over his shoulder, Jane stared at the book in his hands. Rosie had gone shopping, Martha in tow. The boys were with their tutor.

Reverently, he placed it back on the table, stroking the battered leather of the cover. He could feel her hunger for the Book of Hours.

'Read it if you like.'

She didn't wait, sitting, holding it close enough to inhale. He leaned back, watching, thinking. There was still plenty of work to do, to make sure all the pieces fell properly into line and everything was ready at the right time. The plan was there in his head, as much as it could be. Once he had the rest of the details – where to break in and when – he could put the remainder together.

The whole thing was his own machine, a beast that depended on all the parts working perfectly together. Including the new ones he'd ordered from Nate Brooks.

A sigh full of longing as Jane put the book back in its box.

'That'll bring us good money,' he told her.

'I know. I just wish . . .'

'I understand. Believe me, I do.'

If she could take the book to Mrs Shields . . . just for an hour, long enough for the old woman to hold it in her fingers, to look at the letters and the beauty of the pictures. That would be a worthwhile gift – the chance to see and touch something so perfect. It might go some small way towards repaying Catherine for all she'd done. But Jane knew she'd never have that opportunity. It needed to be here, hidden away, until its owner knew it was missing. With regret, she watched as Simon returned it to the secret drawer in the stairs.

Simon left the house in the few minutes of half-light, before the day took on any colour. Nate was an early riser; his apprentices would already have the forge glowing and warm.

The streets were almost empty, the town still quiet. Soon the machines would begin their rumbling for the day and any lingering wisps of peace would vanish. For now, though, there were pockets of silence. He passed an alley where the scent of fresh bread filled the air. A baker at work long before dawn. Simon smiled with pleasure.

He could hear the bellows before he arrived, the wheezing of leather and metal. The heat hit him as soon as he passed through the gate. The furnace was already white-hot. Brooks stood with his arms folded, supervising as the others ran around, readying everything for the day.

'You haven't lost the habit of mornings, then, Simon,' the man said with a broad grin.

'A time when a man can think.'

'And collect his order?'

'If it's ready.'

Four pieces of dull, thin metal, just a few inches long. He inspected the tips, bringing each one close to his face, then nodded approval.

'These look just right.'

'It's easy enough to make a few adjustments.' Brooks picked up a large rasp. 'A little off here or there. Try them and see.'

'I will. Thank you.'

'Like I told you, the shape's very similar to nails, and those are our business. They're thinner, springy, but they'll be sturdy enough for your needs.'

A handshake, a promise of meeting again soon that they'd both forget, and he was gone. Simon tucked the pieces of metal away in his waistcoat pocket. He'd test them later, then file away the edges and corners himself until they were exactly what he needed.

The day had begun. Carts trundled over the cobbles on Briggate. A group of small, ragged boys were throwing stones at a dog. They ran off shouting when it turned and bared its teeth at them.

Leeds. It ran through his blood.

NINETEEN

February turned into the start of March, and the days began to stretch out towards spring. A little warmer, with the pinched faces of the old and sick easing a little. Simon waited to hear from the cavalrymen, the address of the first place to rob.

He went to the Yorkshire Hussar to play cards, but no sign of the ensign or lieutenant. After a week he began to wonder if they'd decided not to trust him.

Then, just as he was leaving, they arrived, dressed in full uniform.

'The tree,' Johnson whispered as they shook hands. 'Eleven tomorrow.'

They moved on, calling out their greetings and preparing to join the card game.

Things were finally going to happen. He found the gap in the wall behind the Green Dragon and slipped through to see Jane.

As she listened to his instructions, she kept sliding her knife over the whetstone, pausing to rub her thumb along the sharpened edge.

'How soon, do you think?' she asked after he finished.

'It's close,' Simon replied. He could feel it. Very close.

He'd been to a gunsmith and bought a pistol, walking out past

Burley to practise. The loading and firing was awkward and slow; it took minutes to make a single shot. At six feet he was reasonably accurate; he'd be able to hit a man. Past that and he'd have a greater chance by throwing the weapon. He was better with a knife. More deadly, faster. But the gun might have its uses. It would be worth carrying at the right time.

His house was quiet. The boys were asleep, and Rosie had settled for the night. From the attic, a soft noise as Martha turned over in bed. She'd been here for more than a week, doing everything that Rosie told her and trying to make herself part of the household. But he'd noticed the longing in her eyes whenever he left. She wanted to be like Jane, to work with him.

Simon felt uneasy with her in the house, as if she was constantly spying on them. That was stupid, and he knew it. She was just a child, barely older than the twins. Martha even played with them a little. Or tried. Like him, the boys were wary and reserved around her. They didn't seem to trust her.

Only Rosie appeared comfortable with the girl. She treated Martha like a daughter, she had from that first night. His wife was happy, as if a young girl completed the family. For her, maybe it did. She'd never said anything before. Perhaps she hadn't realized it until there was one in the house.

He couldn't raise a fuss. He wouldn't object. Maybe he'd warm to Martha once he grew used to her presence. He undressed, hanging his clothes over a chair. Tomorrow things would change. Tomorrow.

Soot fell in showers, smuts that dirtied the collar of his shirt as he walked out along North Street. Warm enough not to need the greatcoat, the first time this year. There was even a hint of sun above the clouds over Leeds.

Simon stood under the big oak tree, staring up into the branches. Buds were growing on the tips. Another month and it would be in full leaf. He turned as he heard the hooves approaching.

Faster than last time, at a trot, the two men grinning at each other. They circled the tree, slowing, jerking back on the reins and slipping out of the saddle in easy movements.

'You've taken your time,' Simon said.

'It needs the right opportunity,' Johnson told him.

'And something worth stealing,' Murdoch added.

'We've done the work for you.' The lieutenant drew a piece of paper from the pouch on his shining leather belt. 'All the details are here. The address, when the place will be empty.'

Simon tucked it away without looking. 'And when I'm done?'

'You sell the items. Make sure you get a good price. We know what they're worth. You have five days to do it all. We'll be in touch so you can pay us.' His gaze was like stone. 'Don't try to cheat us, Westow. We'll know.'

'We have our agreement. Why would I cheat?'

A curt nod and they were back in the saddle, taking off up the road and quickly spurring their beasts to a full gallop. He felt sorry for any soldiers facing a full troop of cavalry; it had to be a terrifying sight. Simon watched until they were close to the horizon, then started back towards town.

He took out the paper. Johnson wrote in a neat, copperplate hand. Exactly as he'd promised: an address, the times of day when he'd be able to enter, and what to take. A set of six silver spoons. Small, very portable. They'd melt down quickly, and that made them easy to sell.

'They went right past where I was hiding and carried on up the road.'

Jane had caught up with him on the Leeds side of Sheepscar Beck.

'They've given me the instructions.' He told her when, and the times the house would be empty. 'I want you to watch the place. Start today. Find out who lives there and see if they've told us the truth. I don't want to walk into a trap.'

'Are you going to do it?'

'Yes,' Simon answered slowly. 'If it's everything they claim. But I'm not taking any risks. Six silver spoons? The value means I'd be looking at the hangman's noose, not transportation.'

'Do you have a plan?'

He gave a half-smile. 'The start of one. We'll see how far it takes us.'

The last few days had been easier, smoother. Working alone, with no Martha dogging her heels. No explanations to give, no need to exchange words for their own sake.

It made this task easier. Sitting out of sight for hours, watching a house where nothing was stirring. It looked as if it had been a small farm at one time, with a stable and two small outbuildings.

She'd wandered by here the afternoon before, out in Headingley. The village had grown since she'd last been here. New villas along the Otley Road mixed with the older buildings. It smelled prosperous these days, filling out with factory owners and the newly rich. The land beyond was still fields, some tilled, others given over to sheep. She watched the first of the young lambs move with awkward legs as they followed their mothers.

The house she wanted stood right in the middle of the village. Not small, but certainly hardly the largest. A long, thin garden extended behind it, with a stable. Finding a spot where she could stay hidden and watch the place would be a task.

It wasn't perfect. Too far away, but as close as she could safely come. Jane was there before dawn the next morning, the shawl gathered tight around herself for warmth as she settled into the long, damp grass.

An hour passed and a trooper arrived, leading a pair of horses. He waited, saluting with absolute precision as a man came out of the house in glistening high boots and elaborate frogged uniform. A moment later the pair rode off.

Through the windows she spotted a woman moving around in the house. Working, cleaning. A servant, practised in her movements. A little later she was there again, upstairs. Another hour later a man strode down the short drive and vanished at the far side of the house. Ten minutes passed and he appeared once more, sitting in the driver's seat of a coach and pulling up outside the front door.

Jane sat upright, concentrating, studying, as the servant came out of the house with another woman. This one was tiny, wearing a brightly coloured gown and a vivid, plumed hat. The driver helped her inside, the servant followed and the vehicle bounced out to the road. It had the feel of habit, a daily routine.

Jane stayed, one hour, two, until the carriage returned. In the house, nothing had stirred while they were gone.

The driver put the coach away in the stable, walked away from the property, and stillness returned. In the early afternoon the woman and her servant left the house again. On foot this time, both carrying baskets. Social calls around Headingley. Jane followed at a discreet distance.

They went to the tumbledown cottages, a few minutes in each before moving on. Charity for the poor, giving out food and old clothes. Then, finally, a slow amble home.

She'd seen what she needed to, but she stayed until dusk, when the officer and the trooper rode straight-backed and proud through Headingley. Once the man was settled, the shutters closed against the night, she rose silently and walked away.

Jane felt Martha watching her. The girl was standing over in the corner, not saying a word. But her gaze was steady. She'd been bathed, her hair brushed, dressed in a frock Jane had never seen. She looked different, with an air of innocence around her, as if all that time living on the street had vanished with the dirty bathwater.

'Do you think it's straightforward?' Simon asked. He paced around the kitchen, hands pushed into his trouser pockets.

'That depends on the locks.'

'The times the house was empty match what the cavalrymen said.'

When the house was quiet, Simon dipped the nib into the inkpot. With his hand above the paper, he paused for a second before writing.

Very soon. Very. Be prepared.

Two folds, a dab of wax to seal it. He put on his greatcoat and very quietly let himself out of the house. A walk along North Street, sliding through Constable Williams's garden. A light burned behind the shutters in an upstairs room. Simon pushed the note under the door and made his way home.

'The same as yesterday,' Jane said. 'Out in the carriage in the morning, visits around Headingley in the afternoon.'

The day had been brighter, the sun often pushing through the clouds as she sat hidden from view. She'd basked in it, the first time this year she'd felt any real warmth in the air when she was outside.

'We'll do it tomorrow, then,' Simon told her. 'I'll call for you before it's light.'

He felt nervous. Christ knew he'd broken into houses before. But never to steal something. And certainly not in the middle of the day.

'The last two mornings the woman and servants were gone for two hours,' Jane whispered as the coach rolled down the drive.

'Let's hope they keep to that today.'

They were at the back of the house, shielded from sight. The door was solid wood, locked, tight in its frame.

Simon's hands were slick and damp. He wiped them on a piece of linen and brought out the metal tools Nate had made for him.

'What are those?' Jane asked.

'Lock picks.' Long ago, an old crook had taught him how to use them. How to insert them and feel his way through the lock.

'Simple enough, boy,' the man had told him with a grin. 'They aren't too complicated. Once you have the knack you can be sitting on a chair and drinking their porter in half a minute.'

It took longer than that. He was rusty, long out of practice. He'd filed these tools down, but they weren't quite as sharp and supple as the ones the old man had owned. Two minutes, close enough, before he felt the tumbler give and they entered the kitchen.

Sweat was running down his face. He mopped it up with the square of linen and took a deep breath.

'He keeps the spoons upstairs.'

Thank God the door to the room wasn't locked. He'd worried when he'd seen it closed. But it turned easily in his hand.

It was a spare and spartan room, very military; for a second Simon felt sorry for the man's wife. But what interested him was the chest at the foot of the bed. He opened it up, hands sliding through papers and spare shirts until he touched metal. The spoons. Out of sight, but not exactly hidden.

Simon drew them out into the light. Silver, a simple design, flowing and elegant. But they'd been neglected. The metal was clouded and tarnished. In need of a thorough clean. Still, it meant the man probably hadn't looked at them in a while. It might be some time before he discovered they were missing.

He stopped. He was thinking like a thief.

The spoons disappeared into his pocket.

Down the stairs, out again through the kitchen. At first the pick kept slipping and the door wouldn't lock behind him. He tried over and over, feeling a trickle of fear down his back. His anger started to rise. After five minutes his patience was wearing thin. He'd lost the knack. He wouldn't be able to do it.

But he dared not walk away and leave it. Simon straightened his back for a moment and calmed his breathing, then bent again and worked the pick back in. Everything had to be exactly as it was when they arrived. Nothing to bring any questions or fuel suspicion.

He swallowed hard and closed his eyes. Feel it. He remembered the lesson; he could hear the old man's chiding tone in his ear. Get it right, boy. It's not a bloody toy, you can't play with it forever.

Finally, just when he believed it would never happen, the click came and the lock fell in place. Simon exhaled loudly and slipped the lock picks back into his waistcoat pocket. A few moments to steady himself, to wait until his breathing and his heartbeat were even again, then he was out on the lane with Jane and walking back towards Leeds.

He showed her the spoons.

'We'll need somewhere to hide these,' he said.

'Why?' A sharp question. 'I thought you were going to sell them.'

Simon grinned. 'Evidence. And a good way to trap our cavalry friends.'

'I don't understand.'

He laughed. 'You will. For now, we'll put these somewhere safe. I have plans for them.' A pause as he let the last of the fear slide out of him. 'Meanwhile, I need to work on my skills with the picks.'

TWENTY

A good hiding place, one that wouldn't put anyone else at risk of arrest. His mind raced through the possibilities, but none of them felt secure enough. He needed somewhere no one would associate with him, a place where the spoons wouldn't be discovered.

'You go on,' he said to Jane. 'I have things to do.'

She gave him a curious look, then turned away towards the Head Row and her home with Mrs Shields. Simon strolled down Lady Lane, taking the bridge over Sheepscar Beck, then followed the line of the stream down towards Crown Point, where it flowed into the River Aire.

New buildings had risen, but one old tree still remained, a large willow whose branches hung low over the water. He'd seen it for years, a gentle, breathing green, so beautiful in leaf. Sometimes he believed he could remember it from when he was very young, before his parents died. Or was that wishful thinking, a dream he had?

No matter.

There was no one around as he used his knife to dig, no eyes watching from the boat yard on the other side of the river. The earth was soft around the roots, coming up easily. A final glance all around before he wrapped the spoons in his square of linen and pushed them into the hole.

Scooping up the dirt, tamping it down and covering it with dead twigs and brush until it was impossible to see that anyone had been there.

A few days. No more than that. And in the meantime, he'd keep the location to himself. No need for anyone else to know, not even Rosie or Jane.

Simon wiped his knife clean and returned it to the sheath before he walked away.

The Yorkshire Hussar was quiet. Behind the bar, Billy Crawford looked bored.

'You're not making any money tonight,' Simon said.

The man shrugged. 'Some days are like that. The good ones make up for the bad.' He limped to the far end to collect an empty glass. 'Brandy, isn't it?'

'Yes. And one for yourself.'

Crawford raised his eyebrows. 'Very generous of you.'

He filled two glasses and pushed one across to Simon. 'Your good health.'

'Who's the commandant out at the garrison?'

'Colonel Fields,' he replied, then suspicion curled his lip. 'Why, have you been having a problem with . . .' He nodded towards the card table. Only three there now, none of them cavalrymen.

'Nothing like that. Curiosity.'

'It killed the cat. Worth remembering that.'

Simon grinned. 'As long as it doesn't try to wound me. Do the officers pay their bills on time?'

'I don't give them the choice. It's cash on the nail here,' Crawford replied. 'I served with so many of them, I know what they're like. If I offered credit, half of them would never give me a penny.'

'Safer.'

'Better for my purse. And how's your business? Many thieves for the taking at the moment?'

'Always one or two,' he said and thought of Murdoch and Johnson. 'They keep the world turning.'

Another half hour, sipping at the brandy, enjoying idle conversation, and he left. A few more customers had drifted in, but not the faces he wanted to see. Simon stayed alert as he walked home, but people kept their distance.

On Swinegate, his shutters were still open wide, light pouring out to the street. Strange. This time of night they should be closed and barred. Inside, Rosie was moving frantically from room to room, and the secret drawer at the back of the stairs hung wide open.

'Thank God you're home.' She stood, hands on hips, hair hanging loose down her back. Her face was like death.

'What's happened?'

'Martha's gone.'

'What? Where?' For a moment he didn't understand. Then the pieces fell into place. 'What did she take?'

'Money and that silver milk jug.' The words poured out, frantic and tripping over each other. She went from parlour to kitchen, back again. Halfway up the stairs then down again with no idea what she was doing. 'I don't know how she could have seen the drawer. I didn't think she'd been around when I opened it.'

Simon placed his hand on her shoulders. Stopping her, steadying her until she looked at him and was quiet.

'How long ago?' He kept his voice gentle, stroking her cheek.

'I don't know.' Her eyes turned wild again. 'I thought she was in the attic. I went up to wish her goodnight, but the room was empty. I started to look, then I saw the drawer and—'

'It's not your fault,' Simon said.

'But I was the one who wanted to take her in.'

'And I agreed,' he told her. Blame wasn't going to help. They needed to find Martha. 'Now, how much money has she taken?'

'About four pounds. She took the coins, but she left the banknotes.'

That was something. For Martha to steal anything was bad enough. But it could have been worse . . . she probably didn't understand the value of paper money.

'And she took the jug. Anything else?' A thought shook him. 'The book?'

'That's still there.'

Of course. The girl wouldn't see any worth in a book. Thank God for that, at least.

'She has my new shawl, too, the heavy one. It was hanging by the door. And she's wearing that coat I bought her.'

Simon pulled her close. Rosie was blaming herself. It wasn't going to help. Martha was somewhere in Leeds. He had to find her and take back what was his.

The girl needed to learn that you didn't steal from a thief-taker.

'You stay with the boys. I'll get Jane and we'll start looking.'

'Yes.' As he turned the doorknob, she said, 'Why do you think she did it?'

'I don't know. Honestly, I don't.' The girl had a warm, safe home here, food in her belly. She was off the streets. Why would Martha want to turn her back on that and steal from the people who'd taken her in? It was something he wouldn't understand if he lived to be a hundred.

'I'm sorry.'

'We'll take care of it. All of us.'

Jane's face was set hard. Her footsteps echoed off brick and stone as she walked down to the river and out along the Calls.

It was no surprise. Mrs Shields had warned her about Martha. And Jane had sensed something about the girl herself, some unease she hadn't been able to name. Yet . . . she let her come around, time after time. She'd fed her, given her a bed. Maybe she'd seen a little of herself in Martha. Or she'd simply been weak. She'd been surprised when Rosie wanted to take her in. Still, she'd never expected Martha would repay them all like this.

The girl had been so grateful for the kindnesses she'd received. From Jane, from Rosie and Simon. What had happened? How could she change so quickly? Had she seen the money and been overcome with greed?

Jane went around the camps where the children slept. No one had seen Martha for days. Not there or on the streets. She'd disappeared so completely, some wondered if she'd died. Vanished into the river and been pulled away to the sea.

'She's still here,' Jane told them. She took out farthings and ha'pennies, passing them to small, eager hands. 'When you see her, I want to know. Come and find me.'

She visited all the places she knew and asked her questions. From there, to all the sheltered spots she could remember visiting when the girl was with her; Martha might have gone to one of those, trying to stay out of sight for the night.

Nothing. Two hours before dawn she was sitting in the kitchen on Swinegate. Rosie looked distraught, running her hands through her hair and clutching a small, dainty handkerchief in her fist. Simon was silent, listening as she listed the places she'd been.

'I didn't have any luck, either. We'll try again in the light.'

'Did she take the book?' It was the question she'd wanted to ask since Simon had come knocking on the door with the news.

'No. It's still here.'

Jane gave a short nod. Inside, she was grateful. Coins, a piece of silver, they could all be replaced. But that tiny book was worth more than anything she could imagine.

'We'll go round all the fences in the morning,' Simon continued. 'Tell them about that silver jug. Make sure they know to send word if anyone tries to sell it.'

'I'll do that,' Jane said. 'What are you going to do about those spoons?'

'Make sure they find good homes.' He ran his hands down his face and covered a yawn. 'We all need a few hours' sleep or we won't be thinking straight.' His hands covered Rosie's and he squeezed lightly. 'All of us. Do you want to stay here?' he asked Jane.

She shook her head. At home she'd rest. If she lay down here, the past would torment her as soon as she closed her eyes.

The streets were empty. The sound of her boots on the paving stones echoed like the crack of a gun. Jane kept one hand on her knife hilt, ready. Martha could be waiting and she had no idea what the girl had in her mind. And Big Tom would be healing. Soon enough he'd be back again.

Tonight, though, there was nothing. A few asleep in doorways, bundled under rags as they tried to keep warm against the March night. But none of them as small as an eight-year-old girl.

Why?

Did the reason even matter? It had happened.

Simon was out early. He needed sleep, anything to stop the thoughts that flooded through his mind. But it refused to come. A few minutes here, a little more there. Then he was awake once again, eyes wide open.

The pavements were dirty. Middens overflowed and spread their stink. Down in Boot and Shoe Yard they'd removed cartload after cartload of manure when they tried to clean the place up. A hopeless task. In some places it had lain inches deep on the flagstones.

People were already moving around. The coffee cart across from the Bull and Mouth was doing swift business. Men on their way to work stopped for a cup and a slice of bread and butter. Simon drank, glad of the warmth coursing through his body, and told John the coffee man to keep his eyes open for the girl.

From there, he walked out to the willow where he'd buried the spoons. No more than a glance as he passed, to be certain the ground was undisturbed. Everything was exactly the way he'd left it.

On to Far Bank, where the ferry crossed the Aire. A word with the man who guided the boat back and forth across the river. From there, he worked his way back towards town. He checked the places he knew, explored others. No sign of Martha.

He'd keep searching for the girl, but he knew Jane stood a better chance of finding her. She was the hunter for this job, the one likely to track down her prey. She knew the places to look, the right people to ask, where a coin might bring the choicest information.

He'd never felt comfortable around the girl, but he'd never anticipated a betrayal. Bloody child. He was going to make her pay.

TWENTY-ONE

From here Jane could look down and see Leeds spread out before her. The sky pierced by chimney after chimney. The river and the canal below, and the quay known as Botany Bay, where they unloaded the barges bringing wool from Australia. The big mill standing by the water. She'd followed the road that wound by the entrance, rising up the hill until she could turn and look. All very impressive. But it didn't help her find the girl.

She turned and marched into Armley.

Martha had said she'd grown up here. She'd run off after she tried to drown her sister; that was what she claimed. There was no reason the girl should return and everything to say she'd stay away.

But still Jane had come. Maybe Martha had found her way back. Even if she hadn't, she could discover the true story; the tale Martha told never rang quite true to her ears. And it might hold some clue to where to find her.

Armley was a place of rich and poor. Behind a long, high wall lay sculpted grounds that seemed to roll on forever, and a grand house standing alone in the distance. Elsewhere, the poor were packed into hastily constructed back-to-backs. They were the ones who took the road to the mill every morning and made the owners their fortunes.

The women. They'd know the gossip and the facts, and the distance between the two. It was a case of approaching the right people.

She began with the woman looking wistfully through the draper's window, wishing for something inside. But she'd never heard of a girl called Martha.

'I only moved here a few months ago. My man got himself a job mending the looms down at the mill.'

The second woman she approached thought she recalled something, but no details. Her face clouded.

'I can't rightly say, but I can't bring it to mind. You'd do best to ask someone else, love.'

An hour passed with no sign that Martha had ever been here. Maybe she'd made it all up.

Then she found someone who knew exactly what had happened with Martha. A woman who'd lived three doors away from the family when the girl disappeared.

'She said Martha had the mark of the devil from the time she was born.' Jane sat in front of the fire, letting it warm her bones as she sipped on a glass of cordial.

'Did she tell you what she meant by that?' Mrs Shields asked. Jane felt the fingers stroking her hair, leaned towards the touch and closed her eyes as she spoke.

'She said there'd been something about her from when she was a baby. As soon as she could crawl she was trying to hurt people. Bite them, pinch them. She was always hitting her sister.'

'What about the story with the kitten?' the old woman asked. 'Was that true?'

'Her father found the kitten and gave it to Martha. He thought it might calm her if she had something to take care of.'

'What happened?'

'The neighbour said the kitten scratched Martha so she drowned it in the water barrel. Her sister tried to stop her, so Martha put her head under the water and held it there. She'd have probably killed her if their mother hadn't come out.'

'Did she run off after that?'

Jane was silent, breathing slowly. 'No. The woman who lived close by said that Martha's parents turned her out. They were scared she'd kill them all. They couldn't control her.'

'Bad seed,' Mrs Shields said.

Jane opened her eyes. 'What does that mean?'

'The woman who told you about it was right. Some people are born that way. No reason for it; it happens, that's all. Have you told Simon and Rosie?'

'Not yet.' The past wouldn't matter to them. All they wanted was the return of the money and the jug. She was the one who was curious, trying to piece together Martha's history. To try and understand how the girl who could leap on an armed man and wound him could be the same one who stole from the couple who took her in.

It made no sense. She couldn't make the pieces fit together.

'You care about her, don't you?' Mrs Shields said.

'Yes,' she said. Then: 'No. I don't know. Not really.'

'She's not like you, you know. Don't try to see yourself in her.'

Maybe that was what she'd been doing, trying to help because there'd been no one to look out for her when she was young and alone on the streets.

Jane finished the glass of cordial and carried it into the kitchen. 'I need to go out.'

'To find her?' Mrs Shields asked.

'Yes. Before someone else does.'

Simon settled at the card table, nodding greetings to several of the players. He hadn't finished playing a single hand before Murdoch and Johnson arrived, taking chairs on either side of him.

'Damn me if it doesn't feel a little warmer now than it did this morning,' the lieutenant said, rubbing his hands together. 'Spring's around the corner. Been out and about much lately?'

'Here and there.' Simon watched as the cards landed face down in front of him. Three, four, five of them.

'Anything interesting?'

'You might say it was.'

'Productive, I hope?'

'Very.' He pushed a coin forward, watching how others bet. It was a poor hand. Reading the faces of the remaining players, he shook his head and dropped the cards with a sigh.

'I trust your business will be concluded soon.'

He turned and smiled at Johnson. 'Another day, two at most. That should see it done.' He stood. 'If you'll excuse me gentlemen, I have a feeling the cards won't run for me tonight.'

He'd passed the information and set everything in motion. Simon would be busy tomorrow, and then . . . the battle to give Laurence Poole some small measure of justice would begin.

He was standing on Nelson Street, buttoning up his greatcoat, when Ensign Murdoch came out of the Yorkshire Hussar, clasping the cheroot tight in his jaws.

'Just a word, Westow.'

Simon cocked his head. 'About what?'

'Don't try to cheat us. We're not kind to anyone who does.'

'We've been through this before.' Exasperated, he stared down the soldier. 'Why would I do that? I'm sure you recall that we agreed our terms.'

The man nodded. 'Just remember that. We'll be watching you.'

Simon shrugged. 'Watch all you like.' He paused as if a thought had just come to him. 'Why don't you be here tomorrow night?'

'Tomorrow?' Murdoch raised an eyebrow in surprise then gave a curt nod. 'Very well.'

'I need Isaac Shadforth,' he told Jane.

The morning had arrived with the hint of blue skies above the Leeds smoke. Definitely a little warmer. Not quite spring yet but edging closer; the promise of it hung clear in the air. Simon leaned on Leeds Bridge, watching men unloading the barges. Bowed double under their loads, they still moved confidently and swiftly, as if they were strolling along solid pavement, not tottering along wobbling planks.

'He's never up this early,' she replied.

'Do you know where he lives?'

'Yes.'

'Tell him to come and see me this afternoon. Three o'clock. I'll have some work for him tonight. I'll need you, too.'

'All right.'

'What about the girl?'

She shook her head. 'No trace of her yet.'

'Has she left Leeds?'

'No. She's still here.' For a moment, she looked as if she was on the cusp of saying more, then pushed her lips together. 'Isaac Shadforth.'

When Jane raised the shawl over her hair, she became one of so many women around the town. No one noticed her. Isaac Shadforth didn't need any help to become invisible. He moved through life without being seen. That and his deft fingers gave him a good living as a pickpocket.

He lived well enough, with rooms on the upper floor of a house on Silver Street, halfway between Hunslet and Holbeck. It was an anonymous address, respectable, but not expensive. It seemed to suit him; he'd lived in the same place as long as Jane had known him.

He'd still be there; it was barely nine o'clock and he never stirred from the house before eleven, as if he was a gentleman, not a thief.

Shadforth looked at her in surprise as he opened the door. For a moment he blocked the way, then stood aside to let her enter. The place was sparse, swept as clean as anywhere in Leeds could be.

'Well, well, a visitor. I'm honoured. You must want something.' But there was warmth to his words and a smile in his eyes.

'Simon does.'

'Ah.' His eyes widened. 'And do you know *what* he needs?'

'He'd like to see you. Three at his house.'

'Is there money in it?' Shadforth asked.

Jane didn't bother to reply. He knew the answer to that question. She looked around the room. There was nothing personal here – he had no furniture of any value. Shadforth kept his wealth close. Portable, so he could leave and move on without a second thought.

The way she'd been until she started living at Mrs Shields's house. Now she had a home, a place she wanted to be. But she understood him all too well.

Most pickpockets worked in teams, three or more, the dip and his accomplices. Shadforth was good enough to do it all alone. She'd seem him walk beside people, shoulder to shoulder, and they'd never noticed him at all.

'I'll be there,' the man answered.

'I'm searching for a girl. She's young. She's been going by the name of Martha.'

'I don't know her.'

'If you hear anything . . .'

He nodded. That was enough. He'd spread the word and pass her any information. She let herself out and wandered back to town. The girl was somewhere close. Deep in her core, she knew it.

Kate the pie-seller hadn't seen Martha. Hardisty the knife grinder thought he might have had a glimpse of her the day before, but when Jane pressed him, he wasn't so certain. It had been outside an empty building up towards the Bank.

Jane went to look. The place hadn't been abandoned for long; it didn't have the stale smell of neglect yet. But she could see where there'd been a fire in the middle of the concrete floor, and scraps of this and that. People had slept here. Martha could have been one of them.

She'd return once darkness fell and keep watch.

'You wanted to see me.'

The parlour was empty, lessons done for the day. A small fire burned in the grate, enough to take the chill from the air. The boys were off visiting with Rosie.

'I have some work if you're interested,' Simon said.

'If it pays, I'm always interested,' Shadforth told him. 'As long as it's worth my while, of course.'

'It will be.'

'Whose pocket needs picking?'

'Nobody's.' Simon smiled as the man's head jerked up in astonishment. 'I need your skills, but in a slightly different way. Let me explain . . .'

* * *

Perhaps spring had almost arrived, but the days remained short and dusk still came early. The temperature fell steadily as darkness approached. The building was empty, only a single door in and out. She found a place where she could see it, and shrank against the wall, keeping one hand on her knife, and she gathered the shawl around herself for warmth.

They began to arrive not long after the church clock struck six. By then there was nothing else for them in Leeds. Most of the shops had closed, and there was nothing left to scavenge from the markets. Only the long, cold night ahead of them, and an empty belly unless they'd found something earlier. She remembered all the pain that hunger brought.

An hour passed, then two. She hadn't spotted Martha entering the building. But the girl was sly; she'd proved that.

Jane stayed deep in the shadows. The light of the fire showed faces. Some she recognized – she'd seen them on the streets. So many that were new. But already their eyes and mouths were hardened by the effort of survival.

No Martha, though.

Quietly, Jane made her way to the boy who seemed to be the leader. The others came to him, asked him questions, wanted his opinion.

'I don't know you,' he said as he glanced at her. 'Fresh, are you?' Then his eyes searched her face more closely and he shook his head. 'Can't be, you've got the look.'

'I'm searching for a girl.' She held up a penny.

The boy raised an eyebrow. 'Go on.'

'She was calling herself Martha. She's somewhere round eight years old.' Jane offered a terse description.

'Last night,' the boy said when she was done. 'She came in by herself, but she knew one or two of them.' He scanned the faces gathered round the fire. 'Her over there with the dark hair, and him at the edge, you see him?'

'What did she do?'

'I don't know. We had someone taken bad. I was trying to look after them.'

'Did they live?' Jane asked and he shook his head.

'That girl you want, she was gone this morning. Go and talk to those two, they can tell you more.'

She passed him a second penny. The fire had warmed the building and children were lying down, using shawls for pillows and blankets as they tried to sleep. The girl with dark hair was beginning to settle as Jane stood over her.

'Martha.'

In the red flicker, she saw the girl tense and stare ahead into the blaze.

'What about her?'

'She was with you last night.'

'Yes. Why?'

'Where is she?'

'I don't know. Haven't seen her since she left here first thing.' The girl's eyes were wide now, gazing up at her. 'What's she done?'

'She stole from a friend of mine. I'm going to find her.'

From the corner of her eye, Jane saw the boy at the edge of the group rise. She darted across, grabbing him by the hair and pulling him down to the ground before he could disappear.

He was smaller than her, but he knew how to slip and squirm out of a grip. She kept a tight hold as he tried, jerking him on to his knees and bringing her lips close to his ear.

'I'm not going to hurt you.' He stopped moving, and she said, 'Martha. You know her. You were talking to her last night.'

'What about her?' Bravado. But the fear showed in his eyes.

'Give me honest answers and there's two pennies for you. You lie and I'll use my knife. How about that?'

He swallowed hard and nodded. But she wasn't about to ease her grip or trust him. His body was tense, ready to slither away and dash off at the first chance.

'Where is she staying?'

'Don't know.'

'Where is she likely to go?'

A shrug. 'She came here last night. First time I've seen her in a while.'

Jane pulled his head back until he was looking at her. 'Who else does she know? Not just here. Anywhere.'

'There used to be a boy and a girl. I don't know their names, but they were always together, like they were brother and sister. She knew them.'

'Where can I find them?'

'I used to see them in the burying ground at the parish church. I don't know where they went at night, though.'

'That had better be the truth,' Jane told him.

'It is.' He swallowed hard before he spoke. 'I swear it is.'

'If you see her, tell her I'm coming.'

'What's your name?' he asked.

'She'll know.'

Two coins tinkled on the ground as she let go of his hair and stalked away. She'd heard nothing to help her tonight, but in the morning, she'd be out by the gravestones, asking questions.

Martha had betrayed her, too.

It was after dark when Simon walked out to Crown Point. He took a careful route, cutting back and forth to make certain no one was behind him. By the willow tree he unearthed the spoons and took them. He tamped the earth down and covered it. No one would know it had ever been disturbed.

He moved through the ginnels and courts, all too aware that he was carrying stolen property that was valuable enough to see him dance the hangman's jig if he was caught. He could feel the thin, chill sheen of sweat on his face, the clamminess of his palms.

To the dark. The words spun in his brain. Laurence, Simon wondered, what were you thinking of when you wrote that? It made no sense at all.

Finally, the church clock tolled nine and he hurried through the night.

Shadforth was waiting, exactly where he'd promised, out of sight on Fish Street, where the air was still heavy with the stink of the day's business.

'You know what to do?' Simon asked.

'Simon . . .'

'Sorry.' He held up his hands in apology, then left.

One more person to see.

Constable Williams was standing in the small space beside Mudie's print shop. He was impossible to identify, the hat pulled down low and his coat collar turned up around his neck. A glint of light caught the pin holding his stock in place.

'Ready?' Simon asked.

'We will be. My men are in place.'

'As soon as they come out—'

'I know.' Williams cut him off. 'It was right there in the note you sent.'

'Good.'

The Yorkshire Hussar was loud, filled with smoke from pipes and cheroots. Simon bought himself a glass of brandy and drifted back to the card table. Johnson and Murdoch were already there, studying their hands, not even noticing him until he took an empty seat.

'Well met, Westow. Business all complete?'

'Very much so.' He raised his drink in a toast. 'Good health to us all.'

The cards ran his way. He didn't even need to work the deal. Luck was smiling on him tonight. It felt like the good omen he needed. As the money grew in front of him, he saw the resentful looks from the other players. One or two glanced at him with envy.

Time to stop playing. He bought a round for the table and put his winnings in his pocket.

'Gentlemen,' he said as he stood, 'I apologize. Sometimes . . .'

They were gamblers. They understood luck, the way it ebbed and flowed, and how it sometimes could favour a man.

The cavalrymen rose at the same time. As they did, Shadforth drifted by behind them. Not a head turned as he passed. Nobody had noticed him plant the spoons on the soldiers. Then he was gone again.

'We've had enough, too,' Murdoch said. 'Can't keep up with him.'

Outside, Simon walked a few yards and felt a hand gripping his arm.

As the soldiers emerged, members of the night watch came out of the darkness to grab them.

'This one's got three spoons in his pocket, sir. They look like silver.'

'Same on this one, sir.'

TWENTY-TWO

'Arrest them,' Williams ordered.

The constable turned to Simon. 'You now, Westow. Let's see what you have in your pockets.'

He wasn't surprised. Williams would take advantage of this to try and catch him, too. Without a word, he lifted his arms and let one of the men delve through his jacket and greatcoat. Fingers checked his waistcoat and trousers.

'No spoons. Nothing that looks valuable.'

'Pity.' The disappointment dripped in Williams's voice. 'But I have men going through your house right now.' A pause and a wolfish smile of satisfaction. 'I'm sure we'll find a few things.'

Just as well he'd been cautious. And that everything vital was still hidden away in the drawer in the stairs. The constable's men would never find that; they'd never even know it existed. He'd hoped the constable would have been happy with their arrangement. But he was greedy. A pity. Still, he'd come up empty-handed at the house.

'Do what you like,' Simon said. 'Have any items been stolen?'

'Six spoons. The adjutant at the barracks reported the theft this morning.'

Adjutant? The cavalrymen were stealing from very senior officers.

Ensign Murdoch tried to shrug off his guard, but the man kept firm hold.

'We're with the garrison,' he shouted. 'You'll have to turn us over to them for a court-martial.'

'Maybe we do, my lad,' Williams told him. 'Maybe not. I'm not about to wake the commandant now. You can spend a night in the cells. Haul them away.'

'You can come with me, Westow,' the constable said. 'We'll see what they've turned up at your house.'

'An escort home?' Simon smiled. 'That's very generous.'

* * *

As they entered, Simon saw Rosie standing in the hall, the boys gathered around her skirts. Her arms were folded, her expression hard, unreadable. She turned and gave him a tiny shake of her head.

'They haven't done too much damage,' she said. 'I've been keeping my eye on them.' She glanced at Williams. 'But then there's nothing to find here.'

'She's right,' one of the men said. 'We haven't found anything at all, sir. Nothing stolen.'

'Right.' The man's voice was tight, frustrated as he told his men to leave. 'I want you at the gaol tomorrow morning, Westow.'

'Why?'

'I want your testimony against the officers.'

Simon shrugged. 'If that's what you need.'

'Be there.' The constable turned on his heel and stalked away, slamming the front door behind him.

Rosie exhaled slowly and hugged the boys close.

'Come on,' Simon said to the twins. 'The excitement's over now. We'll put you two back in bed. Look at you, you're asleep on your feet.' He looked at his wife. 'No problems?'

She arched an eyebrow. 'Not beyond them being in my house and pawing through everything we own. I kept them in line. What happened?'

Simon picked up Amos. 'I'll tell you once we have these two under the covers.'

Jane watched it all happen. She was thirty yards away, hidden deep in the night, ready to run for Rosie in case the constable arrested Simon. She saw the spoons brought out of the cavalrymen's pockets and followed as Williams walked with Simon back to Swinegate.

She was there when the constable and his men left Simon's house, heard the slam of the door and the way he hurried off. The book. The beautiful book. What about that? Had he taken that?

No. It was still there; it had to be. If he'd discovered it, he'd have been dragging Simon off to the cells. Everything was safe. That was what she told herself as she began to walk home. By the time she reached Green Dragon Yard, she believed it.

* * *

'They never found the drawer,' Rosie said to Jane. She spread dripping on thick slices of bread and handed them to Amos and Richard. 'Don't make a mess,' she warned. 'Your tutor will be here in a few minutes.'

'And I need to go to the gaol,' Simon said. He breathed in and rolled his eyes. 'Williams wants my testimony. God knows why.'

'What will happen to them?' Jane asked.

'I don't know. Very likely the garrison will take them, so it'll be a court-martial. Military prison, maybe, then they'll be cashiered.'

'That's hardly justice for Poole.'

'No,' he agreed. 'But it's the best we can manage. You know we don't have the evidence to see them tried for murder. Any sign of Martha yet?'

'No.'

By the time he reached the gaol at the top of Kirkgate, the soldiers had already gone, escorted away by a platoon of men from the barracks.

But Williams was there, sitting behind a desk that looked as ancient as the building.

'Last night was interesting,' he said. 'A very gaudy piece of work.'

'You had Poole's killers in your cells overnight.'

'And no proof they did it. Or did you give it to me and I never noticed?'

Simon shrugged. 'I gave you the men. That was all I had.'

'For whatever good it did.' Williams sat back in his chair. 'How did you manage that, anyway? I had someone inside, watching the card table. You never went near the soldiers.'

Simon narrowed his eyes. 'I knew they'd have some stolen spoons. I told you in the note. That's all there is to it. You're the one who decided to search me and my house.'

'A precaution.' The constable gave a dark little smile. 'And I'd be a fool not to take advantage of the chance.'

'Is that all? I thought you wanted my testimony.'

'It appears I don't.' He held up his hands. 'The commandant of the garrison might need it later. After all, it's a court-martial matter now.'

'I see.' Simon raised his hat. 'Then I'll wish you good day.'

* * *

A boy and a girl.

Jane stood by the entrance to the burying ground. The stone posts were old, leaning in towards each other. Her eyes searched among the gravestones, looking for the pair.

Maybe a brother and sister. She watched.

People passed; elbows jostled her. But she didn't move. A coach rattled by along Kirkgate with the crack of a whip and a shout from the driver.

There. A flicker of faded colour at the edge of a headstone. Jane made her way between the graves, moving slowly and silently. Her eyes were fixed on the spot.

A figure rose and started to run. A girl. For a second, Jane froze, astonished. Then she began to move. Her boots pounded on the dirt.

It was Martha. Jane recognized the dress Rosie had given her and the pale, curly hair.

The girl had almost reached the wall. She was small, slower than Jane. Not as strong. She'd catch her.

Suddenly two people were blocking the path. A boy and a girl, almost the mirror image of each other. The faces, their hair, close to identical. They were both holding knives.

Martha's friends. The brother and sister. Trying to protect her. If she stopped, the girl would have time to escape into the streets around Quarry Hill.

No chance to fight her way through them. Jane lowered her head and kicked down harder on the flagstones. With a grunt, she barrelled into the pair. She had the momentum and the speed to scatter them. From the corner of her eyes she saw them tumble and sprawl.

Martha had vanished. She must have been quick over the wall. But fear would do that. Jane vaulted it easily. As she came down, pain shot up her left leg. So sharp she had to cry out and lean on the stones to keep herself upright.

A patch of blood was spreading across her dress. She sat with her back against the stones, breathing hard, already sweating.

The boy must have cut her. Very gently, she eased up the skirt until she could see the damage. It was above her stockings. A long gash, six inches or more on her thigh, blood trickling out bright red on a grey day. Jane ripped off part of her old petticoat and tied it tight around the wound.

She'd lost all sense of Martha. The girl had gone. But Jane

knew she couldn't have caught her now if she'd been standing six feet away. She forced herself to her feet, gritting her teeth before she lowered her left leg.

The pain screamed through her. A single step and she stopped. No choice. To breathe, bite down on her lip and clench her fist. Another, then another.

She'd made herself pull a dead body. Moved it along street after street. If she could do that, she could walk home.

It was slow. Jane kept her eyes fixed ahead, keeping every other thought from her head. Only a picture of home, Mrs Shields's small house. Up Kirkgate, up Briggate, then the Head Row. Banishing the pain. She couldn't let herself feel. She daren't.

People kept their distance, looking at the blood on her dress in horror.

Finally, she forced herself through the gap in the wall of Green Dragon Yard and opened the door of the house. Now she could let go. She fell to the floor.

'Oh, my word. Child, child, what's happened to you?'

Jane closed her eyes and drifted away.

She woke in bed, not sure how she'd come here, trying to piece together the jumbled fragments in her mind and make sense of them. Low voices came from the other room. She strained to hear. Mrs Shields, she knew that one. But there was another. Familiar, but she couldn't place it for a moment. Then she knew: Rosie.

Rosie? Why was she here? She'd never been to the house before. The questions started to well up. Exhaustion overtook her again.

TWENTY-THREE

'Mrs Shields doesn't understand how Jane managed to reach the house. The cut on her leg is bad.'

Simon sat at the kitchen table and stared out of the window. Another grey day, showers of rain drifting across the sky. He'd be working alone, just when he needed Jane most.

'How bad?'

'I didn't see it myself. Mrs Shields bandaged it up and gave her something to make her sleep before she came down here looking for you and found me instead.'

'I'll go up there. Does she know what happened?'

'I'm not sure. She said that Jane was rambling. It sounds as if she'd completely drained herself with the effort of getting home.'

'There was blood in her stocking. It had pooled in her boot,' Mrs Shields said. She sat in her chair by the fire with a glass of cordial in her hand. 'The cut runs all the way down her thigh.'

'How long before she'll be able to walk again?' Simon asked.

'It will take time, Mr Westow. She's going to need to heal. That won't happen by tomorrow.' She gave a gentle smile. 'Or even next week. She's weak and she lost blood. I really don't know what other damage there is.'

'I need her.'

'Then you'll have to be patient. I'm sorry. The body takes its own time.'

'What has she told you? Have you managed to find out what happened?'

'She saw Martha' – the woman paused and gave him a pointed look – 'and started to chase her. There were two people in her way. One of them cut her.'

'Where did it happen?'

'In the burying ground by the parish church. I don't know how she managed to make it all the way back here. Determination, I think.' She turned her head and looked at the door. 'You know what she's like. She fixed the idea in her head. She collapsed as soon as she arrived. The poor girl didn't have an ounce of strength left in her. I had to treat her right there, then go to your house. Your wife came, and she was the one carried her to the bed.'

Rosie hadn't told him that.

'Can I see her?'

'If you like. She'll be resting for a while yet. I gave her a drink to help. Sleep's the best medicine.'

Jane looked so small in the bed. So fragile. Her long hair was spread across the pillow, the covers pulled up to her neck. Her breathing was low, but at least it was even. She had no colour at all in her cheeks.

'What can I do?' he asked when he was back in front of the fire.

'Nothing,' Mrs Shields said, then corrected herself. 'No, you can find whoever did this.' That smile returned for a moment, then she shook her head. 'You know Jane. She'll ask.'

He had no doubt about that. 'I'll do what I can.'

But he had so much pressing on him. Things no one else needed to know about. Not even Rosie. Sometimes ignorance was the safest course. He counted out money and placed it on the table.

'Anything she needs,' he said. 'Medicines, new clothes, new boots.'

Mrs Shields nodded. 'Let's see her mended first.'

The burial ground was empty. He scoured every yard of it, knife in hand. No surprise; he hadn't expect anyone to still be here. He'd return after dark, once the ghouls came out. One of them would have seen. Or they'd be able to find out. Simon wanted a name. That would be enough to start.

Jane felt dizzy when she opened her eyes, as if she might fall over. She blinked and slowly things began to take form. She was in bed, not sure how she'd ended up here.

Her leg.

She clutched at the sheet and blanket and pulled them back. Her left thigh was bandaged. As soon as she saw it, she could feel its deep, aching throb.

It all came back. The graveyard. Martha. The pair who tried to stop her. The walk back here when she had to push everything from her mind.

'You're awake, child.'

She hadn't heard Mrs Shields enter. The old woman stood there, cradling a cup and Jane realized her throat was dry.

'Drink it.'

It had a thin, fruity taste that refreshed her.

'How bad is it?' Jane asked after she drained the cup. Would she still be able to run? A moment of panic clutched at her. Would she be able to *walk*?

'It's bad enough.' Jane nodded. She knew that. She'd felt it every step of the way home.

'You'll be fine, child, but it's going to take time to heal properly.'

'How long?' She needed to be out hunting Martha. Find her and make sure she paid. For this, too.

'As long as it takes,' the woman said with a smile. She perched on the edge of the bed, hardly any weight at all, and took Jane's hand between her own. 'You can't hurry it, child, however much you believe you can.'

Jane nodded. A wave of exhaustion seemed to tower over her. She yawned.

'Was Rosie here? I thought I heard her.'

'I had to fetch her to help me with you. You sleep now.'

She woke again, opening her eyes to darkness. For a moment she believed she'd lost her sight. Then her eyes started to pick out familiar shapes in the night. Her heart began to calm. She slid to the edge of the bed, teeth pressing down on her lip.

Jane swung her legs out, feeling the bite of chilly air on her flesh. Her feet touched the floor. She tried to stand, supporting herself with her arms. A bolt of pain shot through her, so fast and intense that she gasped and had to press her mouth closed in case she let out a scream. She dropped back on to the bed, panting from the effort. She'd done nothing, but she was drained.

But now she knew.

A few minutes, long enough to gather herself. For her body to forget. She pushed herself up once again. Emptying everything from her mind.

This wasn't going to defeat her.

Jane balanced on her right leg, staring at the floor as she brought down her left foot. A hard, jolting agony. She put weight on it. No. It wouldn't hold.

She fell on to the sheet, gulping in air. Her face was covered in sweat.

She'd try again in the morning.

'You need someone to help you,' Rosie said. 'You know I'm right.'

'How?' Simon asked. 'What about the boys? You have to be here for them.'

'We could send them to stay with Mrs Burton in Kirkstall for a few days. She'd love it. So would they. You know that. Fresh air and no lessons.'

She was right; they'd revel in the change. And Simon needed someone he could trust. Someone who knew Martha. Rosie had worked with him for years before the boys were born. She knew what to do.

'All right,' he said. 'Just . . .'

'I'll be fine.' She stroked his cheek. 'You look out for yourself. None of it's worth your life.'

He knew that. As he walked out into the night he was armed with three knives and a primed pistol in the pocket of his coat. He listened to every noise, straining for the sound of a boot or the scrape of metal.

What he heard was Leeds in the darkness. A coach rattling over the cobbles on Briggate, trying to make up time. The laughter and songs of drunks that turned on a penny to anger.

None of it was a threat to him.

Simon stood at the entrance to the burial ground. Ahead, everything became pure black. But living folk slept there, too; it was as close to a home as some of them knew, down among the headstones and the bones.

To the dark. Poole's words came to him. But he still had no idea what the man had meant.

He started along the path. A knife in one fist, the other hand in his pocket, jingling coins. The money should draw them, the greedy and the curious.

He didn't have long to wait. He could smell them before he saw them, stinking of dirt and decay. A couple, dressed in rags so worn that he couldn't tell if they were men or women.

He explained what he wanted and one scuttled off. The other kept watch on him. Simon caressed the handle of his pistol and hoped to God he wouldn't need it.

Time seemed to stretch as seconds turned into minutes. Finally, a shuffle on the flagstones and a bent old woman stood in front of him, supported on a young man's arm. She looked up with eyes that held years of pain.

'Hester and Robert,' she said. The words came out as croaking and crooked as a curse. 'That what they're called. They were looking after the girl.'

'Where do I find them?'

'Here. They rob. Pick pockets and purses and bring it all back here.'

He put two coins in her hand. The skin was hard as leather, the fingers gnarled, twisted. The woman stared at him until he had to turn away. When he looked back, she was gone. He was alone.

Hester and Robert.

He didn't have a prayer of finding them tonight. But they probably did their work in the day. He'd find them in the morning.

Simon locked and barred the doors and checked all the shutters were firmly closed.

In the morning. Everything would seem clearer then.

The Burtons arrived with their cart for Richard and Amos. Simon and Rosie waved off the boys and closed the door. The house felt empty, drained of all the life and joy.

'Are you sure?' he asked. 'It's not too late to catch up with them.'

'I'm certain.'

He sent her to York Street, the far side of the burial ground, while he moved in from Kirkgate. It didn't take long. The pair believed they were well hidden behind a pair of gravestones. A pathetic idea; their voices gave them away.

The young man sprang to his feet, drawing a knife from his belt. The girl grabbed everything she could reach and began to run.

'Robert.'

Hearing his name made the boy hesitate. For a second. Just long enough for Simon to bring his blade to the young man's throat.

TWENTY-FOUR

'Don't,' he warned. 'Drop it.'

A brief reflection of light as the young man let go of the knife and it fell into the long grass.

Simon found the second weapon in Robert's boot. Then he was helpless, suddenly looking very young and lost.

'Martha,' Simon said. 'The girl.'

'What about her?' A sullen response. Simon laid the edge of the blade against the lad's cheek and stroked down carefully, slicing off the pale down that grew there.

'A close shave feels very satisfying, doesn't it? Now, you can do better than that. Where is she?'

'I don't know. I *don't*. She ran off yesterday. I haven't seen her since.' The pitch of his voice rose as he spoke.

Five more minutes and the lad had given him everything, the words writhing and tumbling out of him. Martha had arrived wanting shelter and protection. Robert didn't know her, but Hester did. The girl had paid them with money she'd stolen from somewhere.

'Have you spent it all?'

The boy shrugged. Simon repeated the question.

'Yes.'

'She took that from me. Empty your pockets.'

Robert didn't try to resist. He was terrified for his life. There wasn't much, just a handful of small coins.

'What about a silver jug?'

The boy's eyes widened and he shook his head. 'No. She never showed us one of them.'

Simon believed him; with the knife at his throat, he was too petrified to lie.

'Yesterday,' he said. 'Which of you knifed the girl who was looking for Martha?'

'Hester.'

'You'd better get out of here while I let you.'

He watched the young man run off. A few minutes and he'd return for his weapons and anything else he'd hidden in the tangle of weeds around the headstones.

On York Street, Rosie stood over the girl. Hester cowered on the ground, her cheek bright red where she'd been slapped.

'She doesn't know anything about the jug,' Rosie said.

'The boy doesn't either,' Simon told her. 'But he says this one stabbed Jane.'

'Me?' Hester raised her head. Tears had made lines through the grime on her face. 'Him. It was him.'

Simon glanced at his wife. Her face was flushed with pleasure. She relished all this. The thrill, the excitement of it.

'Go,' Simon ordered.

The girl didn't hesitate. She scrambled to her feet and darted off, leaving a few bags and purses.

'I asked where Martha had gone,' Rosie said. 'She didn't know.'

'The boy didn't either.'

'She thought Martha might have run to the wolves.' She shook her head. 'Do you know what she means?'

'Oh, yes.' The Wolves were a gang. Young men, and the girls who served them and fed off them. Violent and vicious. He'd had one encounter with them, retrieving some pieces of silver plate they'd stolen from a house. He didn't relish meeting them again. Martha must have been desperate if she'd gone there for protection.

'Are we going to find them?'

'Later.' He didn't want Rosie there. The leaders of the gang were too dangerous, too unpredictable and her skills were rusty.

The leg couldn't hold her. Jane tried until tears of rage and frustration streamed down her face. As soon as she moved, it folded under her weight and she had to grab hurriedly at the bed to stop herself falling.

Finally, Mrs Shields came in, horrified to see her trying to stand.

'You have to heal,' she said as she tucked the sheet around Jane and wiped the sweat off her face. 'Time, child. It takes time.'

But time was too precious to waste doing nothing. She'd try again later, once she'd regained her control. Just now she could feel her body trembling from the effort. Jane closed her eyes . . .

George Frederick. At least that was what he called himself, taking the monarch's name. The leader of the Wolves perched on a chair in the corner of the room, a young man with hungry eyes and legs that wouldn't stay still, relentlessly tapping a quick rhythm on the floorboards.

'What if I do know this girl?' he asked. 'Why should I do anything for you?'

Simon moved his hand and a sovereign appeared between his fingers, glittering in the candlelight.

'Is that a good enough reason?'

'We could take that, and all the others you're carrying.' He nodded towards the other three by the door. Boys in men's bodies, with eyes that had seen too much.

'You could try.' If they did, Simon thought, they'd probably succeed; they could overwhelm him, and they were ruthless in a fight. It was how they'd come by the name. The night watch steered clear of them.

Maybe he'd been a fool to come here. But he wanted information about Martha.

Simon flipped the coin high into the air. While the others watched, he slipped knives into both his hands. The money landed in George Frederick's lap. As the man looked up again, he saw that Simon was armed.

'A clever trick. Distraction.' He held up the sovereign. 'Expensive, though.'

'The girl?'

George Frederick eyed the coin. 'She was here last night. Said someone was after her, begged a place to stay.' He shrugged. 'Paid her two pennies for a place on the floor. Left this morning, and she hasn't been back.'

'How much money did she have?'

'I didn't check. She never said she was running from you, Westow. I wouldn't have let her in if she'd told me.'

Simon snorted. 'Flattery.'

'Truth.'

'I'd like to know if she returns.'

The young man rubbed the sovereign. Simon gave a short nod, turned on his heel and left.

The cool night air calmed him and he breathed deep. Standing in that room he'd felt how eager they were to fall on him.

At least he knew a little more now. But it didn't bring him any closer to Martha.

Rosie was out, too, going from place to place and asking children about the girl. She'd be safe enough with them; she was more dangerous than most she was likely to meet.

At home, he settled in the kitchen and tried to read the latest copy of the *Mercury*. No advertisements needing his services. Not much of anything beyond stories of the wealthy and the council.

Simon poured beer from the jug. Without thinking, he was listening for noise from upstairs, the sounds Richard and Amos made in their sleep. But they were out in Kirkstall, safe with the Burtons.

Another hour and Rosie still hadn't returned. He paced around the house, unable to settle in a chair or at the table; no sooner was he seated than he sprang up again. The minutes passed and his fears grew.

She could look out for herself; she'd always been able to do that. But she hadn't used her talents in a while. Her reactions would be slow. In the hall he shrugged into his greatcoat, primed the pistol and placed it in his pocket. He'd just finished when a key turned in the lock and she was there, beaming broad as noon.

'Have you just come back?' she asked in surprise.

'I was about to look for you,' he said and pulled her close. He hugged her tight, smelling the smoke of Leeds in her hair, grateful to have her with him. 'I was worried.'

As she pulled back, Rosie was grinning. She reached into her coat and pulled out the silver milk jug.

'You found her.'

'She had her eyes open for you and Jane. She wasn't expecting me.'

'Where was she?'

'In an old house near Ellerby Lane. She was with some other children. I made her give me this and what's left of the money she took.'

'How much was there?'

'More than I expected,' she said with approval. 'We're not badly out of pocket.'

'What did you do to her?'

'Nothing. Just let her go back where she came from.'

For a moment, he looked doubtfully at her, then nodded. Maybe it was enough. They'd retrieved the silver and most of the money. That was more than he'd realistically expected. And the girl had learned a lesson. Steal from a thief-taker and he'll pursue you.

TWENTY-FIVE

The shatter of glass made him sit up. His mind snapped awake, already working. Christ, what was it? Simon felt Rosie beginning to stir.

'Stay here,' he hissed as he scrambled into his trousers, took hold of his knife and dashed downstairs.

In the parlour, one of the shutters was hanging loose, a hole through the centre of the wood. A few shards of glass from the window lay on the floor. What was it? A stone? A brick?

No. He felt certain he'd heard something else. The noise that had shocked him from sleep. Simon tried to think back. Was there some sort of explosion? Or had he dreamed it?

The candle didn't offer more than a circle of light. He held it close to the longclock to read the time. Just after half past three. No more sleep tonight.

His heart was still beating like a military drum. Who'd broken the window? It had to be the cavalrymen. Others hated him, but not enough to do something like this. How, though? How could they have done it? They'd been taken from the gaol to the barracks and confined there until the court-martial. Had they escaped? He moved very carefully across the floor. The pane of glass wasn't shattered, just cracked; the hole in it was small and round. But there'd been enough force to break the shutter. He crossed the room and examined the wall. There, right there. Something buried in the plaster and lath. He dug it out with his knife, rested the lead ball in the palm of his hand.

Thank God the boys were away; the parlour was where they had their lessons.

'What happened?' Rosie came up behind him and rested her chin on his shoulder.

'We got a present through the window. A gift from the cavalrymen.'

He could hear voices on the street. Two men holding up oil lamps stared at the damage.

'We've sent for the watch,' one said. Mr Garland. He knew exactly what Simon did for a living and looked down his nose at it. 'I'm surprised it hasn't happened before.'

'It's done now. You can go back inside. You're all safe.'

'How can we be safe when something like this goes on?' another man asked. 'This used to be a respectable street.'

He didn't bother answering. They were scared, and who could blame them? Violence had arrived where they lived. That was enough to terrify anyone. They blamed him for bringing it here. And they were right.

Inside, Rosie lit the lamps and swept up the glittering fragments.

'It's not perfect,' she said as she rubbed her hands together, 'but it'll do until the morning.'

'I'll send for the glazier once it's light.'

And day was close. Already he could see the first streaks of light on the horizon.

Rosie stared at the hole in the wall. Simon could see the fear in her eyes, all the things she was imagining. But she wasn't going to show it to anyone but him.

'How?' she asked.

A simple question. But he had no answer.

'I wish I knew.'

She narrowed her eyes and bit her lip. 'They're not allowed out, are they?'

'No, of course not.' But the ball had come from a military rifle, not some old fowling piece. This was their work; it was their message. If it wasn't them, a friend of theirs had done it.

'Was this a warning, or the start of a war?' Rosie stared at the hole in the wall. 'What do you think?'

'It might be both,' Simon replied.

She gave him a hopeful smile. 'Then we'd better stop them.'

He squeezed her hand. 'We will.'

Before nine there was a new pane of glass fixed in the wood, so clear it put the rest of the window to shame. The carpenter was mending the shutter, muttering to himself as he worked. The parlour had the linseed smell of putty.

Simon opened his watch. A little after the hour. He watched as the man swung the shutter, barred it and opened it once more, then nodded to himself.

A few coins and he packed away his tools and left. Rosie was out at the market. Simon wasn't going to achieve anything in the house.

The day was definitely warmer. Spring was teasing them. He walked with his coat unbuttoned, hands in his pockets holding knives. Ready.

Behind the Green Dragon, Simon squeezed through the gap in the wall. The cottage was starting to show its early green, shoots breaking through in the old barrels and tubs. He tapped on the door and waited until Mrs Shields let him in.

'She won't settle and give herself chance to heal.' Her voice was a worried whisper, and his eyes strayed to a closed door. 'I've given her something to make her sleep.'

'That's probably best.' He knew Jane well enough to understand that she wouldn't accept illness or injury. She'd keep going. The girl was too determined, too eager. Forcing her to rest was the only way.

'She'll need to recover,' the old woman said. 'Do you know how many scars she has on her body?'

'No.'

'Eight. I looked while I was cleaning her wound.' She shook her head as she gazed up at him. 'That's too many for a child her age. Then there are the ones on her arm where she used to cut herself.'

What could he say? Jane had lived on the streets. The miracle was that she'd managed to stay alive, and then flourish.

'How long until she can move properly again?'

'I told you: as long as it takes, Simon. The more she tries things like this, the longer it will be.'

'Will you tell her that Rosie found Martha? We have the jug and some of the money.'

'I will.' She gave him a suspicious look. 'Was anyone hurt?'

'No,' he answered. When she kept staring, he added, 'Honestly, no one.'

'Good.'

'Is there anything she needs?'

'Just time and care. I can give her both of those.'

* * *

Jane could hear the murmur of voices. Catherine's, Simon's. She strained, but she couldn't pick out the words. They were talking about her, she knew that. Why else would he be here? Her leg throbbed; it had become a dull pain that seemed to penetrate all the way to her marrow. She shifted a little in the bed and it eased. The sound was like water, lapping at the edge of her hearing. She drifted away again.

'Are you sure you know what you're doing, Simon?' Mudie asked.

'I hope so.'

'A ball shot through your window by a rifle in the middle of the night isn't subtle.'

'I noticed that. I need you to do something for me.'

'I guessed – you have the look in your eye.' He sighed. 'What is it?'

'They know you at the barracks. I'd be grateful if you could go up there and see if Murdoch and Johnson are still behind bars.'

'They must be. They're going to be court-martialled.'

'I need to know. Can you ask?'

Mudie nodded. 'Seems simple enough. And if they are? That means they have friends who want you gone. That might be even more dangerous.'

'I want to know what I'm facing. And friends who were away from the barracks in the middle of the night? There can't be too many of those.' He grinned. 'You're a journalist. You know how to ask questions.'

'If I have the chance. I'll send word this afternoon. Try to stay in one piece until then.'

Rosie was sitting at the kitchen table, slowly turning the pages in the Book of Hours. Simon watched as she ran her fingertips over the illustrations.

'I hope no one ever says this has been stolen,' she said.

He traced his hand across the leather of the cover. 'They will; they're bound to. It's too valuable.'

'I know, but . . . wouldn't you like to have it here, so we could look at it whenever we wanted?'

'We'd need to keep it hidden,' he told her. 'We wouldn't be able to tell anyone about it in case someone tried to steal it.'

'Yes.' She closed the book. 'I know, but . . . we can dream, can't we?'

'As long as you remember it's *only* a dream. The Atkinsons will be back from their travels soon. They'll be placing an advertisement for the book and the jug and whatever else Poole took.'

'Poor Laurence,' Rosie said. 'We haven't been able to give him any real justice, have we?'

'Having them arrested for stealing the spoons is something.' He shrugged. 'It's the best I can do. Better than nothing, at least.'

The note was brief: *Your cavalrymen are officers, so they have the freedom of the barracks by giving their word of honour not to leave.*

Simon tore the paper into little pieces.

Honour. Neither Murdoch nor Johnson possessed a scrap of that. Still, it gave him the answer. Now he knew with certainty they'd been the ones who'd fired through his window.

They could attack him, vanish back to the barracks, and claim on their word as gentlemen that they'd never left. Short of damning evidence, any jury would believe them.

Richard and Amos might have been in the house.

They'd brought the fight to his home. He couldn't allow that to happen. He needed to keep his family safe.

He needed to be away from here.

'I'm going to the Yorkshire Hussar,' he said. Darkness had arrived an hour before and all the doors and windows were bolted.

'Simon . . .' Rosie began, but he shook his head as she started to speak.

'I have to be seen. I need to draw them out. Make them come to me.'

'It's too dangerous.'

'What else do you suggest?' He checked the pistol, making sure the load was tight in the barrel, then primed it and put it in his coat pocket.

'Let me come with you.'

'But . . .' Simon began. No women would ever be allowed in the Hussar. The look on her face stopped him.

'I'll keep watch while you're inside. Nothing will happen until you come out. They wouldn't dare stride in when they're confined to barracks. This way it'll be the two of us against them.'

He nodded and squeezed her hand. She was right. Murdoch and Johnson couldn't show their faces in a public house. But they might be searching for him, waiting.

'Together,' he agreed.

He hung back until she was hidden in the shadows on the other side of Nelson Street, took a deep breath and pushed open the door.

The place was loud. For a second, the noise overwhelmed him. He had to stand still while it washed over his body. A coin on the counter and Billy Crawford poured him a glass of brandy.

No sign of any military men at all. At the card table Simon sat facing the entrance. Coat unbuttoned, pistol and knives close to hand. Rosie was right; nothing would happen in here. For a moment or two the thought made him feel safer.

He played a few hands but couldn't keep his attention on the game. His eyes kept drifting to the door. Whenever someone came in, he tensed. Half an hour passed, then an hour and he threw down his cards.

'Enough for me, gentlemen.' He rose and put on his hat. Standing by the window, he eased the knife from his belt and gripped it. The other hand was in his pocket, cradling the pistol.

The night held a heavy, damp edge. The pavements were wet; a shower had passed over Leeds. Simon didn't try to pick out Rosie. Instead he walked up towards Briggate, trying to watch everything, ears pricked for the smallest noise.

By the time he reached the market cross, there was still nothing. Just the sounds that filled every evening in town. He turned, walking slowly, eyes scanning the entrances to all the courts. Most of the whores had already gone to their rooms for the night. Business was slow.

He was ready. On Swinegate Simon stared into the shadows across from his house. A single, blank blackness.

The door swung open as he turned the key. No Rosie yet. She'd be home soon, trailing behind. Simon cracked open the shutter and watched the street. There she came, confident, head held high.

'Nobody was watching,' she told him as she removed her hat and patted her hair back into shape. 'Not a soul following. Town was very quiet.'

Later, lying in bed, Simon felt her turn towards him and the warmth of her breath on his neck.

'What if they shoot at the house again?'

'They won't. They've made their point,' he said. 'They wouldn't be stupid enough to try.'

'They're soldiers. They know war.'

'They're not fools.' He put his arms around her and drew her close. 'Believe me, they won't do that.'

Still, he woke with every creak and sigh of the house, lying there and listening. But by morning there had been no broken glass. A perfectly safe night.

Or so it seemed. But no night was going to feel quite safe until he'd taken care of the cavalrymen. How, though? How?

'Did they say when the court-martial would take place?' Simon asked.

'They're still gathering evidence.' Mudie raised his head from the printing press. 'That's what they told me.' He fitted another part back into place and screwed it down.

'How long?'

'Someone said towards the end of next week.' He shrugged and annoyance crept into his voice. 'I don't know, Simon. I have no idea how army law works.'

'I need to stop those two.' They were out there. They'd already shown him that the barracks walls weren't a barrier. They would come for their revenge. And they'd do it before the trial.

'Do you have anything in mind?'

'Not yet,' he admitted.

'Then you'd best come up with a plan. From the sound of it, you're going to need it.'

'I will, don't worry.'

But by afternoon he'd managed nothing at all. A few ideas, but he soon picked them apart. Simon sat in the coffee house – the only customer left in the shank of the day. Finally, he gave up and left.

Nothing worthwhile. Nothing at all.

*   *   *

She heard the mutter of voices through the closed door. Simon and Mrs Shields, talking about her again. Jane had tried twice to ease herself out of bed and put her weight on the leg. The first time she couldn't stand. The second she managed a single step before the pain screamed through her.

It was her own fault. She'd been too slow. She'd allowed herself to be cut and now she was no use at all. She'd failed.

Jane took the knife from its sheath and held it against her arm ready to cut. She thought she'd passed all that. That the happiness of living here was enough for her.

She had to pay. But she found she couldn't do it. She couldn't slide that edge over her own flesh. It wasn't what she needed any more.

TWENTY-SIX

'I saw the report on the broken window. Some of your neighbours called the watch.' Constable Williams looked up from his desk. 'By the time my man arrived, whoever did it had gone. He didn't see anything at all.'

'If he'd come inside, he'd have noticed a ball buried in the plaster and the shutter knocked off. Someone shot through the glass.'

'And do you have any idea who it might have been?' He settled back in the chair, chin resting on his hand.

'One of the cavalrymen you arrested.'

'Ah, but they're confined to the barracks. The commandant's orders.' He gestured at the pile of papers. 'I have a letter from him with the details. It can't be them.'

'I say it is.'

'Then bring me proof.' His voice hardened. 'But you couldn't give me any to show they'd killed Poole, could you? Ferguson and Brady are still pestering me about that.'

'I gave you the cavalrymen as thieves.'

'You did,' Williams agreed. 'That's something. But that's not what I needed. It's not enough.'

'What if you had the chance to arrest them for attempted murder in Leeds?'

'Whose murder?' His eyes were alert, glittering. The man was interested.

'Mine.'

'What did he say?' Rosie asked.

'I have to send him a note once a meeting's been arranged and he'll have his men there.'

'Do you believe him?'

'I do,' Simon said after a moment. 'Something like that will keep him secure in his job.'

'Will he keep us alive?'

'I hope so. Although I don't imagine he'd lose much sleep if I died.'

'And me?'

'The constable probably hasn't thought about you at all.'

She'd be there. He wouldn't be able to keep her away. They'd started out together. And if it ended, there were arrangements in place for the boys. The Burtons would take them, and there was enough money to ensure they'd never want for anything.

Anger flared in her eyes and she took a deep breath. 'He needs to start thinking, then. If anything happens to you, I'll kill him myself. Are you certain this is a good idea?'

'I hope so. I don't have any others,' Simon admitted. 'Do you?'

'No. You said their trial begins later next week, so we still have a few days. Maybe something better will come.'

'Maybe.' But he wasn't hopeful.

Simon tramped halfway to Chapel Allerton, walking two miles up the Harrogate Road before cutting on to a track and following it through dense bushes to a small stretch of moorland. There was no one else around. It was just scrub, not farmed, not used for anything. There were only thick tufts of grass and stumps where trees had been felled.

The perfect place to practise.

Drawing and throwing the knife at a target. There was a time when he'd been accurate at this. That was years ago. He'd lost the knack and it took an hour or more until his movements began to flow. A second hour and he was hitting the target eight times out of ten. Much better, but not good enough. He needed to be exact every single time.

Simon rested his arm and took out the pistol. He was a clumsy shot at best. If he hit anything, it was luck. But a gun worried people, it threw them off their stride. Another two hours of loading, aiming, firing. Repeating it until he'd improved a little.

He stayed until he couldn't take any more. His shoulder ached and his hands cramped from gripping the knife and pulling the trigger. No matter – he'd regained his technique with the blade. When he encountered the cavalrymen, he'd have a surprise for them.

He was close to the road when he heard the hooves. Too many of them for a coach. A band of men, ten or twelve of them from the sound of it. He ducked back, hidden by a thicket of hawthorn bushes, and watched the cavalry troop pass.

No Murdoch or Johnson. Not a single face he recognized among the officers or the troopers. Probably none of them would have given him a second glance. But his heart was still thumping hard as he leaned back against the tree.

Christ, he was a fool. Deluding himself. If the sight of a uniform could make him feel like this, what was he doing offering to take on two professional killers?

There had to be another way to seek proper revenge for Laurence Poole. There *had* to be.

Finally, he began the walk back towards Leeds. He took the bridge over Sheepscar Beck and along North Street. He'd just started climbing the hill when a voice made him turn. Alderman Ferguson.

'I thought that was you, Westow. Been out for a stroll? Or are you chasing someone?'

'A little of both,' he replied. It was true enough.

'You heard that Williams did some proper work for once and arrested those cavalrymen?'

'Yes.'

'Helps him keep his job a little while longer.' A flicker of annoyance crossed the old man's face. 'Then the fool let the army take them for a damned court-martial. Never mind, it's just a matter of time before he's gone. He was lucky with them.'

Luck? That hadn't been any part of it. But Simon kept his mouth shut. Ferguson wouldn't care about the truth, anyway. Let the constable enjoy his small triumph.

'How about you, Westow? Been keeping busy?'

'Busy enough. Do you know the Atkinsons who live out by Sunny Bank?'

'Of course.' Ferguson sounded surprised. 'I grew up with the father.'

Naturally, Simon thought. The rich crowded together.

'Do you know when they'll be back?'

'Due next week, I think. Why? Do you have business with them?'

'Someone mentioned them, that's all. Said they hadn't seen them for a few months.'

'They'll be here soon enough.' As they approached the Moot Hall he snapped open his pocket watch. 'Now, if you'll excuse me, I have a meeting of the finance committee.'

Simon sat on the very edge of the bed, feeling large and awkward.

Jane was awake, staring at the ceiling, her face showing nothing at all. Exactly the way it had been as long as he'd known her. At least she was awake, with a hint of colour in her cheeks.

The room was small, with barely space for more than the bed. Still, he thought, it was enough for her; she'd never needed much.

'I found the two who hurt you,' he said. She didn't move. 'And Rosie caught Martha.'

'Mrs Shields told me. What did she do to her?'

'Let her go.'

That brought a sharp, accusing look. 'Why?' Her voice was bitter, filled with the pain of betrayal.

'There was no sense in hurting her.'

'You got the jug and the money from her?'

'Yes, most of it. She hadn't spent much. She'd been with the Wolves. Just for one night.'

A short nod. Jane knew them. 'The two in the burial ground,' she said. 'What did you do to them?'

'Nothing,' Simon answered.

Her eyes narrowed. 'You should have killed them.'

'I scared them off,' he said.

She opened her mouth as if to speak, then closed it again. Nothing.

'We're making plans for Murdoch and Johnson.'

'I want to be there,' Jane said.

'No. You can't walk yet.'

'I will. Soon.'

Wishful thinking. Catherine Shields had told him about the number of times Jane had tried to stand.

'You know how she is, Simon. She won't give up, it's just not in her. But it's going to be a while yet, whether she likes it or not.'

'How's the wound?' Simon asked her.

'It's starting to heal. There's no infection. But it takes time.'

'I know,' he agreed. The scars on his body stood testament to that.

'I'll look after her.' The old woman sighed. 'But she needs to learn patience.'

'She's young yet.'

'There are times when I worry she won't live to be much older.'

'She's clever,' he said.

'I know. But . . . she doesn't always think. She plunges straight in.'

It was perfectly true. He'd seen it often enough in the three years he and Jane had worked together.

'She has time to think now.'

The woman nodded. 'Yes. That's not always the best thing for her, either. She broods. She starts to blame herself for things.'

Simon had seen the scars on Jane's arm. Mrs Shields was right.

'Look after yourself,' he told Jane as he stood up to leave. 'There'll be work for us both once you're well again.'

'How did she look?' Rosie asked.

'Angry,' he answered after thinking for a few seconds. 'She wants to be out of bed.'

'She won't be able to help us with the cavalrymen. I've written to Mrs Burton to ask if she can keep the twins a little longer. I sent a note to the tutor, too.'

'Good thinking.'

'Simon . . .'

He turned to stare at her. 'What?'

'Let's walk away from it all. Please. Murdoch and Johnson are going to be court-martialled next week. You know they'll be found guilty.'

'And in the meantime, they can come and go from the barracks as they like and fire a bullet through our window at night. Next time it could be one of us dead.' He breathed in. 'No. We have to do this. Don't you see?'

He'd expected argument. But she was silent. Unhappy. She'd thought it through, she knew it all as well as he did.

They had no choice. The cavalrymen had given their warning.

Jane stood and lowered her leg. The pain reared through her body, but she forced her foot down to the floor, standing until the agony began to recede. Cold sweat chilled her face and arms, but she made herself take a single, shuffling step. Just one. That was enough for now. She'd proved to herself she could do it.

The wound screamed, but it hadn't beaten her. She'd been the stronger one. Jane opened her mouth and took a deep, slow breath. She shuffled back, willing herself to consider every tiny fragment of movement. She let herself fall back on to the bed and pulled up the blanket.

She'd done it. Barely, but it was a start. Mrs Shields had said that she needed more time to heal. But waiting never won anything. She *had* to be able to walk again. To help Simon, and to put an end to things with Big Tom. Once that was done, she'd teach Martha her own lesson. They both had to pay.

He needed the right place. As he walked around Leeds, searching, Simon felt a constant prickle in his back. He was exposed, on his own, too easy to attack.

He kept one hand on his knife, the other in his pocket, cradling the butt of the pistol.

Down by the old ferry landing downstream on the river, out beyond the Quaker burial ground in Holbeck. Here and there, but none of them right.

Finally, he crossed the Neville Street bridge, gazing down at the water.

And stopped.

Someone bumped into him, cursed and pushed him. Simon barely noticed. He was staring . . .

He walked around, climbing over debris and rotted wood. The remnants of the old water wheel, all in pieces now, everything worthwhile long since scavenged.

So close to home and he'd never even considered it.

Cynder Island had everything he needed, bounded on one side by the river. Out by Flay Crow Mill there were places to hide and keep out of sight. Too much rubble on the ground for the cavalrymen to gallop their horses.

Not even three minutes' walk from his house. Perfect.

Simon paced around, trying to find fault and pick out the problems in the terrain. A few, but it was better than anywhere else he'd seen. If he had to meet the cavalrymen, he'd do it here.

TWENTY-SEVEN

'When did it come?' Simon asked.

'A boy brought it about an hour ago. He said a man had given him a ha'penny to deliver.'

'A man or a soldier?'

'A man, Simon.' Rosie's voice was brittle. The flesh was drawn tight over her face. Her hair spilled from a white cap, loose down her back. She was wearing an old dress of cheap undyed muslin, under an apron stained from cleaning the kitchen.

He looked at the note again. It was short, one glance and he already knew it by heart: *Meet or be hunted. It's up to you.*

He crumpled the paper and put it in the range to burn.

'Did the boy mention anything about an answer?'

She shook her head. 'Simon . . .'

He knew what she wanted him to say. But they didn't have a choice. It was there in the note. Meet or be hunted. And it was better to stare your enemy in the face than to always be looking over your shoulder.

'They're killers,' Rosie said bleakly. 'That's who they are, it's what they've been trained to do.'

'I'm not going to give them the chance.'

'How?'

'It won't be just you and me there.'

'Who else?' She threw it out like an accusation. 'Jane can't even walk.'

'Williams and the night watch.'

'For whatever they're worth.' She spat out the words. 'You said it yourself: it would be a convenience to him if you died before he catches the cavalrymen. Do you honestly want to rely on someone like that?'

Simon gave her a bright, confident smile. 'I'll have to stay alive to spite him, won't I?'

'Words are all well and good . . .'

'I'll come through this,' he said, 'and I'll do it in one piece. We both will. I'm not going to let men like that get the better of me.'

'Good.' Her voice was fierce. 'I'll say this – these two aren't worth dying for. Laurence Poole, whoever else . . . I'll be there with you. I gave you a promise, Simon. But the only ones who matter are those two boys of ours.'

'I know that.' He sighed and put his arms around her. 'I know.'

But they couldn't step aside from this. They had to face it.

Simon would make certain it was on his terms.

'They'll have to be on foot,' he said. 'They can't ride their horses on to here.'

On Cynder Island there was broken glass, and the paths close to Flay Crow Mill were littered with sharp stones. A small bridge of rotted wood that would collapse at the slightest weight. Even the air smelled abandoned and musty. Dank and dead. The river lapped at the shore, stinking and dirty.

Simon watched as Rosie assessed the ground. She'd been reluctant to look, but now she was here she was coming alive, as if seeing the place helped her believe they could win.

'Without the horses, they don't have any advantage,' he said.

'They still have swords.'

'If they can't get close enough to use them, swords won't help.' In a blur of movement, he pulled the knife from his boot and aimed it at a post. The blade quivered in the wood and he grinned.

Rosie handed it back to him. No smile on her face. She stared at him. For the first time since they'd met, he couldn't read her expression. Finally, a nod of acceptance and she started to walk around again. She examined corners and places to hide.

'It might work,' she agreed eventually. 'How long has the mill been empty?'

'Years. They keep talking about rebuilding it, but nothing ever happens.'

By the time they left Cynder Island, he had a plan. He'd paced it out and gone over it with Rosie. She'd added ideas of her own, refinements that left them safer, more protected.

She put her arm through his as they walked back to Swinegate.

'We will beat them,' he told her.

'*If* Williams and his men are some help,' she said again.

'Yes,' he agreed. 'If.'

He sat in the same room in Williams's house. The fire burned bright. The constable stood, lit a spill from the flames and brought it to his pipe.

He'd listened closely as Simon explained the idea.

'Why should I believe you, Westow?' He stood in front of the hearth, toying with a china figure on the mantelpiece. 'You promised you'd give me the pair of them for Poole's murder. That never came to anything, did it?'

'And you know as well as I do that the evidence wasn't there. If you catch them doing this, they won't be able to haul them back for a court-martial. This will be a hanging matter.' He paused for just long enough to make Williams turn his head. 'Succeed and they'll never be able to dislodge you as constable.'

The constable's eye glittered at that prospect.

'Murdoch and Johnson are supposed to be confined to the barracks until their trial next week,' Simon continued. 'But we know they haven't been keeping to that.'

'So you say.'

'The window.'

'You don't have any proof that would connect them to it in court.'

'I don't have to. I told you about the note they sent. Now, do you want them or not?'

The constable puffed in silence, his head wreathed in tobacco smoke.

'How many of my men will you need?'

'Three. And you in charge to make the arrests.'

'At Flay Crow Mill,' Williams said.

'There's plenty of room on Cynder Island for your men to hide.'

'It's not that big, Westow.'

'Large enough for what we need.'

'When?' he asked after a pause.

As soon as he spoke, Simon knew the constable was in. 'I'll send them a letter. Make it two nights from now.'

'What time?'

'Eight.' It would be fully dark long before that, with a cold breeze blowing off the river. Few people strayed around there at night. Only the building across the street looked down on the area.

'I'll have my lads in place an hour before that.'

'If anything changes, I'll let you know.'

A handshake and Simon left, pulling up the collar of his greatcoat against the chill before striding for home.

Rosie was sitting at the kitchen table, held in a flickering circle of candlelight. She was turning the pages of the Book of Hours and put it down to look up at him.

'Williams will do it.'

'Will he help, or just watch?'

'Help, I think.' Christ, he hoped so.

He saw the relief, the way her face softened.

'We'll be fine,' he told her.

'Will we?'

'Yes,' he promised. 'We will.'

It was dark, the kind of chill that came in the middle of the night. Jane lay in the bed, gripping the sheet in her fists. She eased herself to the edge of the mattress and swung around.

Think.

She watched as she lowered her legs. The right first, feeling the cold flagstones through the sole of her foot. Then the left, slowly putting her weight on it, before she tried to stand. The pain was intense. She bit her lip, keeping the cry inside.

You never showed the hurt. You never let anyone else see you were in pain. That was one of the first lessons she'd learned once she was on her own.

She kept her face firm and empty, and made herself push forward, one hand gripping the wooden frame of the bed. The wound sang and howled, but she made herself take one pace. She'd done that before – she could manage it again.

Her arm was shaking. She swallowed hard. A second step. Tentative at first, but Jane pressed down. For a moment she believed she'd faint. The world seemed to shimmer and fade. Then it passed and she was still standing.

Two steps. That was progress.

Back in bed, she pulled up the blanket, trying to stop herself from shivering. Inside, she was pleased. Little by little. It didn't matter what anyone said. She'd force herself. She could do it.

Simon turned in the bed. He couldn't sleep, but he'd never expected that he would. Being here was better than sitting in the kitchen all night. At least he could let the darkness envelop him and pretend he was resting.

He felt Rosie shift. He knew she was awake, too. Just lying there, silent, trying not to think ahead.

'How will you let them know where and when?' she asked. Her voice sounded very small in the night.

'I'll ask George to deliver a message.'

'He might refuse, you know. He'll want to know what it's for.'

'Then I'll pay a boy.' He was silent for a long time. 'I'll go over to Flay Crow Mill again once it's light.'

'I'll come with you.'

Good. He wanted them both to have every foot of the ground imprinted on their minds.

A thin drizzle was falling, the air warm and damp, a proper spring day. The wood and the old, rusted metal were wet under his touch. The river passed just a few yards behind him, washing up debris. Old clothes, the bloated, rancid corpse of a cat. A pall of smoke filled the sky, fed by the factory chimneys.

Simon breathed and began to pace out distances. He pulled and tugged, picked things from the ground and tossed them aside. He needed to be able to move quickly, without thinking or looking where he was going.

He was going to need weapons hidden around the mill. Every advantage he could manage. He'd go into this prepared. He was going to win.

Rosie walked across the whole of Cynder Island, clogs crunching over the dirt, bending to examine this and that. She looked like a scavenger hunting for bits and pieces that might keep her alive for a day or two.

'Well?' Simon asked when she'd finished. 'What do you think?'

'We should block some of the tracks.' She pointed. 'That one there, and that, over to the right. If we do that, they'll never be able to come at us from the sides.'

Her ideas made sense. It restricted the lines of attack. There were still too many of them for his liking, but he couldn't close them all. And there were ample places for the constable's men to remain out of sight.

'Now do you believe we can beat them?' he asked.

'Yes.' But he saw the uncertainty which still sat at the back of her eyes. She wanted to believe it, she needed to believe it. But she couldn't, not completely. Not yet.

He squeezed her hand. 'I promise you. Then we'll have the boys back.'

She tried to smile, but it was a weak, wan effort.

For a moment he was overcome by her. That Rosie was willing to sacrifice everything for him. He turned away and blinked hard, feeling the sharpness in his eyes.

'I'd better go and see George. Send that note.'

'No.' Mudie shook his head. 'I'm not letting you kill yourself that way. And I'm damned well not going to let you sign your wife's death warrant.'

'Williams and his men will be there.'

'I don't care if you have a bloody platoon of sharpshooters with you.'

'I'm not doing this for any kind of honour,' Simon told him. 'You know me better than that. If I don't end it now, then one night they'll be there, waiting for me.'

'They have their trial. They'll be cashiered, in disgrace.'

'And they're officers,' Simon yelled. He paused for a heartbeat and started again, his voice calm again. 'For God's sake, George, we both know that means there won't be any sentence of hard labour for them. That would affect the *honour* of the regiment. Yes, they'll be quietly cashiered. All that means is they'll be free and ready for revenge. They'll come after me and Rosie. This is my chance to stop them.'

'No,' Mudie repeated. 'I'm not going to do it, Simon. As simple as that.'

'I'll find someone else who will.'

The man shrugged. 'I can't stop you. But I won't be a party to it.'

Mudie could have put the note straight into their hands. As it was, Simon gave a boy a penny and watched him dash off, clutching the paper. Now he had to hope the lad actually delivered it to the garrison and that the guard at the gatehouse passed it on. Too many maybes for him to feel comfortable.

The knife-seller on Kirkgate seemed surprised to see him, but danced attendance as Simon tried the balance of blade after blade, finally selecting four of them.

'Sharpen them for me.'

'Gladly, sir. If you can call back in an hour . . .'

By afternoon they were hidden at Flay Crow Mill. Out of sight but quickly to hand.

TWENTY-EIGHT

One step. A second and Jane was gasping for breath at the effort. A third, forcing her foot down, riding over the pain yelling in her leg. She stopped, letting the waves subside, turned and walked very slowly back to the bed.

Six steps in total. Six.

She was still shaking from the effort as she pulled the blanket around her body.

Six steps. Jane smiled as she closed her eyes.

* * *

'Do you think they'll spy out the ground beforehand?' Rosie asked. The Book of Hours lay on the table in front of her, but she hadn't opened it. Her fingertips moved over the leather, stroking the surface as if it offered her some comfort.

'Probably,' he replied. The cavalrymen were arrogant and confident, but they weren't fools. They'd been through a war. Let them come and look at Cynder Island and reconnoitre the battlefield. It wouldn't help them. Whatever they did, he'd make sure they lost.

'None of this feels real,' she said. 'Just waiting and wanting the hands to turn on the clock. It's not the way things should be.'

'No,' Simon agreed. It felt as if their entire existence had been suspended, all the ordinary tasks vanished, leaving them here as the minutes passed too slowly.

And there was still the night ahead.

They needed to sleep, to be fresh and alert for tomorrow. But rest seemed like a distant, hazy country.

From the window, Simon watched Rosie leave, walking out to Kirkstall to spend a few hours with their boys. He understood. She needed them close for a while. He wanted to go with her, but he wasn't sure he could take the pain of leaving them again. If he held them, he knew he'd let his plans crumble. They were worth more than any of the risks.

But the only way he could be sure of a safe life with Amos and Richard was for the cavalrymen to be arrested. Tried and then hung.

He stayed at home, sharpening his knives and cleaning the pistol. Simon paced from room to room, the same path over and over until he believed he must be wearing a rut in the floorboards. For Christ's sake, he still had more than twenty-four hours of this ahead of him.

Simon put on his greatcoat. Damp, warm air against his face as he walked up Briggate. A coach skittering out of the Talbot yard brushed close enough to knock off his hat before disappearing around the corner on to the Head Row.

He hadn't been paying attention. People died every week, hit by coaches or carts. His mind had been on tomorrow, not the here and now. Stupid.

The lamps were glowing in Mudie's print shop, and a bell tinkled over the door as Simon entered.

'Are you still going ahead with your damned idiocy?'

'Tomorrow night. Williams and his men will be there.'

'You always were a fool, Simon, but this time you've lost your senses.' He wiped ink from his hands and filled a small glass with brandy. 'Don't,' he said. 'You don't have to do this.'

'I do, George.'

'Pride.' He spat on the floor. 'Stupid bloody pride.'

'No,' Simon began, then stopped. Mudie was right – pride was one small part of it. That determination not to be beaten by anyone. But it was much more than that. He had no choice. He was doing this to keep himself and his family safe for all the years ahead. That wasn't pride.

That was desperation.

'No,' he continued with a sigh. 'Honestly, George, it isn't just that. Believe me.'

'Then you'd better be prepared. I've watched those cavalrymen go through sword drills. They're deadly.'

Rosie had been crying. He could see the tracks down her cheeks. Simon held her close, keeping her pressed against him until she slowly pulled away.

'How are they?' he asked.

'Blooming.' She smiled, but it never reached her eyes. 'They love the country; they can run around and the air is fresh. We should move out there.'

'Maybe we will,' he said. But they were talking to fill the silence, nothing more.

'We can find a tutor in Kirkstall. I could have a garden and grow some of our food.'

But she was a town girl to the soles of her feet and they both knew it. Rosie had never grown a thing in her life. Maybe she could start, but he doubted that. This was their home, surrounded by all the smoke and the dirt that was Leeds. They belonged here. At the moment, she needed to cling to dreams of the future. To have something in sight beyond tomorrow.

He slept. He must have slept. He opened his eyes in that strange time before dawn arrived when the world seemed full of hope. Simon lay there, listening as Rosie breathed softly and evenly.

The next he knew, pearl light leaked through the shutters and the rest of the bed was empty. He stirred, washed and brushed at his teeth, then selected his clothes. Trousers that didn't fit too tight on his legs; he needed to move quickly and in comfort. A thick woollen waistcoat. Simon attached a knife sheath to his forearm and slid the blade in place. Finally, his work jacket, always grubby and worn, but with plenty of pockets.

In the kitchen he nuzzled against the back of Rosie's neck, but she barely seemed to notice him. Lost in her thoughts. She picked a shawl off the back of the chair and wrapped it over her shoulders and her hair.

'I need some air.'

'Cynder Island?'

Rosie nodded.

'I'll come with you.'

Another check. The first of many to come during the day.

The river looked bleak and dirty, the stench strong enough to make him cough for a minute. But it passed.

Simon tried to think of the problems he hadn't already imagined, everything that might go wrong. So much, so very much.

'There won't be any light tonight,' Rosie said.

Simon looked up, studying the sky. Above the pall from the factories, the clouds were pale. Off to the west, they seemed to be thinning. It would be a three-quarter moon.

'Maybe some flashes,' he answered.

'Very dark down here.'

'It'll be the same for them. We'll come down early, our eyes will have adjusted,' he reminded her. 'We've walked it all, we know it. They'll have to blunder around while we have a good position by the mill. That gives us the advantage. The constable will have his men here, too. They'll stop everything before it begins.'

She was scared. Terrified. So was he, but he couldn't afford to show it. He had to stay strong, to let her see that. Her body almost hummed with fear. But still she continued, picking her way around, covering the same ground again and again until she'd be able to do it without thinking once the fighting began.

Arm in arm, they strolled home. But there was no joy about them. People glanced at their faces and hurried to keep at a distance.

Simon escorted her inside and left again. He had people to see and arrangements to make.

A note to Williams to make sure his men would be there by seven, out of sight around Cynder Island. He prayed that the man wouldn't let him down. Why would he? An arrest like this would make him untouchable in the constable's job for years to come.

Down the hill, over Sheepscar Beck and over to the far side of Quarry Hill. Nate Brooks looked astonished to see him again. He wiped the sweat off his face with a broad hand.

'Found a taste for good company, Simon?'

'I'm here to spend a little more money.'

Brooks pursed his lips. 'I never turn away a customer. What is it, more of those picks?'

'Easier than that.'

The smith grinned. 'Those are the kind of words I like to hear. Come on, I need a drink, you can tell me more.'

Half an hour and Simon left with metal jingling in his coat pocket. He'd enjoyed watching the men work, so swift and confident around the molten metal. Each with his task, even the boy on the bellows. For a few minutes, seeing them move with such precision, the weight of everything that lay ahead had been lifted.

He walked back to Cynder Island, staying alert; Murdoch and Johnson might have slipped out of the barracks and be scouting the place. No sign. The only person he saw was a ruin of a man with one arm strapped up, looking as though he hadn't washed in a week. The smell rolled off him. Big Tom Bailey, Simon realized with surprise. He looked as if he'd lost all his bravado. He'd deflated to nothing. Tom studied Simon with angry eyes, spat and shuffled off.

Not a threat. Just another man damaged by life.

Simon reached into his pocket and pulled out a handful of small metal pieces. Brooks and his apprentices had made caltrops, small metal objects with sharp points, just long enough to cut into a horse's hoof. He spread them around. In the darkness they'd be invisible.

It was insurance to make certain the cavalrymen didn't try to use their mounts. He needed them on foot, where they'd be vulnerable. Ten minutes and the paths were littered. The few that remained he scattered across the island. They might do some damage through the sole of a cavalry boot.

In the kitchen, he picked at his food. Rosie hadn't even set a plate for herself. After five minutes, he pushed it away. 'We should go and see Jane.'

He needed to visit her, and being outside was better than sitting in the thick, brooding silence that pressed down around them.

Simon's eyes moved from face to face as they walked. He was aware of people on the other side of the street, of the ones walking behind them. Carts rumbled by on Albion Street, weighed down by their loads. They passed the grand buildings of Albion Place, houses for Surgeon Hey and his children. A pair of servants stood gossiping on the pavement, cackling with laughter.

Behind the Green Dragon, Simon held Rosie's hand as she slipped through the gap in the wall, then followed. They hadn't exchanged a single word on the way here. Somehow conversation seemed too fragile, too precious to waste.

Jane looked a little stronger today, Simon thought. Still with little to say for herself, but when did she ever speak much? Rosie told her about their preparations for the cavalrymen and watched the emotions parade across her face. The anger, the frustration that she couldn't be with him.

Finally, he stood.

'I'll come back tomorrow and tell you about it.'

He hoped he could keep that promise. No, he'd be safe; both of them would be. He was ready, and he had no choice but to trust that Williams would have his men waiting.

'She won't give up,' Mrs Shields said. 'She thinks I don't hear her. She stands and tries to walk.'

Simon smiled. He couldn't help himself. That was Jane.

'How many steps has she managed?'

'Six so far,' the woman replied. 'She needs to rest, but she'll never listen.'

'At least she has you.' He meant it. Somehow, Mrs Shields had been able to reach Jane. It was more than he and Rosie had ever managed. The girl had changed. Not too much, perhaps, but for the first time, she looked as though she might be able to accept herself and her life.

Jane stared at Rosie, wondering why she was still here after Simon had gone. She began to open her mouth, but Rosie held a finger to her lips, waiting until the door clicked shut.

She reached into the pocket of her dress. Jane tensed. What was she doing? Bringing out her knife? But all she saw was a hand that vanished under the blanket before pulling back.

'I've brought you something.' Rosie kept her mouth close to Jane's ear. 'It might help. Don't look until I've gone.'

A quick, awkward smile and she turned.

Jane listened to the voices, not even trying to pick out the words. Then there was silence. She moved her fingers, touching leather, then bringing the present into the light. For a moment she felt that she couldn't breathe.

The Book of Hours.

The longclock ticked away the minutes. Simon felt sure that the sound grew louder as the day passed. He could hear it up in the attic as he stood by the window, staring down at the street.

Nobody was watching the house. Off in the distance he could make out part of Flay Crow Mill. It was nothing more than a wasted jumble of wood sitting at the water's edge. No sign of anyone there yet. He eased up the sash and smelled Leeds. Smoke, oil, dirt and decay. The noises rushed in: all the rhythms of the machines, one on top of another, coaches, carts, voices. How could a man hear himself think with all that? A snap of the wrist and the window was closed again. The world was muted.

Down in the kitchen he sat across from Rosie, his hands holding hers. No words. After so many years together they didn't need them. She was terrified, but she was coming with him. She'd do it because he was there. His battle was her battle. He'd do it for her, for the boys, so they'd all be able to live in peace.

A knock on the door. A boy with an assurance from Williams: *We'll be there*. Simon gave the lad a penny and watched him dash off with a grin on his face.

Rosie looked at him questioningly. Simon put the paper on the table.

'The constable,' he said. He felt lighter, all the tightness around his chest gone. This would be fine.

'The cavalrymen aren't under arrest yet,' she reminded him.

'I heard you stir,' Mrs Shields said. She carried a bowl of warm broth and placed it on the stool beside the bed. 'How do you feel?'

'I'm getting better,' Jane lied. 'I want you to sit on the bed.'

'Why?' The old woman looked puzzled.

Jane reached under the pillow and brought out the Book of Hours.

'Take a look at it.'

One page, then two and three, the ecstasy growing on Catherine Shields's face, suddenly replaced by fear.

'Where did you get this? You didn't—'

'Rosie brought it.' She was too weary to tell the whole story.

'It's exquisite. You see the way their faces look, they're real. And the colours are so bright.' Her eyes were wide with wonder and pleasure. It was worth everything just to give her this moment. She deserved it.

Catherine's bony fingers touched her hand and lightly squeezed the fingers.

'Thank you for . . .'

'I'm glad you like it.'

'I . . .' With a handkerchief she dabbed at the tears rolling down her cheeks. 'Thank you, child.'

Rosie stood on the step as he locked the front door. He'd done it thousands of times before, but suddenly it felt like a very final act.

Simon pulled her close and whispered 'I love you' in her ear. Then he stood back and smiled. 'Ready?'

'Yes.' Her hand was shaking as she squeezed his fingers. But she was there, beside him.

TWENTY-NINE

Away in the distance, the clock in the parish church struck half past six. Simon moved around the mill. He remembered the paths, reaching out and touching the sodden wood. A knife here, another over there; everything was as he'd left it.

To the dark. Laurence Poole's words rattled through his mind.

Here he was, caught in the pitch black, and he still didn't have a clue what the man had meant.

He heard the rustle of fabric as Rosie moved. A simple, warm dress of plain brown wool under a dark cloak, the hood covering her hair. She held a knife gripped tight in her hand, eyes searching in the darkness.

A few minutes and Simon heard the sound of boots. Four or five men, he thought, coming closer. He slid behind a part of the mill wheel, hardly daring to breathe in case they heard him.

A hissed command. Simon exhaled slowly. He knew the voice. Williams. He'd arrived, exactly as promised. Now Simon had to hope the men had enough brains to keep silent and out of sight and then appear when they were needed.

The clock struck the half hour. Time had flown by. Thirty minutes until the cavalrymen were due. He squeezed behind Rosie, hands on her face, his lips brushing the soft down of her cheek. Her skin was cold and she flinched at the contact.

'We'll soon be home again,' he promised. She smiled, but there was nothing behind it, just a simple reaction to hearing him speak. Rosie didn't look as if she'd even heard what he said, lost in her thoughts.

Simon walked. Slow, even paces, listening for any sound and hearing only the water lapping close. The air grew colder, the dampness pushing down into his throat.

A single chime from the church. A quarter to the hour. Once again, he checked his knives were ready. On the belt, in his boot, in the sheath up his sleeve. Reaching without thinking. Then up and down the line once more, feeling for the weapons waiting there. Hand going into the pocket of his greatcoat and caressing the metal of the pistol.

Eight o'clock. The bell pealing. Simon stood, waiting. This was the time he'd set with them. Had the boy delivered the note?

His heart was beating fast, hammering against his ribs. Simon tried to catch his breath. The seconds passed. No sound of hooves. No noise from boots on Cynder Island. Nothing more than the emptiness of the night around them.

Ten minutes. A quarter of an hour.

They weren't coming. On the island, he could hear men stirring, shuffling, a few whispers. Williams and the night watch growing restless.

But no sign of the cavalrymen.

Simon wasn't leaving. Not yet. They might still show themselves.

Half past eight. He heard the constable talking to his men and the tramp of feet as they left.

'Simon.' Rosie touched his arm. 'It's time we went, too. We've been out here long enough. Let's go home.'

'Not yet. Give it until the top of the hour,' he replied.

'Do you really think they'll come?'

Maybe. He was prepared for this. He was ready to fight, and he wasn't going to walk away until he knew beyond a shadow of a doubt that there would be no battle. Deep inside, Simon still believed they'd arrive. They were hungry for revenge. They needed this as much as he did.

'Just a little longer.' He was listening, straining to pick out anything at all. But with the constable's men gone, Cynder Island stayed silent.

The bell began to ring the hour. Time to admit the cavalrymen weren't coming. Or they weren't coming here. They might be waiting to ambush on the way home. Simon collected the knives from their hiding places and slid them into his pockets.

'Do you think they're scared?' Rosie asked. 'Is that why they never arrived?'

'No,' he replied after a moment. 'Not scared. They're wary. We'll probably get another note in the morning.'

They'd barely covered twenty yards when he froze.

'Get back,' Simon hissed as he turned and pushed her ahead of him. He handed her two of the knives. 'It's them.'

Hoofbeats. Horses cantering through the streets, drawing near. Johnson and Murdoch had timed it well. It would be just the two of them against the cavalrymen.

'Keep out of sight for as long as you can.'

The beasts slowed, shoes ringing on flagstones as the riders guided them closer. Then a loud, screaming whinny, a muffled voice trying to control the animal. Simon smiled. The caltrops had worked. Murdoch and Johnson were here, but they'd be forced on to their feet. Exactly what he wanted.

'Ready?' he whispered.

'Yes.' Rosie's word drifted on the air.

Simon waited, standing with his back to the ruin of the mill wheel. He watched the darkness, waiting for movement in the deeper shadows. The knife blade was cold and ready in his fingers.

There. He heard scuffling on the ground. Simon tensed, straining his eyes to pick out a shape. Nothing. They were watching, he could feel their eyes trying to pick him out.

Then it came, the flare and fizz as the trigger was pulled. Light burst from the muzzle of the rifle. The brilliant explosion of shot. It came nowhere near him, too high and wide, heading for the river.

But it gave him a target. He drew his arm back and took aim in a single fast motion, then let the knife fly.

He heard a grunt of pain and smiled. First blood. No telling what damage he'd done. Simon was already moving, bent double as he ran. A second rifle cracked; the ball whined off the wood where he'd been standing.

That was all the shooting they could do. It would take far too long to reload; they'd be vulnerable the whole time. That left them with swords. Their main weapons. They'd be deadly with them – if he gave them the chance.

Simon caught a trace of movement at the edge of his vision and threw another blade towards it. Just a clatter as it fell to the ground.

A wasted attempt, but it would keep them wary about attacking. He'd already managed to wound one of them.

Simon brought out the pistol. The polished wood of the butt felt slick against his palm. He hooked his finger around the trigger. One chance, that was all he'd have with the weapon. He wouldn't shoot until he was certain.

The seconds passed. He couldn't see Rosie, but he wasn't worried. She had a good head, she never panicked. And she would fight like one of those tigers from India, tooth and claw and blood. She'd destroy anyone who came at her.

If he allowed them long enough, the cavalrymen would be able to load the rifles again. Crouching, he moved behind the old mill wheel, close to the water's edge. Feeling around, he scooped up a stone the size of his palm and tossed it into the blackness. Then a second and a third. They wouldn't do any damage, but they might make the soldiers careful.

Had someone gone running for the watch after they heard the gunshots? And even if they had, would any of the constable's men return? Williams had given up the evening as a bad job; he was probably back in the warmth of his parlour now, sitting by the fire with a glass of wine.

There was only one way that he and Rosie would ever make the walk home.

The church clock chimed the quarter hour. How had the time passed so quickly?

The soldiers were staying quiet. If they were moving, they were doing it silently.

A sudden yell, and a dark outline emerged from the night, dashing straight at him. Simon raised the pistol and waited. Ten feet. He breathed and steadied his arm. Eight feet. Close enough to see the face. Ensign Murdoch. Simon took another breath and made sure of his aim. Six feet.

He squeezed the trigger. The ball exploded from the muzzle and hit the cavalryman in the middle of his chest. He was too close to miss, almost touching the man's skin.

Murdoch was moaning, trying to turn and crawl away. But second by second, his strength was fading. Another minute and the ensign would be dead.

Only Johnson left to worry about. He'd be very cautious now. He might even try to run, to save himself.

Simon ducked and scuttled along until he reached Rosie. 'Move to the centre,' he said. 'I'm going to ease around behind him.'

'What about the one you fired at?' she whispered.

'It was Murdoch. He won't be giving anyone a problem now.'

She nodded. 'Be careful.'

'If Johnson comes at you, don't spare him.'

She bared her teeth. 'Don't worry.'

He knew the paths. He'd walked them so often in the last two days that they were ingrained in his brain. But he stopped constantly, looking, checking. Johnson was here. Close. Very close. He was clever. And deadly.

A turn to the right, three paces. Halt and listen. To the left. Six steps and pause again. Left again and he was by the entrance to Cynder Island. He could smell the horses.

One of the animals snickered as he approached. Simon stroked its neck and felt in the saddle bag. Perfect. A length of rope, the type of thing any good cavalryman would carry. A couple of knots and both animals were hobbled. They wouldn't be leaving quickly.

He began to ease back towards Flay Crow Mill.

He took his time about each step. Lowering the heel first, then gently pushing the weight towards the toes. Not a sound, moving slowly enough that he could feel any caltrop before it hurt him.

He had time. If Johnson attacked, Rosie could hold him off for a few seconds. And if he didn't, Simon would find him.

He moved silently across the wasteland of Cynder Island. The church bell rang again, marking the half hour. Simon wiped the sweat from his palm. He needed a second knife.

As he ducked to reach into his boot, he heard the swish of a blade and let himself fall to the ground. The sword missed, slicing through the air above his head. Simon rolled, coming up holding both his weapons.

Johnson was already running. He was breathing hard, making too much noise, beyond caring, simply wanting to get away. So easy to follow. Simon was the hunter now, letting the other man make the pace and wear himself out.

The cavalryman must have realized his friend was dead. He didn't know this place, he was panicking, making mistakes, taking wrong turns, blundering and hoping to chance across the way out. He was desperate.

Simon was happy to keep his distance. He had time. He had all night. Let Johnson thrash around.

A sound carried across the darkness. Something splashing into the water. It made the lieutenant stop. Simon knew exactly what it was. Rosie had tipped Murdoch's body into the river. By morning he'd be halfway to Hull, nibbled at by the fish and the other creatures that lived down there. Two days and no one would know him at all.

So easy to disappear . . .

Johnson began to move again. One step, then he paused again, turning his head to the left, then the right. As if he heard something, sensed something. Then he was running full tilt. As if his life depended on it.

What was it?

Simon listened. There, he could feel the vibrations in the ground. Then he could hear it. Hooves. More than two horses, a whole troop of them.

No wonder the lieutenant had run. He didn't want the soldiers to catch him out here.

The horses were still tethered and hobbled. Simon heard footsteps echoing off the buildings. Johnson had gone, vanished into the night.

He whistled, two short, low blasts, the signal he and Rosie had always used. A minute and she was by his side. Simon raised his eyebrow in a question and she answered with a small nod. Everything was fine. He smiled and squeezed her hand.

All he had to do was wait.

The horsemen reined in a dozen yards away, six mounted men. The officer in charge dismounted and walked towards them, one hand resting lightly on the hilt on his sword. He was in his late thirties, trim, dark hair turning grey at the temples.

'I'm Major Harvey. Do you know where they went?'

'They ran off,' Simon replied before Rosie could answer. 'They came for us but we beat them back.'

The officer looked doubtful. He stared at Rosie with respect. 'You held off both of them?'

'We did.'

'But—' The type of women the major knew would never have to fight for their lives. And they'd never need to push a dead body into a river.

'We were prepared,' she told him with a sweet smile.

'Where did they go?'

Simon shook his head. 'I don't know. What brought you to this place?'

'They're supposed to be confined to barracks. When we couldn't find them, we questioned the men at the gate . . . it all came out. Even where they'd be in Leeds.'

'Do you know who I am?' Simon asked.

'You're the one who found them with the spoons. The

thief-taker.' He touched the brim of his hat in a salute. 'I'm the camp adjutant. They belong to me. I'm grateful.'

No need to mention that Simon had also been the one who stole them.

'What will happen when you find them?'

'The cells until their trial. If they tried to kill you, we might hand them to the constable. Did they hurt you?'

'No,' Simon replied.

'Madam?'

Rosie shook her head.

'Do you know where they might have gone?'

'I don't.' At least he could be honest about that.

The adjutant raised a gloved hand. 'Simpson, take these two horses back to the barracks.' He looked at Simon and Rosie once more. 'Might I call on you tomorrow and discover what happened? We should have them by then.'

'On Swinegate.'

'I'll be there in the morning.' A few strides and he was back on the horse, pulling on the reins as he led the troop away.

'Why did you say they'd both run?' Rosie asked once the soldiers had gone.

'It's better than saying we killed one of them, isn't it? If anyone ever asks, tell them that they fired their rifles. I shot my pistol and missed. If there's any blame, we can let Johnson take it.'

'Where do you think he's gone?'

'I wish I knew.' A wave of exhaustion broke over him. 'We're safe for tonight, that's what matters. He's going to be too busy trying to save himself to come after us. Let's go home.'

One gone, but the other was still out there. He wanted Rosie to feel easier, yet he knew that neither of them would be completely free until Johnson was caught or dead.

Standing on the doorstep, Simon looked up and down the dark street. A couple crossed the road, the woman clutching the man's arm. He watched until the darkness swallowed them.

Sleep, he thought. He was drained, completely empty. Tomorrow he'd start looking for Johnson. Tonight, though, he needed to rest.

But as soon as he closed his eyes, the images came. The shot, Murdoch charging towards him, the shot, sensing the man fall.

He'd killed a man. The first time.

It was kill or die. He knew that. In his head there was no doubt about it. Simon had done it to save his own life.

Yet the weight was there, heavy in his mind and in his soul. It would always remain, seared into him. He'd seen the man's face, lit by the flash of the pistol.

Simon lay in bed with his eyes open, aching for sleep. It wasn't going to come. There were devils playing in his head. Sin and God and guilt. All those things they'd talked about in the services at the workhouse. He thought he'd left that behind when he walked out of the place, but it had burrowed under his skin, deep inside.

Why? He'd done what he had to do. Nothing more.

He'd wounded men, hurt them badly. But he'd never needed to cross that line. Someone else had always done it for him. Jane. Rosie. Tonight he'd been God and it sat heavily.

There would be many more sleepless nights ahead. He could feel it.

THIRTY

'Child. Child.' Mrs Shields's voice hissed and her bony hand gently shook Jane awake. Morning, but still early from the thin light coming through the shutters.

She blinked, already fully alert as she pushed herself up in bed. The old woman was white, hand shaking as she clutched a grubby piece of paper.

'What? What's happened? Are you all right?'

She took a moment or two to gather breath. 'That man.'

Jane didn't need to ask. All it took was those two words and she knew exactly who it was. Big Tom.

'What about him?' She didn't understand. Why would he send her a letter? There was no point in looking at the writing; she couldn't read. But whatever it said, it had terrified Catherine Shields.

'He says he has the girl.'

The girl? What girl? Then she understood. 'You mean Martha?'

Catherine nodded, as if saying the name would make it all too real. 'He sent something. To prove it.'

'What? Where?'

The woman closed her eyes. 'A finger.'

The girl had stolen from Simon and Rosie. But it didn't matter what she'd done, she didn't deserve this. Jane forced down the bile in her throat. What had Tom done to her?

She needed to think.

'What does he want?' she asked.

Mrs Shields looked at the note as if she hadn't already memorized every word. Her face was grave, the lines seemed to be carved deep around her mouth.

'He says he'll kill her unless you go and meet him tonight.'

That was a promise Big Tom would enjoy keeping. Easy to kill a young girl you have as a prisoner. He'd probably . . . she pushed the thought to the edge of her mind. There was nothing she could do about that.

'Where?' Jane started to push herself out of bed. 'When?'

'Child.'

But she couldn't stop. Jane bit down on her lips as she stood. She kept one hand on the bed for balance. The pain seared through her body as she put her weight on the leg. But she could walk. She could make herself do it. She had to.

'You see?'

'Child,' Mrs Shields repeated. Her eyes glistened with the beginning of tears. 'You don't—'

Jane turned her head to stare at the old woman. 'I *do*. She helped me.' The words tumbled out of her. 'Martha saved me once. I have to go. Where does he want me? What time?' The woman was silent, staring down at the ground. 'Please. Tell me.'

'Tonight. At seven o'clock.'

'Where?'

'Child . . .'

Jane made herself move, shuffling across the floor. It hurt, each small step an agony, but she didn't stop. Very gently she took hold of the old woman's hands and looked into her face. 'Please. Where?'

'The mill pond on Skinner Lane.'

If she didn't go, Big Tom would kill Martha. He'd use her, hurt her, kill her. Jane had no doubt about that. He'd relish every second of it. He'd love the feeling of power over someone helpless.

This time she had to kill him. Even like this, slow, wounded and dragging her leg, she could beat him.

'He says you have to go by yourself. If he spots anyone else, she'll be dead.'

Jane nodded.

The silence swelled in the room.

'Jane.' Mrs Shields's voice was fragile, close to crumbling into tiny fragments. 'You know you've become like my . . . granddaughter.'

'Yes.'

'I can't ask you to let someone die.' She breathed slowly. 'But isn't there something . . .?'

'No.' Jane snapped out the word. Then, quietly, 'No, there's not.'

Her leg burned, but she barely noticed the pain now. Her mind was racing ahead with ideas, trying to make a plan. The mill pond. She'd been out there before, but she didn't know it. She'd need a spot where she didn't have to move. To make him come to her. Anything else and he'd have the advantage. She couldn't afford to give him that when she was like this.

Did Big Tom know she was hurt? She considered that; safer to believe that he did. Let him think she was weak.

Jane tied her petticoat around her waist. She reached for her dress, gasping as her weight shifted and a bolt of agony reared up her leg. She waited until it passed, hardly daring to breathe, then put on the rest of her clothes.

She had to do this. Alone. She couldn't ask Simon and Rosie—

Jane stopped. They'd had their own meeting last night. She hadn't given them a thought this morning; she didn't know if they were alive or dead. She had to go there, to find out.

'I need to see Simon.' She heard her voice, apologetic, begging.

'You can't walk that far.'

'I have to.'

A gale of emotions blew across the old woman's face. Finally, she nodded.

'I'll come with you, then. You can lean on me.'

They made a strange pair, the old supporting the young. Jane kept her hands tight on Mrs Shields's arm, trying not to drag against her. She knew people were looking at them. For once, she didn't care.

Her leg hurt, the pain turning from white heat to something dull by the time they reached Boar Lane. Slow progress, very slow, each step a deliberate effort of will. But she was moving. She'd reach Swinegate.

What would she find?

Every time she wondered, she felt as if the ground was opening up and she was falling and falling, with nothing below to stop her.

'Do you need to rest?' Catherine asked. But she shook her head. If she stopped, she might never start again. She had to get there, to know.

Simon watched Jane. She looked as if coming here had taken everything she possessed. She seemed to drop as she sat. Catherine Shields perched on the chair next to her, face filled with concern.

'What happened?' Jane asked. He'd seen her relief when he answered the door, Rosie right behind him, a knife ready in her hand.

'Murdoch's dead.' It felt strangely easy to say after spending the night being tormented by his conscience. He hadn't made his peace with killing someone, but he accepted it. He had to do it. If he hadn't, he'd be dead himself and floating down to the sea.

Jane's face was as pale as a corpse, the skin taut across her face. He could see she was waiting for more. Finally, Simon said, 'I shot him.'

She didn't blink, simply kept staring at him.

'Rosie put the body in the river,' he continued, hearing Mrs Shields draw in a sharp breath.

'Johnson?'

Simon shook his head. He hadn't had a chance to find out yet today. 'He ran off before the troopers arrived. I don't know if they've caught him yet. You—?'

'A letter,' Mrs Shields said. She had it tightly folded in her hand and pushed it towards Simon. Rosie picked it up, frowning as she read it, then handed it to him.

'The finger . . .' he began.

'It was real,' Mrs Shields said, and rubbed her eye. He felt sorry for her, pulled into a world she didn't want to know. A deadly, brutal place where there was little forgiveness. So different from everything she knew.

'We'll be there,' Rosie said. Her tone made it clear: no discussion.

'He wants me. By myself. You saw.'

'You can hardly walk,' Simon told her.

'I can still kill him.'

'No, you can't,' he said, and saw the fire start to blaze in her eyes. 'The way you are right now, you won't have a chance against him. I saw Big Tom yesterday. He looks ill, but you're worse. Let us help. It's quite a distance out there.'

'He'll kill Martha.'

'He won't know we're there until it's too late,' Rosie said. 'I promise.'

'No.'

Simon looked at his wife. He needed her patience and good sense now. At his best, Big Tom wasn't much of an opponent. But even as he was now, he'd destroy Jane. Then he'd murder Martha. No evidence left to damn him. Simon couldn't let that happen.

'We all want you alive,' Rosie said. 'Me, Simon, Mrs Shields. We care about you.'

'But—'

'We won't give him the chance to kill you or Martha,' Rosie continued. 'I know who Big Tom is. The world would be better without him.'

'I need to be the one to do it,' Jane said. 'I started it all.'

Simon frowned and stared at her. He didn't understand what she meant. Started it all? Maybe it didn't matter.

'You will be,' he agreed. 'Why don't you rest for a few hours? We'll come for you in plenty of time.'

Hesitation, then a nod of agreement. 'At home,' Jane insisted. 'Home.'

She struggled to rise. Even with Catherine Shields's help, the first few paces were an effort of iron will that took its toll.

Simon brought a walking stick from the parlour. 'Use this. It might help.'

Rosie guided her to the front door. He hung back with Mrs Shields.

'I'm sorry,' Simon said.

'It's done, and we can't change it,' she answered with a sigh of resignation. 'Please look after her. Please. She's all I have. Take care of the little girl, too.'

'We will.'

'It sounds as if you have your own problems.'

'With a little luck, the army will have taken care of those.'

'For your sake, I hope they have.' The old woman gave him a tight smile and left.

Major Harvey looked worn and dusty. The lines on his face stood out in sharp relief.

'I've had men out searching all night, but we haven't found either of them yet.'

Good. That meant they hadn't fished the ensign's body from the river, Simon thought. He should be a fair distance downstream by now, hopefully unrecognizable.

'Are the constable and his men looking, too?'

The adjutant nodded.

'They might have left Leeds, Major,' Rosie said. 'Have you considered that?'

'It's a possibility, madam.' He grimaced, the same way he had the night before when he'd had to talk to her. 'But we have their horses. None have been stolen from any of the stables. And they haven't taken a coach. My officers have checked round all the inns.'

'Have you asked at the Yorkshire Hussar? They used to go there.'

'The landlord will send a message if he sees them. All they have is what they were wearing. No money except for a few coins.'

'I know we have a lot of manufactories in Leeds, Major, but there's a great deal of countryside surrounding the town,' Simon said. 'I'm sure you're aware of that. It's easy to stay hidden out there.'

'Of course.' A small cough, hesitation or embarrassment, he wasn't sure. 'I take it you know Leeds very well, given your profession?'

'Yes.' He glanced at Rosie. 'We both do.'

'I'd like to hire your services to help track down our renegades, sir.'

He'd never expected this. First the constable, and now the British Army, paying him to find the man who wanted to kill him. Things turned on themselves in the most unexpected ways.

'You already have Williams and the watch,' Simon said.

Harvey's back was ramrod-straight.

'The commandant and I want these men found as soon as possible. They've already brought disgrace to the regiment. We'll hire whoever is useful.'

No need to haggle about the fee; this was too perfect to refuse.

'I accept. We both do.'

They were the hunters. It was official. Simon smiled at Rosie as he locked the door behind them. The air outside was dirty, smudges of soot falling like drizzle. But there was the warmth of early spring, the promise of something better ahead. It was almost enough to make him smile. And for a brief time, he could banish the memory of the dying face from last night.

'Which way?' she asked.

'Flay Crow Mill,' he said after a moment. 'It seems like a good place to begin.'

Johnson wasn't there, of course. The man wasn't a fool. But it gave Simon the chance to retrieve the last of the knives, to see the dark patch of Murdoch's blood in the dirt. Rosie was staring out over the water.

'He's gone.'

'Yes,' she said and turned to him. 'Where now?'

It was a good question. He'd been racking his brain, going over his conversations with Johnson and trying to recall any place the lieutenant had mentioned. Nothing.

'Welling Court,' he said suddenly. 'Laurence Poole lived there. It might be somewhere Johnson could hide.'

But the room had already been rented. A woman stood at the door, three young children gathered around her skirts. She shook her head at any mention of a cavalryman.

Where else could he be?

'Come on,' he said, and led the way over Timble Bridge, between the houses and the businesses, then one turning and another until they were on Paradise.

'There,' Simon said, pointing at an old house. 'Charlie Harker, the fence, lived there until he ran off. Johnson had dealings with him.'

'Where do you want me?'

'The back. It opens into the ginnel.'

She nodded and began to walk. The knife appeared in her hand.

Simon waited until she was out of sight before he walked to the front door. Unlocked, and inside everything had been ransacked. If Charlie Harker had left anything of value, it was long gone. Salvaged or smashed for firewood.

He could hear Rosie moving around the kitchen, and darted upstairs. Johnson wasn't here now; it was impossible to tell if he'd been in the place at all.

Rosie shook her head as she saw him. 'It's all guesswork, isn't it?' she said.

'Yes,' Simon agreed. 'But what else can we do?'

The stick helped. Jane could put her weight on it as she walked. But it was still draining. By the time she reached Mrs Shield's house, her leg felt as if it was on fire, that her fingers might be burned if she tried to touch it. Her arm ached from forcing herself along with the cane and her face was shining with sweat. She'd done too much. But there was more ahead. She had to be ready for that.

'Cordial,' Catherine said.

Jane drank. The liquid cooled her, soothing and satisfying. She was exhausted. The idea of standing and shuffling her way to bed seemed too large to imagine. She'd need all her strength for later. Jane placed the empty mug on the floor, leaned back and closed her eyes.

Simon had talked to almost everyone he knew. George Mudie, Barnabas Wade, Kate the pie-seller and so many more that his voice was hoarse. None of them had noticed Johnson, but they'd pass the word. A web of people would be watching. This was a time he could have used Jane's help, talking to the children and sending them running around Leeds to search.

That made him think about Martha and what Big Tom might be doing to her. The girl had stolen from him, she was sly. But he wasn't going to let anyone rape and maim a child. There was only one justice for that.

Jane believed she could beat him. She didn't understand how weak she really was. One glance gave it all away. Her face was gaunt, hollowed-out and bone-weary. She looked as if a puff of wind could topple her. But she believed determination was all she needed. That willpower was enough.

This time she was going to need more than that.

Tom would prey on her injuries. That was his way. She might damage him, but he'd kill her. Then he'd take his pleasure over the death of the little girl.

Simon wasn't going to let that happen. Neither would Rosie.

Twice he saw patrols from the barracks, just two men in each, riding around the streets of Leeds, their necks craned. The watch was out, too, moving around slowly in small groups.

They were all looking, but no one was finding. There had to be a better way. Finally, Simon marched into the Moot Hall and up the stairs to the council offices.

Constable Williams was there, sitting at his desk and smoking a pipe as he gazed out of the window. He glared when he saw Simon.

'What are you doing in—'

'Do you want to find Johnson?'

'Of course. Last night . . .'

Simon shook his head. 'Last night doesn't matter any more, does it? You waited, you thought they weren't coming, and you left. That's perfectly fair. In your shoes I'd have done exactly the same thing.'

'You beat them,' Williams said.

'I made them run.' He wasn't about to give the constable the truth of what happened. That would go to the grave with him. 'They're still out there.'

'I already know that. My men are looking for them.'

'You, the cavalry. Me. We're all searching and getting nowhere. You need to talk to the adjutant and make a plan so you're not all covering the same ground.'

Williams nodded. 'What about you?'

'I'll keep my eyes open.' He looked around the office. Old wood panelling, a high ceiling, portraits on the wall. Still a grand room, even if its best days were long in the past. 'Remember,' he said, 'if you arrest them, no one will listen to Ferguson or Brady about removing you from office.'

'I haven't forgotten, Westow. Anything you hear . . . I'd be grateful.'

'I'll let you know.'

And he'd be glad to pass on the information. Let Williams and the army fight Johnson. He'd gladly miss that battle.

Jane ran the blade over the whetstone. Time after time, in a quick, practised rhythm. Finally, it was sharp enough to satisfy her. She laid the blade along her arm, above the scars that climbed up her skin. She breathed slowly, feeling the calmness creep through her body. Like this, she was in control. It was so easy to imagine the cut, the first bubble of dark red blood and the release it brought her. A way of paying for her failures.

She didn't move the knife. The blade was cold against her flesh. Finally, she placed it back in the pocket of her dress. Tonight, she'd either kill Big Tom or be dead herself.

'Child.'

Jane turned her head. Mrs Shields stood in the doorway, sad, scared.

'Please look out for yourself.'

'I will,' she said. 'I promise.'

'Good.' The old woman tried to smile. In the end she pressed her lips together and left. In pain.

But the whole world hurt, Jane thought, and every single person in it. That only ended when you died.

She pushed herself to her feet, resting on the cane.

She was ready. For anything.

THIRTY-ONE

The water in the mill pond was dirty and dark, slimy green weeds floating at the edge.

Jane picked her spot, with her back against the broad trunk of a tree. It was still far shy of seven o'clock but the light was beginning to fade. She wanted the chance to know the ground, to see it, even if she couldn't walk it all.

Simon and Rosie had helped her out here. Even with someone to lean on, someone to keep watch, it had taken over an hour, slow as a snail. But Jane had no sense that anyone was following them.

The tree was in the perfect place. Close enough to the water that Big Tom wouldn't be able to creep up on her. He wasn't likely to do that, though. He'd have Martha with him. He'd want Jane to see the girl's suffering. The thought would arouse him.

She sat with her legs stretched out in front of her. The last few days had been dry and the ground was hard. Plenty of stones close at hand. She gathered a few, weighing them in her palm. She couldn't move well, but these would help. Without thinking, she turned the gold ring on her finger, the one Mrs Shields had given her to keep her safe. It hadn't helped with her leg. Perhaps it would keep her alive tonight.

Rosie and Simon were out there. Well-hidden and patient. Waiting if she needed them.

'I started all this with him,' Jane had told them as they walked out along Sheepscar Lane. 'It's my fault he has Martha. I need to be the one who ends it.'

'You will,' Rosie assured her. 'We'll look after Martha. You don't have to worry about her.'

'Are you sure—' Simon began, but she cut him off.

'Yes.' Abrupt as she stared ahead. She could do it. She had to do it, for Martha, for herself.

Darkness fell and she gathered the shawl around her shoulders. No need to pull it over her hair – she wanted him to see her. To know she wasn't afraid.

She was barely aware of time creeping by. A few people crossed on the track over the grass. None of them noticed her sitting by the tree, so still that she'd become a part of the landscape.

By full night, her eyes were sharp enough to pick out movement. A big dog fox that started to trot, then stopped, picking up the scent of humans before darting off again. The snuffling of animals hidden in the undergrowth.

Then she felt it. Someone was coming.

Big Tom.

Far away, off in town, she thought she heard the clock booming the hour. Maybe she imagined it. But he was close.

Jane forced herself to stand, ignoring the agony in her leg, skirt rustling softly as she rose. The stick helped. Once she was upright, she placed it behind her, leaning against the tree trunk, out of sight.

She could see him now. He had something with him, half-carrying, half-dragging it.

Martha.

The girl didn't try to resist.

Jane moved, shifting her balance, making certain he'd spotted her. When he was ten yards away he stopped and let the girl drop to the ground. Martha had a dirty bandage wrapped around her left hand. Jane caught a glimpse of the girl's face. Nothing but pain and terror.

'She lives. You die,' he said.

'All right.' She didn't hesitate. He was thinner than the last time she'd seen him, his bulk pared away. Not so big any more. The arm she'd wounded was pulled close against his chest.

That was a weakness; she could use it. But Jane needed him to come to her. If she tried to move, she was certain to stumble, to fall, and he'd be on her. Like this, with her back against the tree, she was strong. But he could advance and retreat while she was rooted to this spot. She needed to make her first strike count. Deep and hard.

'Come on,' she said. Her fingers were tight around the knife. 'You wanted this.'

Simon and Rosie were out there. She trusted them. They'd be watching, coming to help if she needed it.

But she wanted Big Tom for herself. He took one pace forward, then two. Still not close enough for her to hurt him.

Jane kept her eyes on Tom. Staring into his face and seeing all his hate and anger. Watching the way his hands and his feet moved. He gave away what he was going to do. He might as well have shouted it out loud. She knew; she could shift and stop him.

One minute and neither of them had struck a blow. She could feel his patience beginning to fray. Good. Let the frustration rise. He'd make mistakes and she'd pounce on them.

Her mind was clear, utterly sharp. She couldn't even feel the pain in her leg.

He was going to attack on her left. He'd glanced that way. Now he was on the balls of his feet, ready to dart forward. Jane kept still, as if she hadn't noticed. Waiting until he committed himself.

As soon as he moved, her hand flashed out. The knife drove through his coat. Jane saw his eyes widen as the blade pierced his skin. She pushed it home, pressing it into his side with every ounce of her strength before pulling it out again.

He almost fell. Big Tom staggered, clutching at the wound. He roared. Jane didn't hear him. She was concentrating on his face. Behind the pain, there was slyness in his eyes. She'd hurt him badly, but he knew she couldn't move forward to finish him.

The clouds shifted and moonlight caught the sheen of sweat covering his face. He was struggling, but he wasn't done yet. He had the strength for one more attack. Jane tightened her grip on the knife.

He needed to make his move very soon. His trousers were already dark with blood and his leg was sagging.

As he started to lunge, he toppled as something clutched at his ankle and dragged him down. Martha. She'd slid across the ground, inch by inch, lost in the night, until she could reach him.

The knife fell from his hand and clattered on stone. The girl was fast. She grabbed it and hurled herself at him, stabbing over and over in a frenzy. She continued even when he was no longer moving, chopping down on his fingers, pushing the blade into his groin as she sobbed and screamed.

She carried on, bringing the knife down time after time after time until exhaustion arrived. Finally, she plunged it into his chest and let it go, with the hilt sticking out of his ribs. She knelt by the body. Her tears didn't stop. Maybe they never would, Jane thought.

Rosie slid out of the shadows and put her arms round Martha's shoulders. A few whispered words in her ear, then she helped the girl to her feet. She was slow, shaking with hate and terror as she tried to move. She was lost in a place filled with hurt and she might never find her way out of it again. Jane had seen it happen, people who wandered all their lives in another world.

Rosie guided her gently away. Jane stared at Big Tom's body. It was done. She'd wanted to be the one to kill him, but perhaps it was better this way. There was real justice, as much as there could ever be.

How long had it taken? It felt like an hour. Time stretched; she'd experienced that strangeness before. It had probably taken barely more than two minutes from the moment he'd arrived until Martha had finished with him. She could recall every single heartbeat.

He'd never touched her. He hadn't even come close.

'Do you want to leave him here?' Simon asked. His voice was soft; she hadn't heard him approach. Jane wiped the knife on her skirt and slid it back into the pocket of her dress.

'Yes,' she answered after a moment. Her voice was dry, as harsh as gravel. 'Let them find him in the morning.'

They'd never connect him to her. They probably wouldn't even spend much time on it. One more murder where they didn't find the killer. Maybe it would serve as a warning. But the people who needed to hear it would never take notice.

Jane took hold of the stick and began to walk. Each step was painful. But she didn't stop, didn't look back at Big Tom. It was over, it was a part of history now. He could never hurt anyone else.

She forced herself on. Feeling the pain, accepting it. That was what you did. You carried on. You kept going. It was the only way.

'You can lean on me,' Simon said. Jane shook her head. She didn't want to lean on anyone.

'Child.' Mrs Shields took hold of her and drew her inside. Her hands patted Jane all over, feeling for wounds. 'Are you—'

'I'm fine. He never came close to me.' She didn't want to talk about it, didn't want to think about it ever again. She could put it away in a box in her mind and leave it there.

'Martha?'

'Rosie is looking after her,' Simon said. He tipped his hat and eased out of the door.

'Where is she?'

'In the attic,' Rosie replied. 'She fell asleep as soon as she lay down, poor little thing.'

'How badly did he hurt her?'

'He took two of her fingers. I've washed her hand and put on a fresh bandage. The wounds look clean.'

'What about the rest?'

She shook her head and bit her lip. 'I haven't asked her. We can guess.'

'Yes.' He stroked the hollow between her neck and her shoulder. 'Do you trust her? Remember what happened last time she was here.'

'She's in no state for that, Simon. She won't be for a long time yet. If ever.'

'I hope not.' He sighed and it turned into a yawn. 'I need to rest. It's been a long day.'

Mudie looked up as Simon entered the printing shop.

'Have they found the cavalrymen yet?' he asked.

'Not that I've heard. I'm just on my way to the barracks.'

'They've probably run off. Anyone sensible would.'

'Very likely.' Could it be true? There was nothing in Leeds now for the lieutenant. Soldiers and the night watch were hunting him, and the constable was ready to charge him with attempted murder. Leaving would be the obvious solution. Still . . . he wondered. Of course, one was dead, but only he and Rosie knew that.

'Did you hear about the body?'

'What body?' For a second his heart leaped into his mouth. Had they pulled Murdoch from the river?

'Down at the mill pond in Sheepscar. People are saying it's Big Tom Bailey.'

Simon breathed slow and steady. 'Good luck to whoever did it. He's had it coming for a long time.'

'He was stabbed over thirty times. Whoever did it cut off his fingers, too. That's quite a crime.'

'You know what he was like, George, it's no loss. Do the watch have any idea who was responsible?'

'From what I hear, not a clue.'

'Hardly a surprise.' If they'd suspected Martha or Jane, they'd have put out the word straight away. They were safe. Some good news, at least.

A warmer morning as he walked out along North Street. The earth was slowly coming alive after winter. It was always hard to judge with the town all around him. Everything was stone and brick and slate. Barely a tree to be seen. And Leeds was growing bigger every week.

More houses, more factories, more chimneys to pour their smoke into the sky. Year on year it grew worse. Every breath he took was full of soot and dirt. But there was nothing to be done about it.

A guard escorted him from the gatehouse of the barracks to the adjutant's office. As soon as he saw Simon, Major Harvey raised his eyebrows.

'Do you have something?' he asked hopefully.

'No,' Simon replied. 'I was hoping you might.'

The adjutant could only purse his lips and shake his head. 'My patrols haven't found any sign of them. We'll give it the rest of today, but my guess is that they've run. If you hear any hints . . .'

'I'll let you know.'

'Thank you, Westow.'

'They've vanished,' Constable Williams said. 'The pair of them. Probably changed their names and run halfway to London. That's what I'd do in their place.'

Maybe one of them had done precisely that, Simon thought. The other was certainly gone, but in the water, dragged down to the sea by now.

'It's possible,' he agreed. Yet whatever Williams and the adjutant said, Simon wasn't entirely convinced. Part of him wondered if Johnson was still somewhere around Leeds. He was keeping out of sight and craving a final revenge. The man had nothing; that meant he had nothing to lose. And Simon was the one who'd put him in that position.

He went around the inns and the beer shops, but no word of the lieutenant. Finally, he made his way home. Rosie was in the kitchen, kneading bread dough on the table.

'Where's Martha?'

'Still sleeping, the last time I looked.'

But he checked the secret drawer in the stair before he sat in the parlour to think.

He'd carry around the weight of killing for the rest of his days. The sound of the pistol firing would always be a cannon explosion in his mind. The astonished expression on Murdoch's face, the way he fell; he'd never be able to erase them.

Simon had had to do it. He knew that, he understood it. It was the only way to remain alive. But his heart was still full of sorrow and guilt for what he'd done.

'How's your leg?' Simon asked Jane.

'I can't stand on it today.'

She'd pushed herself too far, too hard. Now she had to begin again. She'd rested, she'd slept, eaten the food and drunk the potions Mrs Shields fed her. It helped. When she was awake, she and the old woman looked at the Book of Hours. That was a joy they could share, one which would never fade.

'What about Martha?' she asked.

'Rosie's looking after her. She thinks it'll be easier if a woman does that.'

Jane nodded. 'Have you found Johnson?'

Simon nodded towards the window and the fading afternoon light. 'He's still out there.'

'I can't help you. Not yet.'

'I know. Williams wants him. If he can take him up, his job will be safe for years.' Simon smiled at her. 'Get yourself well. Spring's almost here, crime will be picking up. We'll soon be busy again.'

No point in going out into the night and searching. If anyone saw Johnson, Simon would hear.

At home, Rosie and Martha were talking up in the attic. The girl's voice was halting and tentative. She'd woken an hour before, trapped in a nightmare, screaming and sitting up in the bed. Rosie had hurried up the stairs, soothing her and easing the girl into slow wakefulness.

Simon was brooding over killing a man. Martha had far worse demons dancing in her head.

'What do you think?' Rosie asked as they sat at the kitchen table eating bread and cheese for their breakfast. 'Should we bring the boys home? Is it safe?'

He took time before he answered. 'Yes.'

He needed their noise, their high spirits and games. They made the place into a home. He craved the return to normality that their presence meant. Back to being a thief-taker again. Not hunting men, not being a killer. The simple act of retrieving stolen items and collecting his fee.

'Yes,' he repeated with a smile. 'Let's have them back home.'

Another hour and Rosie left to collect them, driven by their neighbour in his cart. Martha was with her, staying close like an infant. The girl was pale, not quite steady on her feet yet and hiding the bandaged hand. What was going to happen to her? he wondered.

The knocking at the door roused him. Simon blinked and looked around. He must have dozed; for a moment, as he blinked, he wasn't sure where he was. His mind cleared and he stood.

The boy was small, maybe six or seven, and thin as a farmer's rake. He was dressed in a shirt made for a child three or four years older and the hem of his trousers dragged on the ground. No shoes. He held out a piece of paper in a grubby hand.

'From Constable Williams, sir.'

Simon dug a farthing from his pocket, took another look at the boy and made it a ha'penny, watching as the lad hurried away with a smile across his face.

We have one of them trapped on the top of Richmond Hill. The army is here, too.

They'd found Johnson. All credit to whoever did that; it was more than he'd managed. Simon checked his knives, put on his coat and hat and slammed the door as he left.

He darted through the streets, walking quickly and slipping between people. He ducked out of the way as a coach roared up Briggate. Along the Calls, over Timble Bridge, then Mill Street and the sharp climb up Richmond Hill.

It was bare and bleak up here, looking down on Leeds and the haze over the buildings. Nothing to see bar a few farmhouses and Ellerby Lane winding off into the distance.

Hands on hips, Simon caught his breath and stared. He could pick out a group of men a quarter of a mile away, easy to spot in their red military coats. A few were on horseback, the rest on foot.

A thin dirt track led towards them. As he drew closer, Simon started to hear the voices and the shouts to someone out of sight. Two of the men knelt, rifles at their shoulders, aiming towards a small mound.

Constable Williams stood to the side, talking with Major Harvey. The adjutant was standing, holding his horse by the reins.

'Westow,' he said, right hand waving a faint salute.

'You have him?' Simon asked.

'On the other side of that mound. The ground slopes away behind it. I have men stationed below. He can't get away, but he won't surrender.'

'He? Just one of them?'

'Lieutenant Johnson,' Harvey replied. 'We haven't seen Ensign Murdoch.'

Nor will you, Simon thought. 'How did you find him?'

'One of the watch,' Williams answered with pride. 'Spotted him and sent word, then followed him up here.'

'What weapons does he have?'

'Just his sword. That's what my man said,' Williams told him.

'I want him alive,' the adjutant said.

'For the honour of the regiment?' Simon asked.

'Exactly, sir,' Harvey replied.

'It should be easy enough to take him. How many is it – ten against one?'

'We're going to have to go in and drag him out.'

'Then why don't you?'

'I'd rather he surrendered,' Harvey said. 'We can wait.'

And come darkness he'd be able to slip away again. Simon looked around in disgust. Soldiers, the watch, and all of them too scared to do anything. They had Johnson cornered. He didn't want to be a part of this, but it was time for this business to be over and done.

Simon drew his knife and took a second from his boot.

'Then I suppose we'd better take care of it,' he said, and stared at Williams. 'Are you coming with me? You're the constable.'

He spoke loudly enough for everyone to hear: Harvey, the troopers, the constable's men. Williams could do his job for once and show a little mettle. Shame him in front of everyone.

'Well?' He waited. The constable's face showed nothing. He hadn't moved. Finally, he looked around at all the faces and grimaced.

'Fine,' Williams agreed. The constable wouldn't want to give any ammunition to Ferguson and Brady. He drew his sword and strode past Simon with a bitter glance.

Just the two of them and the sighing of the wind.

'Do you like being a hero, Westow?' The constable kept his voice low, half the words whipped away to East Yorkshire.

'It's your job to catch people who break the law.'

'He'll give up in time. He can't escape. All those men from the barracks can wait. They don't have anything better to do.'

'If you catch him, the aldermen can't touch you.'

'And if I'm dead, I'm no use to man nor beast.'

Simon veered to his left. Two steps and he'd forgotten Williams was there. He was thinking about the lieutenant, trying to anticipate what he might do.

A glance behind him. Harvey had mounted his horse, keeping it still and watching.

Ahead, the ground fell off sharply. And there was Johnson.

Seeing him was a shock. He was dirty and unshaven, his hair wild around his head. As if the veneer of civilization had been stripped away from him. The only thing that mattered to him was survival.

Johnson glanced at Simon with contempt, as if a knife wasn't a weapon to worry him. He turned his head quickly to face Williams. Surprised, frightened, the constable took a step back.

That was all the lieutenant needed. He sensed the weakness, the possibility of freedom. He flew up the slope, sword poised to strike.

The constable managed to parry him twice. Simon was running, shouting, screaming, anything to catch Johnson's attention. But he might as well have stayed silent.

It wasn't a fight. It was destruction. Williams had no idea how to use his weapon. Simon wasn't going to reach them in time to save him. There was only one thing he could do.

The cavalryman had his back turned to Simon. A rough glance at the target and he sent one blade through the air, then a second and the third.

They all hit. Two dug into Johnson's shoulder, the other caught him in the waist. But too late for the strike on the constable. The point of the sword slid between his ribs and straight into his heart. He was dead before his body hit the ground.

Johnson turned. His knees were sagging, he had a rictus smile of pain, but he was still standing, ready to take a pace forward.

That was all he managed. Major Harvey spurred his horse forward. It leaped towards the lieutenant, and the adjutant's sword sliced down. He only needed a single blow and Johnson crumpled.

Over. Finally, it was over.

The constable lay on his back, staring up at the sky. Blood was pooling under his body. Simon knelt and closed his empty eyes. He gestured to one of the men from the watch.

'Take him back to town.'

No need to look at Johnson's corpse. He never wanted to see him again.

'I only did what I had to do,' the adjutant said. Christ Almighty, why did he think he needed to explain himself?

'You did,' Simon agreed. 'I'll testify to it if you need me.'

'What about the other one?' Harvey asked. 'Ensign Murdoch.'

He stared at Williams's body. 'I doubt he'll trouble you.'

'Are you sure?'

'Yes.' Simon began to walk, following the path down the hill. He wanted to think, to be alone. He'd goaded Williams, wanted him to prove he deserved to be constable. If he'd said nothing, the man would still be alive.

Was it his fault?

No. If Williams had been worthy of his position, he wouldn't have needed to be pushed. Responsibility came with a job like that, and he'd ducked it for too many years.

At least the constable would be remembered as a hero. Maybe he deserved it; in the end, he'd done his best. He hadn't run off. He'd stood his ground and raised his sword.

A brave end, but Alderman Ferguson would be content, too. He'd be able to appoint his own man as the next constable.

The taste of Leeds caught in his throat, made him hawk and cough. Back at home, he downed a pint of weak beer to wash it from his mouth. Three days, four deaths. His only regret was Williams.

He was still sitting there when the front door opened and the boys burst in like a gale, upending every thought. He caught hold of them, smelling the freshness of the countryside in their hair and on their skin. Having them here made him feel whole again. It pushed everything else away.

Rosie stood in the doorway, smiling as Amos and Richard overwhelmed him. They giggled and squirmed and tried to climb all over him as he tickled them.

'Enough,' she told them after a few minutes. 'Take your things up to your room.'

Even with the boys upstairs and out of the way, the house felt full. Lived in and happy.

'People are talking about it all over town.'

'I was there. I saw it,' Simon told her.

She raised an eyebrow. 'What now?'

'Nothing,' he told her. 'It's finished. Life can go back to normal.'

Even as he said it, he wondered – what was normal now? Everything had changed. He'd killed a man. He wasn't the same person he'd been before it happened. Things had shifted and he needed to become used to the idea. To understand what it meant.

A sudden thought hit him. 'Where's Martha? Didn't she come back with you?'

Rosie smiled, a soft, peaceful curl of her lips. 'She's going to stay with the Burtons. They always wanted a daughter and they took a shine to her straight away. It'll be good for her, Simon. Quiet, a routine, people who care.'

He nodded. Somewhere different might help. 'She needs to' – he hunted for the right word – 'recover.'

Above their heads, young voices sharpened and reached a crescendo.

'I'll be up there in ten seconds,' Simon called out. 'I'd better find absolute silence.'

'Still glad to have them back?' Rosie grinned and raised an eyebrow.

'Oh, yes. As happy as I can be.'

THIRTY-TWO

She could walk without the stick. Jane still limped, but every day it was easing; another week and it would be gone completely. It didn't stop her working. Simon had been right. Warmer weather meant business for them. In the last week alone, she'd traced two men who'd stolen from houses and retrieved the items they'd taken for Simon to return to the owners.

The end of April already. The month had started with fair weather, but the last fortnight had seen drizzle and showers almost every day. Each evening she returned soaked through to Mrs Shields's house.

'How is Martha? Have you heard?' Mrs Shields asked when they sat down to eat. Beef stew tonight, with rich gravy that left Jane warmed and satisfied.

'No.' Simon had told Jane the girl was living with a family in Kirkstall. She hadn't asked anything more. What did it matter? Martha had gone.

Long ago, she'd learned it was always safer never to find out what had happened to people. They disappeared. They faded away. In time, she knew, Catherine Shields would die and Jane would be alone again. There was nothing she could do about that. For now, though, she had family. That was enough.

Jane had enjoyed the attention Martha had given her. She admitted it. She'd liked the idea that someone believed she was worth something and wanted to be like her. It was flattering. But the girl was better away from all this. She'd survived for a while, but sooner or later she'd have broken. This way she'd have a chance of some sort of life. Maybe find a husband and have a family.

'Those men you went after, child . . .'

Big Tom, she meant, and the ones who'd come before him. The ones she'd never mentioned, though the woman knew.

'No more,' Jane promised.

'Thank you.' Catherine reached and placed a hand on Jane's

arm, lightly stroking the scars. Line after line, a ladder of them on her flesh. Something else she'd put away, maybe forever.

After they'd eaten, Jane brought the Book of Hours from the stool beside her bed and they sat looking at each page. There was always some new detail to astonish them. The expression on an angel's face, the pattern of colour around a capital letter.

She'd heard that the Atkinsons had returned. It was only a matter of time before they'd discover the book and the silver jug had been taken. God only knew what else was missing, too. Simon would return what he had, and the book would vanish. She'd never see it again, and all she'd possess would be these memories. But those were better than nothing at all. She'd seen it, she'd touched it and marvelled at it. For the rest of her life she'd still be able to conjure it up in her mind.

The world settled into a steady rhythm. Simon answered the advertisements in the *Mercury* and the *Intelligencer*, people who'd lost items and offered a reward for their return. Most things he and Jane managed to recover with few problems; a nagging few evaded them.

Williams received a grand funeral, with a medal struck in his honour and a pension granted to his grown children for his service to Leeds. Ferguson's man, Porter, quietly assumed the post of constable. Simon's guilt over Murdoch's death began to recede. The jagged edges became dulled and blunted.

To the dark. He turned the words over in his mind; he'd done it so many times, and he was still no closer to understanding what Poole had meant. No matter now; it was all done.

He'd heard that the Atkinsons had returned. Each day he looked for an advertisement, but none appeared. Instead there was a discreet note delivered by a servant. A request to attend Robert Atkinson at his house on Cankerwell Lane.

The front door this time, and a liveried servant to answer his knock. Inside, the sounds and smells of people living here. Fires in all the grates to take off the chill in the building. All very different from the last time he was here.

Atkinson was a small, dimpled man wearing a dark coat, a bright yellow waistcoat, and pale fawn trousers. He was younger than Simon had expected, probably no more than forty, with broad hands and jowly cheeks. His curly hair was receding on the top of his head.

'Thank you for coming.' His hand was extended and he sounded welcoming enough, but there was little pleasure on his face.

An entire silver coffee set had been stolen, he explained: milk jug, sugar bowl and tongs, as well as the pot itself. The servants had discovered its absence in the days after the family's return. They'd already seen the missing pane of glass at the back door.

'I'll do what I can,' Simon said. 'But I have to warn you, I can promise very little. You were gone over two months?'

Atkinson nodded. 'Almost three. We left at the start of the year.'

'If the theft happened soon after that, he's had plenty of time to sell the items. They could be anywhere by now. Melted down, maybe.'

Atkinson winced. 'Good God, I hope not. It's a rare set. A Leeds silversmith. My grandfather bought it from him. Every piece carries his hallmark. It's BB.'

'I'll do what I can. My fee is ten per cent of the value of whatever I return.'

'That's fine.' The man didn't even try to haggle.

'Was that all he took?'

'The only thing we've found.' Atkinson cocked his head. 'Why?'

'Sometimes people don't discover things until later.' A quick, professional smile.

'I hope you can find it.'

Simon took the silver jug from the drawer in the stairs and placed it on the table. Rosie and Jane were sitting there. The boys were in the parlour, the drone of their tutor's voice seeping through the house.

'It was part of a set,' Simon said. 'Four pieces in all. It seems that Laurence Poole did well for himself at their house.'

'It's strange, though,' Rosie said. 'He died with nothing. He was scrambling to find money to leave Leeds, remember?'

'We're never going to know what really happened,' Simon said. 'And we're never going to find the rest of the set now. I'll take this to them tomorrow.'

'And charge him the full fee?' Rosie asked.

He grinned. 'Of course.'

'What about the Book of Hours?' Jane asked. She'd brought it with her. Mrs Shields had carefully wrapped it in oilcloth and tied the package with string. It sat in front of her.

'He didn't say anything about it. I haven't seen any advertisements asking for its return.'

'Faster than I expected, Mr Westow.' Atkinson caressed the jug, sliding his hands across the smooth surface.

'I suspect the rest has long ago left Leeds.'

The man pursed his lips and sighed. 'I suppose this is better than nothing at all.'

As Simon slid his fee into his pocket, he said, 'Have you looked again to see if anything else was taken?'

'I checked last night,' Atkinson said. 'Did it myself. Everything is there.'

He found Jane at the corner of Briggate and Boar Lane.

'The book,' he said.

She looked up at him with fretful eyes. 'What about it?'

'I don't know where it came from, but it seems to be yours now.'

She smiled, put the shawl over her hair and disappeared into the crowd on Briggate.